FANTASY ILLUSTRATED

ASTOUNDING
50TH ANNIVERSARY CATALOG

Collectible Pulp Magazines, Science Fiction & Horror Books

Catalog #31

by
DAVE SMITH

Fantasy Illustrated
Silvana, WA 2019

INTRODUCTION

Greetings and welcome to Fantasy Illustrated catalog #31. I started putting catalogues out about the same time I opened Fantasy Illustrated in 1979. The last one was published in 1999 so it has been 20 years since that one came out. After that the internet took over as the main conduit for selling mail order so I ceased doing print catalogues. I have always loved the look and feel of a good catalog so to celebrate my 50th year in the business I felt that issuing this catalog was a great way to celebrate. Although it has been a lot of work, it truly has been a labor of love to produce and get it into your hands.

In a way you could call this my 50th and 40th anniversaries. Let me explain. I started out working at the age of 14 for a book store called the Book Sail in old downtown Anaheim in the summer of 1969. This is where I got my first education in old books, comics and pulp magazines. It was here that I saw my first pulp (Amazing Stories #1) and learned about such pulp heroes as the Shadow and Doc Savage. In 1979, I opened my first comic store, Fantasy Illustrated, about a mile and a half south of Disneyland. Thus, I have been in the business for fifty years and on my own as Fantasy Illustrated for forty years. Although the store started out as a basic comic book store, I gradually added pulp magazines vintage paperbacks and hardcovers to the inventory. My specialty was and will always remain vintage material.

Along the way I opened two other locations in California, one in the city of Orange and another in Costa Mesa. In 1994, after selling the store contents and location to another comic dealer I moved to Washington State and bought Rocket Comics in Seattle, while retaining the Fantasy Illustrated name for my mail order business. In 2001, I closed down my last brick and mortar store going full bore into mail order and shows. I also started revisiting my roots by putting a greater emphasis on pulp magazines and collectible books.

I want to take this opportunity to thank all my customers over the years that have made it possible to work this unusual job for all these decades. From the customers at my first store in Garden Grove California to the new ones I made friends with in Seattle and now to all the ones I ship books and pulps to and sell to at shows. Thank you all.

Along the way I have met some wonderful dealers at the various shows I set up at. It's an amazing friendship to bond over the printed word. So many of you have been so generous with your time. I am especially grateful for the dealers that are part of Colorado Antiquarian Book Seminars. I spent a week there (CABS class of 2019) this past summer and learned so much from people that were so very generous sharing their deep knowledge of the book trade.

I want to single out a few people specifically. Russ (Rusty) Peak was one of the first employees I hired back around 1980. He worked his way up from bagging and boarding comic books to managing the Garden Grove store. When I relocated to Washington State he followed me up and helped me run Rocket Comics also.

If you ever see me selling at the Windy City Pulp show or the Seattle Antiquarian Book Fair you can't help but run into John Hutchins. John was a customer of mine at Rocket Comics who became a good friend and is now a huge help when I do shows. He does way more than help carry boxes for me. His knowledge of the items I sell is deep. He is a great example of an autodidact in this regards. I am so very grateful for my friendships with Russ and John and what they have added to my life.

I also want to acknowledge the memory of John McLaughlin owner of the Book Sail who hired me way back in 1969. This turned out to be a life changing event for me.

Lastly, but most importantly much thanks to my wife Kelli who for 17 years has been my helper going to the various shows and trying to explain to her friends what I do for a living. She now has a deeper appreciation then she ever had (or expected to have) of science fiction and pulp magazines.

It has been an amazing ride these past 50 years. There have been a lot of ups and downs and speed bumps along the way both business-wise and personal. At times the hours have been very long and stressful but I wouldn't trade these past years for any regular 9-5 job in the world. As I turn 65 about the time this catalogue is being published I am very grateful and feel really blessed and look forward to continuing in the business as long as I am able because I'm certainly willing.

I really hope you enjoy reading this catalog as much as I did in creating it. Best, Dave Smith.

TABLE OF CONTENTS

SHOWS

We are scheduled to set up at the following shows in 2020

Printed by Northwest Bookworks, a division of Arundel Books.
Visit us at northwestbookworks.com

Tiger! Tiger!

Chesley Bonestell

Dark Carnival

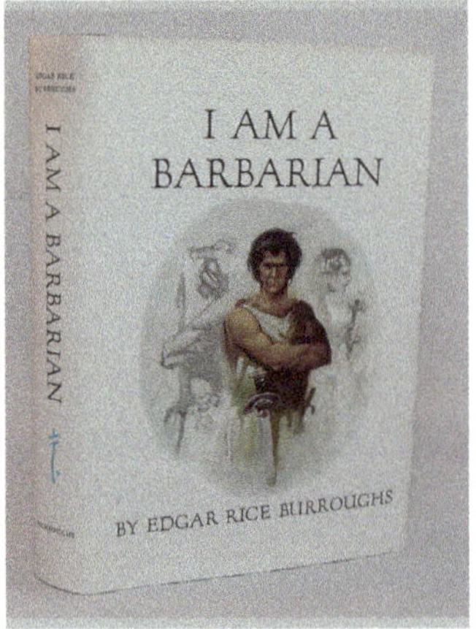
I Am Barbarian

Books

[Astounding Stories]
Rogers, Alva
Requiem For Astounding.
Chicago, IL: Advent Publishers: 1967. First paperback edition. Near Fine, solid spine, light toning to covers.   50.00

Bester, Alfred.
Tiger! Tiger!
London: Sidgwick and Jackson, [1956]. Octavo, boards. First edition. Published in the U. S. the following year as The Stars My Destination (Anatomy of Wonder 1976, 4-65.) Dark blue boards with gilt lettering. A fine copy in very good dust jacket with a few short tears, slight loss at edges and folds and back panel, with old small tape repairs that have stained and bled through. (Inv. 4168.)   1,100.00

[Bonestell, Chesley] Miller, Ron.
The Art of Chesley Bonestell.
London, England, Paper Tiger 2001. First Edition. NF, NF. Very mild wear to ends of spine, appears to be unread. Scarce. Jacket unclipped. Foreword by Arthur C. Clarke. (Inv.#4499.)   350.00

Bradbury, Ray.
Dark Carnival.
Sauk City: Arkham House, 1947. First edition. Bradbury's first book and the 24th Arkham publication. A very good book in a good to very good priced-clipped dust jacket with general wear to extremities and some chipping, mainly to crown and foot of spine. Mild foxing to pastedowns and end papers. 3000 copies printed so stated. (Inv. 4157.)   800.00

Burroughs, Edgar Rice.
At the Earth's Core
Canaveral Press, New York, 1962. Hard Cover. Mahlon Blaine (illustrator). 1st Thus. NF in VG+ price clipped dust jacket, light wear to the top of the spine and light bumping to the head and heal of the spine, First Canaveral Edition.   60.00

Burroughs, Edgar Rice.
The Cave Girl.
New York: Canaveral Press, 1962. First Canaveral Press edition. 21cm x 14.5cm. Pale yellow boards with black lettering, 323pp. Illustrated dust jacket by Roy G. Krenkel [and Joe Orlando] Book appears unread in near fine condition with mild pushing to spine ends. Dust wrapper is near fine with mild wear to extremities. Price sticker (presumed by publisher) of $3.50 to front flap. According to Canaveral editor Richard Lupoff, this book can have various binding colors as they allowed the printers to use different cloths as a money saving device. Zeuschner 85 (Inv. 4482.)   95.00

Burroughs, Edgar Rice.
Escape on Venus.
New York: Canaveral Press 1974. Green cloth with black lettering . Art by John Coleman Burroughs. FN/FN appears unread. A reprint of the 1963 edition. Zeuschner 127 (Inv. 4521.)   60.00

Burroughs, Edgar Rice.
I Am Barbarian.
1967, 1st edition. A fine copy in a fine dust jacket. Maroon boards with gold lettering. Print run was 2,000 copies. Zeuschner 571. (Inv. 3606.)   250.00

Burroughs, Edgar Rice.
Jungle Tales of Tarzan.
1919 (reprint edition 1950.) . Interior illustrations by J. Allen St. John. Endpaper maps, front board illustration and title page decorations are by Rafael Palacios. Bound in orange boards with illustration and lettering in brown. Dust jacket flap has the publisher's price of $1.00. Near Fine in very good plus dust jacket, illustrated by C. E. Monroe, Jr, with mild edge wear. Zeuschner 223. (Inv. 3711.)   75.00

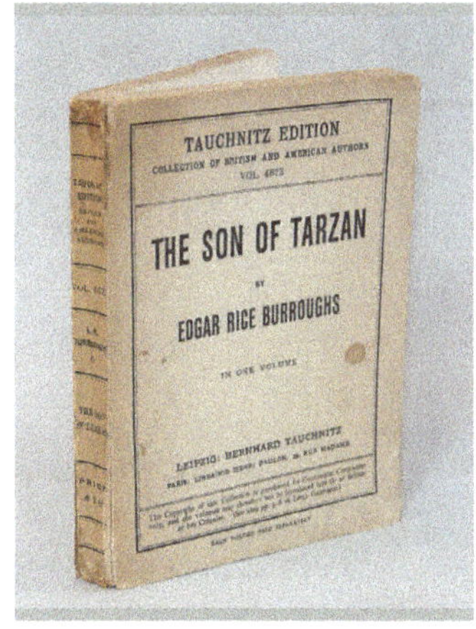

Llana of Gathol   **Son of Tarzan**   **Tales of Three Planets**   **Tarzan and the Castaways**

Burroughs, Edgar Rice.
Llana of Gathol.
1st Edition. A fine copy in a near fine dust jacket. First Edition stated on the copyright page. Blue boards with red lettering. Slight
rubbing mainly at the bottom of the DJ in the spine area, else fine. Zeuschner 280. (Inv. 3602.)   400.00

Edgar Rice Burroughs.
The Moon Men.
New York: Canaveral Press 1962. Reprint of The Moon Maid. Orange cloth with black lettering. Art by Mahlon Blaine. Has $1.50
Book mark sticker over original price. Spine ends pushed on book with corresponding to dust wrapper and very mild chipping to crown
of spine. NF/NF. Zeuschner 344 (Inv. 4520.)   60.00

Burroughs, Edgar Rice.
Pirates of Venus.
New York: Canaveral Press, 1962. First Canaveral Press edition. Tan boards with dark brown lettering, map endpapers. Book is FN with NF dust
jacket with a hint of chipping to crown and spine and very mild wear mainly to folds. Contains four plates from the original edition by J. Allen
St. John. $2.95 price sticker over unclipped original $ 2.75 price, thus making this a 1963 release. Zeuschner 412. (Inv. 4517.)   65.00

Burroughs, Edgar Rice.
Son of Tarzan, The.
Leipzig: Bernard Tauchnitz, 1925. Condition: GD+. Tauchnitz edition. Very scarce edition in original wrappers. General moderate wear,
some spine splits, small stain to front wrap, pencil drawings to first page and last two pages. Some corners folded over to first few pages.
Still a presentable copy of this very hard to find edition. (Inv. 3926.)   400.00

Burroughs, Edgar Rice.
Tales of Three Planets.
Canaveral Press, New York, 1964. First edition, first printing. FN/VG+, bound in blue cloth with black lettering. An anthology collecting
three stories, Beyond The Farthest Star, The Resurrection Of Jimber-Jaw, and The Wizard of Venus. Dust jacket and interior illustrations
by Roy Krenkel. Zeuschner #517. (Inv. 3611.)   200.00

Burroughs, Edgar Rice.
Tales of Three Planets.
Canaveral Press, New York, 1974. Second printing. FN/FN, bound in lavender cloth with black lettering. An anthology collecting three
stories, Beyond The Farthest Star, The Resurrection Of Jimber-Jaw, and The Wizard of Venus. Dust jacket and interior illustrations by
Roy Krenkel. Zeuschner #518. (Inv.4518)   200.00

Burroughs, Edgar Rice.
Tarzan and the Ant Men.
1924 (reprint edition 1950.) Endpaper maps, front board illustration and title page decorations are by Rafael Palacios. Bound in green
boards with illustration and lettering in black. Dust jacket flap has the publisher's price of $1.00. Fine in NF dust jacket, illustrated by
Betty Monroe with mild edge wear. Zeuschner 538. (Inv. 3713.)   85.00

Burroughs, Edgar Rice.
Tarzan and the Castaways.
Canaveral Press, Inc. New York. 1964 First edition. $3.50 price on unclipped flap. Dark green boards with black lettering, FN/NF with
publishers label affixed to copyright page. Mild tanning to jacket. Frank Frazetta art, Zeuschner #546. (Inv. 3612.)   325.00

Burroughs, Edgar Rice.
Tarzan and the City of Gold.
Edgar Rice Burroughs, Inc.,1933 (reprint 1948.) Grey boards with dark blue lettering. Some chipping to extremities of dust wrapper
and some loss of paper near top of dust wrapper spine and corresponding spine of book. VG/VG. Zeuschner 559. (Inv. 3700.)   40.00

Burroughs, Edgar Rice.
Tarzan and the Forbidden City.
1938 (1948 reprint.) A fine copy in a very good plus dust jacket. Grey boards with dark blue lettering. Zeuschner 571. (Inv. 3605.)   150.00

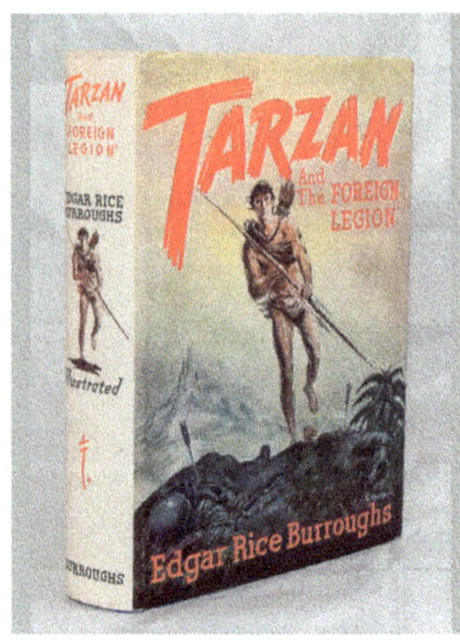

Tarzan & the Foreign Legion

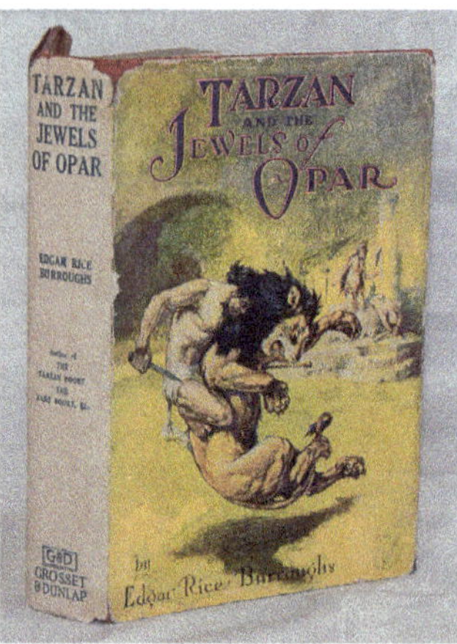

Tarzan & the Jewels of Opar

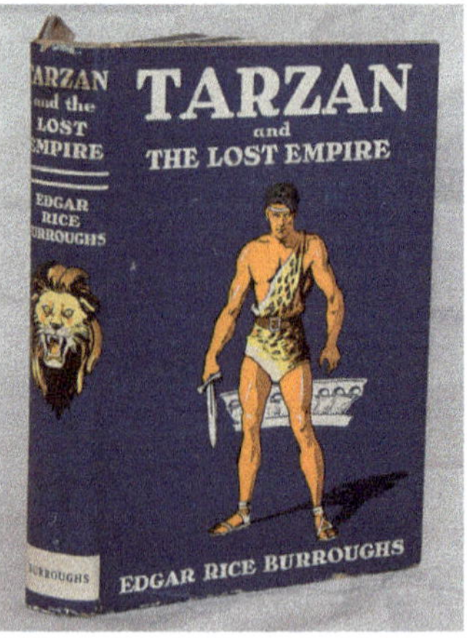

Tarzan and the Lost Empire

Tarzan and the Madman

Burroughs, Edgar Rice.
Tarzan and the Foreign Legion.
1947 first edition. Illustrated by John Coleman Burroughs. The last Tarzan story written before Burroughs passed away. FN/FN. Blue cloth with orange (red?) lettering. A beautiful copy! Zeuschner 578. (Inv. 3610.) — 275.00

Burroughs, Edgar Rice.
Tarzan and the Golden Lion.
Grosset & Dunlap, 1923 (Circa 1958 reprint). Hard Cover. Book Condition: NF/NF. Reprint. Gray boards with decoration depicting Tarzan standing on an elephant's back, arms raised, spear in hand. Dust jacket flap price of $1.50 intact. Front panel has Monroe illustration of lion attacking native, with Tarzan in background, knife in hand. Back panel of DJ has ads for nine Zane Grey "Adventure Stories for Boys." Price of 150150 on upper corner of front flap. Zeuschner 592. (Inv. 036.) — 45.00

Burroughs, Edgar Rice.
Tarzan and the Golden Lion
Edgar Rice Burroughs. Grosset & Dunlap, New York, 1923 (1949 reprint). Dark orange boards with black lettering and figure of Tarzan on an elephant to front board. Book NF with mild rubbing to spine ends, dust wrapper also NF with mild rubbing and a 1/4" tear, 332 pages. Map end papers.100100 on the front dust jacket flap. Zeuschner 592. (Inv. 3687) — 55.00

Burroughs, Edgar Rice.
Tarzan and the Jewels of Opar.
Grosset & Dunlap, New York.1918 (circa 1935-1940 reprint.) Hard Cover. Book Condition: VG/VG. Some staining to front board and chipping to edges and folds of dust wrapper. 38 titles listed on back panel and 29 listed near back of book.
 Zeuschner 607. (Inv. 039.) — 75.00

Burroughs, Edgar Rice.
Tarzan and the Jewels of Opar.
Grosset & Dunlap,1918 (reprint edition cir 1952-54) Front board illustration and title page decorations by Rafael Palacios. Bound in green boards with illustration and lettering in black. Dust jacket flap has the publisher's price of $1.00. Fine in NF dust jacket, illustrated by Monroe with mild edge wear. Zeuschner 609. (Inv. 3714.) — 85.00

Burroughs, Edgar Rice.
Tarzan and the Lost Empire.
Grosset & Dunlap, New York, 1929. (reprint from cir 1933-1937.) Hardcover. Book Condition: VG+/G Third Printing (?) Little wear at spine edges and corners of dust jacket, some chipping at folds and three inch tear in DJ, top edges green. 39 ERB titles listed on back flap The dust jacket and frontispiece art is by A. W. Sperry. Zeuschner 640. (Inv. 037.) — 65.00

Burroughs, Edgar Rice.
Tarzan and the Lost Empire.
Edgar Rice Burroughs, Inc.,1928-1928 (reprint from 1948.) Grey boards with dark blue lettering. Book has mild wear near spine and dust wrapper has mild chipping to extremities, VG+/VG+. Zeuschner 642. (Inv. 3698.) — 85.00

Burroughs, Edgar Rice.
Tarzan and the Madman.
1st edition, Canaveral Press, 1964. Black lettering on light grey cloth boards. Print run between 3,000 and 4,000 copies. Book is fine with just slight pushing to spine ends in like dust jacket Zeuschner 649. (Inv. 3683.) — 300.00

Burroughs, Edgar Rice.
Tarzan At the Earth's Core.
Edgar Rice Burroughs, Inc. Publishers, Tarzana CA, 1948. Hardcover. First Burroughs edition. Bound in tan/gray boards with lettering in blue. Frontis and wrap-around dust jacket art by J. Allen St. John. VG+/VG+ Appears to have some tape staining at extremities of dust wrapper and minor to top edge of book. No tape remains so we are led to believe that some sort of protector was taped on at some point. Zeuschner, #669. (Inv. 3715.) — 85.00

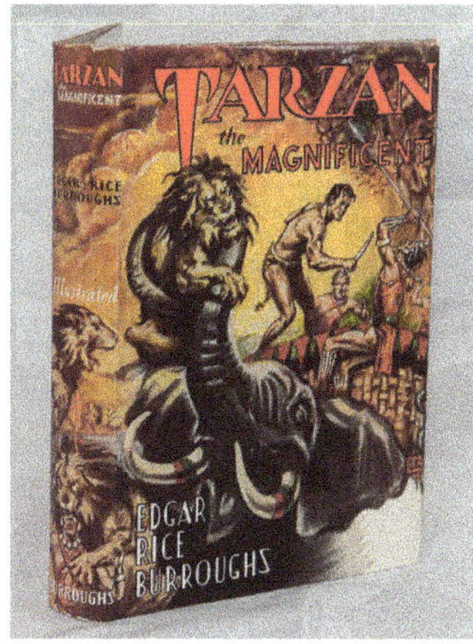

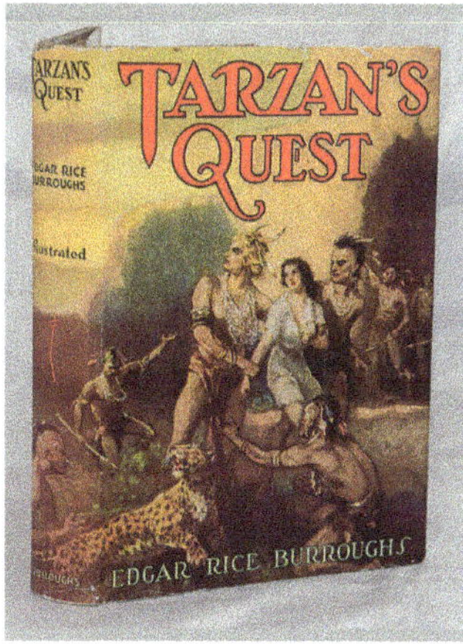

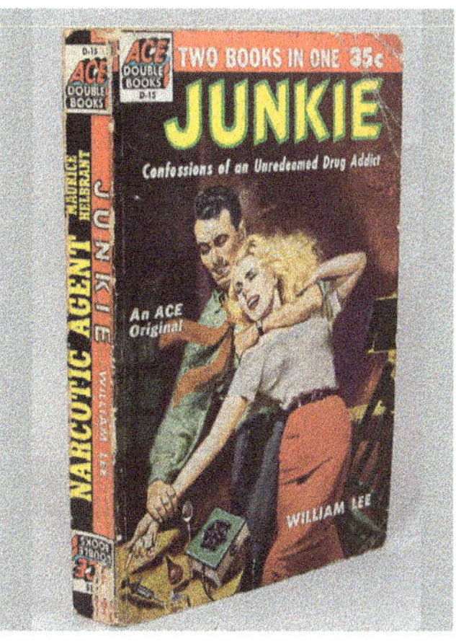

Tarzan the Magnificent   **Tarzan's Quest**   **Junkie**   **Stories of Your Life**

Burroughs, Edgar Rice.
Tarzan Lord of the Jungle.
1928 (reprint edition 1948-1953.) Endpaper maps, front board illustration and title page decorations are by Rafael Palacios. Bound in green boards with illustration and lettering in black. Dust jacket flap has the publisher's price of $1.00. Fine in NF dust jacket, illustrated by C. E. Monroe, Jr., with mild edge wear. Zeuschner 689 (Inv. 3712.)   85.00

Burroughs, Edgar Rice.
Tarzan the Invincible.
Tarzana, California: Edgar Rice Burroughs, Inc. Publishers, 1931 (this edition 1948.) Frontispiece and DJ cover with illustration by Studley O. Burroughs, original tan boards, front and spine panels stamped in blue, top edge stained blue. Later edition. About fine in a very good DJ with wear to folds, some minor creasing to front panel. Zeuschner 736. (Inv. 027.)   95.00

Burroughs, Edgar Rice.
Tarzan the Magnificent.
Tarzana, California: Edgar Rice Burroughs, Inc. Publishers, 1939 (1948 reprint.) A fine copy in a near fine dust jacket. Grey boards with dark blue lettering. Zeuschner 750. (Inv. 3603.)   150.00

Burroughs, Edgar Rice.
Tarzan the Terrible.
New York: Grosset & Dunlap, 1921 (1949 reprint). Grosset & Dunlap. Cloth; near fine. Dust Jacket near fine with very mild wear to extremities in black decorative binding with Tarzan on elephant on front board, map of Africa endpapers. Art by Monroe with the 100100 flap price. Zeuschner 761. (Inv. 3709)   65.00

Burroughs, Edgar Rice.
Tarzan Triumphant.
1932 (1948 reprint) , Tarzana, CA: , 1948. 8vo. 318 pp. Beige boards, blue lettering, w/ d. J. Cover art by Studley O. Burroughs. Slight edge wear, couple very slight closed tears, still NF/VG+ with former ownership stamp on ffep. Early Burroughs edition of this Tarzan title published under the author's imprint. Zeuschner 788. (Inv. 017.)   85.00

Burroughs, Edgar Rice.
Tarzan's Quest.
Tarzana: Edgar Rice Burroughs, Inc. 1936 (reprint edition 1948) Grey boards with blue lettering, FN/VG+ with lite wear to extremities. Zeuschner 798. (Inv. 3608.)   150.00

Burroughs, Edgar Rice.
The Warlord of Mars.
New York: Grosset & Dunlap [1919] 1920. The frontispiece is black-and-white, and is a reproduction of the color dust jacket cover. The copyright information on this reprint shows only information as to the first printing by McClurg, in 1919, although this G&D edition was published in cir 1920-1923. Three ERB titles on back panel with lists of Zane Grey and Jack London books also. Tan cloth with black lettering. Wrinkling to spine cloth and general wear to book and dust jacket, VG-/VG-. Zeuschner 296. (Inv. 033.)   75.00

[Burroughs, William S.] William Lee
Junkie
New York, Ace Books Inc. 1953. First edition, 16mo. Original wraps. Some creasing to both covers, mild spine abrasion, pages have typical age toning. About VG condition and better than many we have seen. William S. Burroughs first book. An Ace double D-15 backed with Narcotic Agent by Maurice Helbrant. (Inv. 4509.)   550.00

Chiang, Ted.
Stories Of Your Life.
Tor Books, 2002. Hardcover. Condition: Fine. Dust Jacket Condition: Fine. 1st Edition. Spine ends lightly pushed. Appears unread. First printing of first edition with complete number line (1-10). Small black remainder dot on top of text block. The basis for the movie Arrival. (Inv. 4501.)   375.00

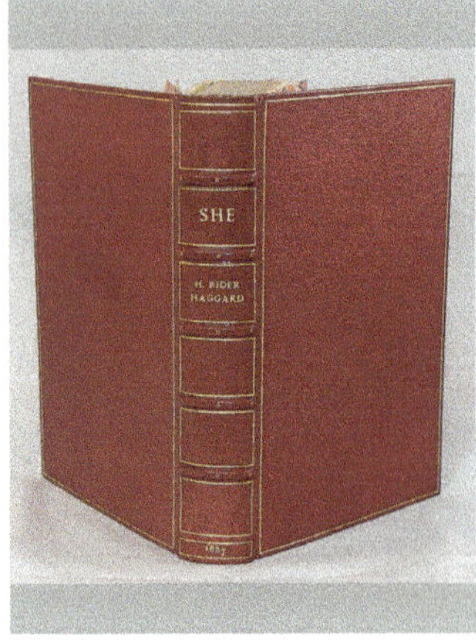

A Scanner Darkly	**She**	**The Man Who Sold the Moon**	**Puppet Masters**

[DE MILLE, James]
A STRANGE MANUSCRIPT FOUND IN A COPPER CYLINDER.
London : Chatto & Windus, 1888. First British edition : with advertisements dated 1887 and possibly pre-dating the New York edition
published in 1888. A posthumously published novel from the Nova Scotian professor of classics and fantasy writer - lost world in a
volcanically heated Antarctic, lost races of prehistoric people, plants and animals, and an utterly reversed moral order - "the outstanding
example of the lost race subgenre" (Barron). Crown 8vo (19cm). [2], viii, (292) + 32pp advertisements dated December 1887. Nineteen
plates by Gilbert Gaul (1855-1919). Original pictorial cloth in a design of sea-monster, copper cylinder, etc; spine just a
touch darkened; faint wear and mild rubbing at extremities; some light spotting to prelims, but otherwise very good. (Inv. 3679.)   500.00

Derleth, August.
Night's Yawning Peal.
Sauk City]: 1952. First edition, signed by the author on the front free endpaper. Book is very good plus with pushing to crown and foot
of spine in a very good dust wrapper with some tape repairs to verso and some chipping. 4,500 copies printed. (Inv. 4161.)   200.00

Derleth, August.
Thirty Years of Arkham House 1939-1969. August Derleth. Thirty Years of Arkham House 1939-1969. Sauk City: 1970. First edition.
Fine book is tight and sturdy in near fine dust wrapper with some very mild stain spots. Print run of 2,000 copies. An essential reference
work for the Arkham House collector or dealer. (Inv. 4162.)   50.00

Dick, Phillip K.
A Scanner Darkly
Advance review copy with slip laid in. New York, DoubleDay & Co Inc. First edition with G51 gutter code to page 216. Tan boards
with black lettering. Spine ends very slightly pushed, previous owners stamp to front past down & erasure mark to ffep. A near fine copy
in fine dust jacket with Doubleday review copy slip laid in dated January 21 1977. A movie based on this book was released in 2006.
"An affecting, powerful novel." (Anatomy of Wonder, Barron 2004.) (Inv. # 4510)   1,000.00

Haggard, H. Rider (Sir Henry Rider)
She: A History of Adventure.
London: Longmans, Green & Co., 1887. First edition: the so-called "first issue" with all the misprints noted by Scott and Whatmore –
although these would appear to be common to the whole of the edition. Endlessly reprinted ever since and the basis of at least eight
film versions: in Margaret Atwood's phrase, Ayesha (She-Who-Must-Be-Obeyed) has become "a permanent feature of the human
imagination". Crown 8vo (186 x 114mm). [viii], (318) , [ii]pp. Two color plates. Bound in a smart later (late twentieth-century) full
crimson morocco, banded and gilt, by Bayntun-Riviere of Bath; all edges gilt; marbled endpapers; original decorative cloth gilt bound
in at rear; a few slight and minor marks, but a very good and handsome copy. (Inv. 3681.)   1,200.00

Hamilton, Edmond
Collected Captain Future, Volume One.
Haffner Press, Royal Oak, MI, 2009. First edition. Octavo, cloth. Collects the first four Captain Future adventures. Introduction by
Richard A. Lupoff. In new unread condition still in publishers shrink wrap. Seller Inventory # 4466.   325.00

Heinlein, Robert A.
The Man Who Sold the Moon.
A rare staple bound booklet published by Malian Press in Australia in 1952. An outstanding copy with just a hint of wear to the
predominately black covers. VF. From the estate of Robert Weinberg. (Inv. 4171.)   550.00

Heinlein, Robert A.
The Puppet Masters
New York. Doubleday & Company Inc. 1951 First Edition. Bookplate to ffpd, mild edge staining to top and bottom extremities
of book and dust jacket which may have been caused by perished tape, three paper pulls to top edge of jacket and one to bottom of
the back panel, text block toned. VG/VG. "An effective, if rather hysterical, invasion story, and a prime example of paranoia in
1950's sf." Nicholls, The Science fiction Encyclopedia, 1979.   900.00

Pulpwood Editor

Always Comes Evening

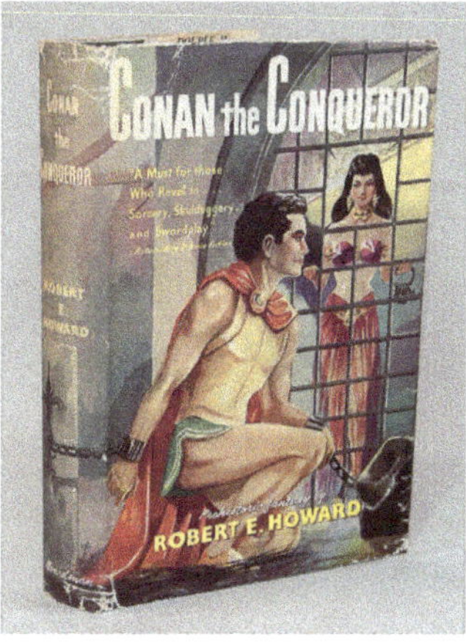

Conan the Conquerer

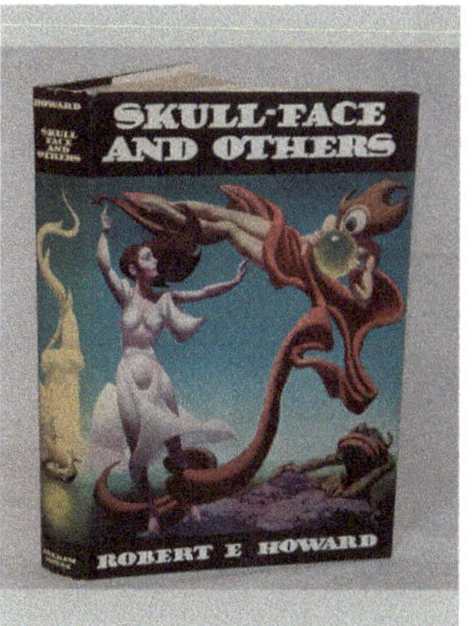

Skull-Face and Others

Herbert, Frank.
The White Plague
New York, G. P. Putnam's Sons. 1982 limited signed edition. First edition, specially bound and signed by the author, numbered 488 of 500. Slipcase shows minor wear and a very small split to one corner. Book is fine in as new condition . (Inv. 4462)   500.00

Hersey, Harold B.
Pulpwood Editor
New York Frederick A. Stokes 1937, 1937. First Edition. Very good with mild darkening where the pastedowns were glued to the covers with some off setting to the end pages. Dust jacket about very good with some loss at folds, spine ends and some tape mends. A very scarce book in original dust jacket. A nicely written and very important book for anyone who is a student of pulp fiction magazines. (Inv. 4516)   550.00

Hodgson, William Hope.
The House on the Borderland.
Sauk City: Arkham House, 1946. First edition. Mild damp staining to boards and spine of book and evident to spine of dust jacket. Some foxing to past-downs and front and rear fly leafs. VG-/VG-. 3000 copies printed so stated, actually 3,014. (Inv. 4154)   300.00

Howard, Robert E.
Always Comes Evening: the Collected Poems of Robert E. Howard
Compiled by Glenn Lord. Arkham House: Publishers, Sauk City, WI, 1957. First edition. First state binding with author and title on the spine running bottom to top, European style. 636 copies printed. A collection of Howard's poetry. One page sticks out just a tad from text block with a ¼" closed tear and couple of pages with mild bends to top corners. NF in NF dust jacket. From the estate of Glenn Lord, his file copy. (Inv. 4167.)   1,100.00

Howard, Robert E.
Conan the Conqueror.
T. V. Boardman & Company. NF/VG+. First UK edition from 1954 which is much scarcer then the Gnome Press editions. Publishers file copy with sticker to front fly stating "NOT FOR SALE Sample complete copy Proof Copy Manuscript" Brilliant silver lettering to spine, dark blue boards with very mild bumping to corners, great paper quality. Dusk jacket is unclipped with mild creasing and rubbing with tape mends to verso. A remarkable file copy and quite possible the only one like it of this high demand Howard title. From the estate of Robert Weinberg. (Inv. 4166.)   2,000.00

Robert E. Howard.
Crimson Shadows, the Best of Robert E. Howard Volume One.
Burton MI: Subterranean Press, 2009. FN/FN in slipcase. Limited signed edition signed by the artists Jim and Ruth Keegan and limited to 750 numbered copies. (Inv. 4519.)   175.00

Robert E Howard.
The Dark Man and Others
Sauk City: Arkham House,1963. First edition. Collects fifteen macabre and fantastic stories, most first published in WEIRD TALES. A fine copy in a nearly fine dust jacket with just hints of rubbing mainly to spine ends and folds. A beautiful copy. 2,000 copies printed so stated, actually 2029. (Inv. 4155.)   400.00

Howard, Robert E.
Skull-Face and Others.
Sauk City Wisconsin: Arkham House, 1946. First edition. Sm 4to, black cloth with gilt lettering. FN/NF. Small glue stain to lower right corner of rear board, very mild discoloration to pastedowns due to binding glue, trivial damp staining to spine of jacket. Unclipped price. Howard's first book published posthumous several years after his suicide, being an anthology of his work featuring such characters as Conan, King Kull, Solomon Kane and others. Jacket art by Hannes Bok, limited to 3,000 (actual 3004) copies. (Inv. 4498.)   1,600.00

Typewriter in the Sky

The Lathe of Heaven

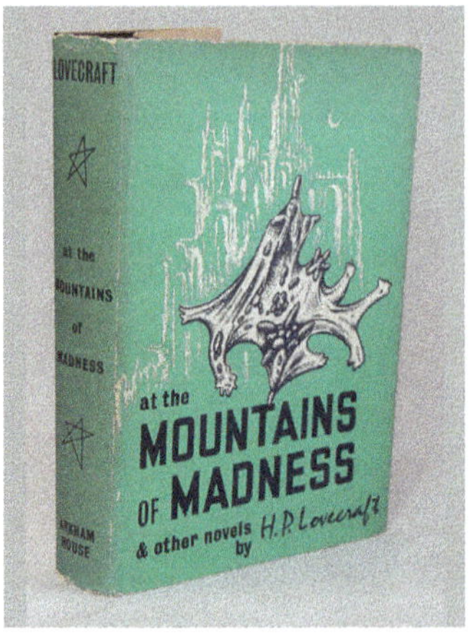

At the Mountains of Madness

Dreams and Fancies

Howard, Robert E.
The Pride of Bear Creek.
West Kingston, RI: Donald M. Grant Publisher, 1977 Condition; near fine; dust jacket near fine. More western adventures of
Breckinridge Elkins. Illustrations by Tim Kirk. Collects 7 stories.   45.00

Hubbard, L. Ron.
Typewriter in the Sky.
London: Cherry Tree Books No.409 (Fantasy Books) 1952 First UK Digest Paperback Edition, 1952. Soft cover. Fine condition. Very mild
surface creasing, clean & bright throughout. Appears to be unread. From the estate of Robert Weinberg. Cover art by Ron Embleton. (Inv. 4169.)
                                                                                                                                       175.00

Keyes, Daniel.
Flowers for Algernon.
Magazine of Fantasy and Science Fiction. Magazine of Fantasy and Science Fiction April 1959. Contains the very first published appearance
of Flowers For Algernon by Daniel Keyes. In publishers wraps near fine condition appears unread with slight mild tanning to supple paper. 100.00

Le Guin, Ursula K.
The Lathe of Heaven.
New York. Charles Scribner's Sons. 1971 First Edition, Code A-10.71 (C) Curry, Science fiction and Fantasy Authors 1979. Spine
ends mildly pushed and very slight lean. Text block sound with nice paper. White wrapper presents very well with two 1" and one ¼"
closed tears to back panel. NF/NF. Blends parallel worlds with psychology. Barron, Anatomy of Wonder 2004 II-642. "Imaginative
 territory which is generally associated with Philip K. Dick". Nicholls, Science fiction encyclopedia, 1979. (Inventory #4514.)   650.00

Lovecraft, H. P.
At the Mountains of Madness.
1964. First edition, first printing. Collects many of the major horror novels of Lovecraft, in addition to the title novel, the collection also
includes The Shunned House, The Case of Charles Dexter Ward and others. Near fine book with mild pushing to spine ends in a like
near fine dust jacket with mild wear to folds. 3,000 copy print run so stated. (Inv. #4164)   450.00

[Lovecraft, H. P.] S. T. Joshi.
Collected Essays Volume 1: Amateur Journalism. H. P. Lovecraft
New York, Hippocampus Press 2004, First edition. Sm 4to. 440pp. Black cloth with silver lettering. Fine in fine dust wrapper,
Appears unread.   300.00

[Lovecraft, H. P.] S. T. Joshi.
Collected Essays Volume 5: Philosophy Autobiography & Miscellany H. P. Lovecraft.
New York, Hippocampus Press 2008, First edition. Sm 4to. [300pp ?]. Black cloth with silver lettering. Fine in fine dust wrapper, still
sealed in original shrink wrap (Seller inventory # 4484)   200.00

Lovecraft, H. P.
Collected Poems.
Sauk City Wisconsin: Arkham House 1963.First edition. Book in fine condition with near fine dust wrapper with toning and mild
staining. 2000 copies printed so stated. (Inv. 3618.)   175.00

Lovecraft, H. P.
Dreams and Fancies.
Sauk City Wisconsin: Arkham House 1962. First edition. A collection of letters written by Lovecraft to his friends in which he discusses
his dreams, followed by eight stories. Fine with very slight pushing to spine in a near fine dust wrapper. 2,000 copy print run so stated.
(Inv. 3622.)   325.00

Lovecraft, H. P.
The Dark Brotherhood and Other Pieces.
Sauk City, Wisconsin: Arkham House 1966. First edition. Book in fine condition with fine dust wrapper with just mild pushing to foot
of spine. $5.00 unclipped jacket. 3500 printed so stated but in actuality 3460 copies printed. (Inv. 3621)   300.00

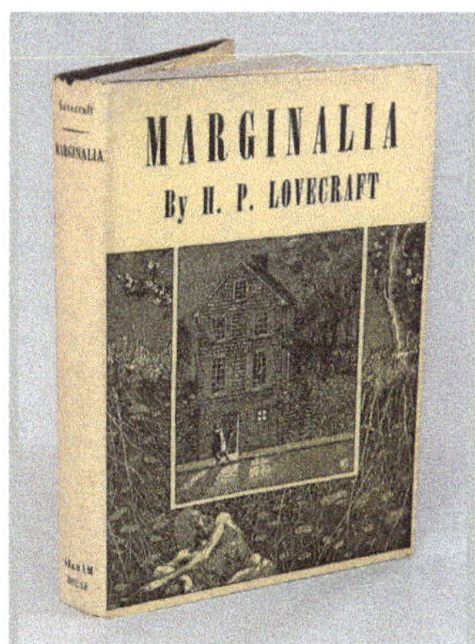

Marginalia

The Shuttered Room

Something About Cats

The Abominations of Yondo

[H. P. Lovecraft] S. T. Joshi.
H. P. Lovecraft Letters from New York S. T. Joshi.
San Francisco, Night Shade Books. 2005 First edition, sm 4to. Black cloth with silver lettering, FN/FN with just very mild bumping to spine ends, appears unread. This is the second volume in the Lovecraft letters series edited by S. T. Joshi and covers his time period of living in New York. Seller inventory #4500.   185.00

Lovecraft, H. P.
The Lurker At the Threshold.
Sauk City Wisconsin: Arkham House, 1945. First edition. A near fine copy with previous dealers sticker to front paste down in a nearly fine dust jacket with a touch of rubbing to the corner tips and spine ends. 3000 printed so stated, 3041 actual. (Inv. 3680.)   200.00

Lovecraft, H. P.
Marginalia.
Sauk City, WI: 1944. First edition. Book is VG with mild spotting to boards and spine with previous owners name to front paste down in a NF dust wrapper with mild wear to crown and foot of spine. It is a collection of Fantasy, Horror and Science fiction short stories, essays, biography and poetry by and about H. P. Lovecraft being the third collection of Lovecraft's work published by Arkham House. 2,035 copies were printed. (Inv. 4160.)   400.00

Lovecraft, H. P.
The Shuttered Room and Other Pieces.
Sauk City: 1959. First edition. Arkham House, Sauk City, 1959. Hardcover. FN/FN. Illustrated by Richard Taylor (illustrator). First Edition; First Printing. The Shuttered Room and Other Pieces by H. P. Lovecraft. First Edition, 1959. 313pp. Publisher's gilt titled black cloth; grey endpapers. Unclipped $5.00 price. Very slight pushing to head and tail of spine otherwise a wonderful copy. 2500 copy print run so stated, actual print run is 2,527 copies. (Inv. #4163)   400.00

Lovecraft, H. P.
The Shuttered Room and Other Pieces.
Sauk City Wisconsin: Arkham House 1959. First edition. 313pp. Publisher's gilt titled black cloth; grey endpapers. Unclipped $5.00 price. Binding is tight, slight bumping to head and tail of spine. Dust jacket with minor wear. 2500 copy print run so stated. (Inc. #3616)   350.00

Lovecraft, H. P.
Something about Cats.
Sauk City Wisconsin: Arkham House 1949 First Edition. Ronald Clyne (illustrator). Publisher's black cloth boards with gilt-lettered spine, gray endpapers, five inserted illustrations, including the frontispiece portrait, 306pp, in first printing dust jacket with the 3 dollar price on the front inner flap. Book in Fine condition with just the slightest of bumping to spine. Minor toning to fine dust wrapper. 3000 printed so stated. (Inv. 3617.)   300.00

Merritt, A.
Burn Witch Burn.
Neville Spearman, London, 1955. Hardcover. First British edition with red cloth boards and spine stamped in black, 223 pps. A fine unmarked copy, some toning to front and rear flys in jacket that has some paper perished from crown with mild wear to extremities.   85.00

Smith, Clark Ashton.
The Abominations of Yondo
Sauk City Wisconsin: Arkham House, 1960. FN/NF. 1st Edition. Collection of Fantasy/Horror stories. Two thousand copies published so stated. Near fine in near fine jacket; very minor rubs to jacket and spine ends. (Inv. 3682.)   200.00

Smith, Clark Ashton.
Genius Loci
Sauk City. Arkham House, 1948. First Edition. Near Fine in Near Fine dust jacket. Previous owners name on front paste down. Slight dulling to spine title. 228 pages collecting 15 stories, most reprinted from Weird Tales. 3000 copies printed so stated.   225.00

| **Spells and Philtres** | **Tales of Science and Sorcery** | **Jumbee** | **The Secret of Saturn's Rings** |

Smith, Clark Ashton.
Spells and Philtres.
Sauk City: 1958. 519 copies printed. Arkham House, First edition. Octavo, jacket art by Frank Utpatel, cloth. Poetry. A fine copy with just a hint of rubbing to book spine and very mild rubbing to foot of spine in a fine gorgeous looking dust jacket. Not priced-clipped.   850.00

Smith, Clark Ashton.
Tales of Science and Sorcery.
Sauk City, Wisconsin: Arkham House 1964 First edition. Collects fourteen stories and a memoir by E. Hoffmann Price. Fine in fine dust wrapper with just a hint of rubbing to spine. 2500 copies printed so stated though some sources indicate the run was 2482. (Inv. 3620.)   225.00

Stevens, Dave.
The Rocketeer.
Graphitti Designs, 1985. Hardcover. FN/NF condition. Limited to 1,000 Copies. Signed by Dave Stevens. Bound in brown textured cloth with gold lettering, decor to front and spine. Unclipped dust jacket with very mild edge wear to extremities.   275.00

Taine, John.
The Crystal Horde
Reading, Pennsylvania: Fantasy Press 1952. First edition. Orange boards with gilt lettering to spine. Spine ends slightly pushed, mild wear to two bottom corners in great looking dust jacket, NF/FN. Originally appeared in Amazing Stories Quarterly in 1930 as "White Lily [as] an account of alien invasion reminiscent of Merritt's The Metal Monster…" Barron, Anatomy of Wonder, 2004. (Inv. 4525.)   75.00

Taine, John.
The Forbidden Garden
Reading, Pennsylvania: Fantasy Press 1947. First edition. Orange boards with gilt lettering to spine. Spine ends slightly pushed. Moderate chipping to spine ends and some wear to edges of front and back spine panels. NF/VG. Four inserted plates in b&w. "An extravagant romance…based on bizarre mutational effect" Nicholls, The Science Fiction Encyclopedia, 1979 (Inv. 4526.)   50.00

Taine, John.
Seeds of Life
Reading, Pennsylvania: Fantasy Press 1951. First edition. Orange boards with gilt lettering. Bottom of spine is gently pushed, else a wonderful copy in similar dust jacket, FN/FN. "A mutational romance first published in Amazing Stories Quarterly in 1931, in which an overdose of radiation transforms an ineffectual human into an enterprising superman…"Barron, Anatomy of Wonder, 2004. (Inv. 4524.)   75.00

Walton, Evangeline.
Witch House.
Arkham House, Sauk City, 1945. Hard Cover. Book Condition fine; dust Jacket condition fine. First Edition. First book in the Arkham House Novels of Fantasy and Terror series. This copy has been signed by the author on the title page. Limited to 3000 (actually 2949) copies. 200 pages. A sharp book with the scarce signature of the author. (Inv. 375.)   300.00

Whitehead, Henry S.
Jumbee and Other Uncanny Tales.
Sauk City: Arkham House,1944. First edition. A collection of macabre stories set in the West Indies of the early 20th century. Previous owner's book plate on front pastedown. A near fine book in very good plus jacket. Dust jacket has some rubbing to corners and mild chipping to crown of spine. 1,559 copies printed. (Inv. 4158.)   450.00

Williamson, Jack.
Darker Then You Think.
Fantasy Press, 1948. Hardcover. 1st Edition. Near fine book with slight toning to crown of spine and small spot to back cover with similar toning to dust wrapper with mild edge rubbing. (Inv. 3703.)   175.00

Wollheim, Donald A.
The Secret of Saturn's Rings.
Philadelphia, John C. Winston Company. 1954, First edition. 8vo. Authors first book and 22nd in the Winston series. Book in fine with mild pushing at spine ends, dust jacket has some edge wear most notable at foot of spine for VG condition   300.00

ANC
STARTLING
STORIES
SEPT.
25¢
EARLE
BERGEY
FEATURING
THE CYBERNETIC
BRAINS
A Novel of
Men and Machines
By RAYMOND F. JONES
THE HARPERS OF
TITAN
A Captain Future Novelet
By EDMOND
HAMILTON
A THRILLING
PUBLICATION

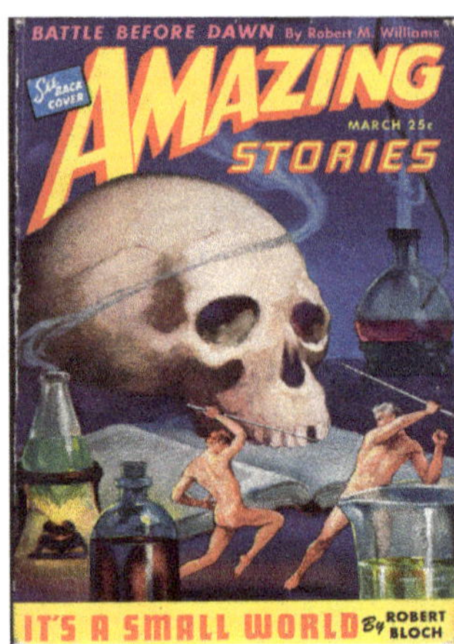

Amazing Stories 1944 Mar

Amazing Stories 1950 Feb

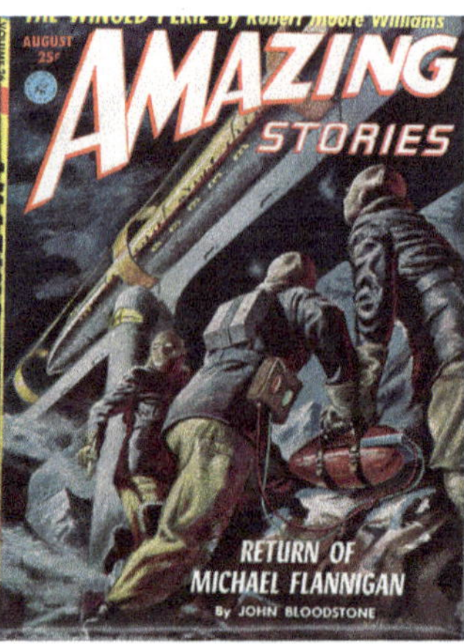

Amazing Stories 1952 Aug

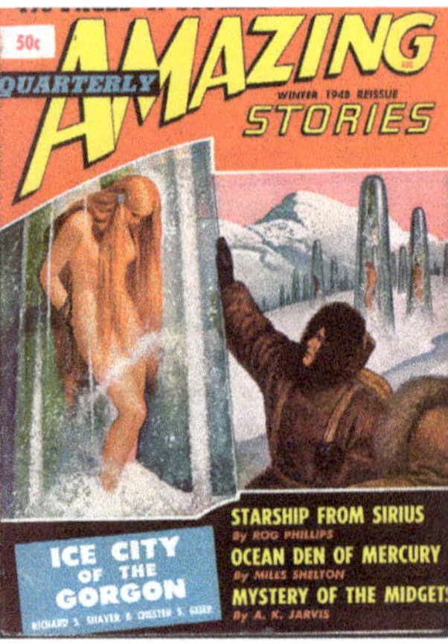

Amazing Stories Q 1948 Win

The Story of the Yakima Pedigree Pulp Collection

In the late 1990's, I put on two pulp and paper conventions at the Seattle Center; which is where the Space Needle is located. It was at one of these shows that a guy struck up a conversation with me and told me of a pulp collection. He told me how great the condition was and how beautiful the paper was, unread perhaps. I wasn't convinced at first, as people had been using the same kind of descriptors for decades on how great their collections were and almost without fail overstating the virtues of them. He was from Yakima, a city on the other side of the Cascade Mountains in eastern Washington. To go there and back would be a day of my life to an area I really didn't care much for. Still something nagged at me that I needed to go check it out. What if…it were true?

Sometime later I grabbed some money, my check book and headed out. I really didn't hold out much hope of it being as he described but if I didn't go and it turned out to be true that would haunt me for years to come.

When I got there he took me into a back room and turned me loose. The pulps were in many homemade wood boxes. After going thru about half of the first box it started to dawn on me that I may just be looking at one of the finest condition pulp collections that had ever been discovered!

After going thru several of these boxes I was almost shaking at what was before me. Most of the pulps were in immaculate unread condition. Not just nice paper but truly white. I really don't think they could have been any whiter on their publication. I started making mental comparisons to the Mile High/Edgar Church collection of comics. Surely this had to be the "Mile High" pedigree of pulps!

I don't remember a lot of the details of our negotiations, it being a bit of a blur after all these years. I do remember that it didn't take too long of a time and we were able to reach a deal fairly quickly. There were a lot of pulps there; guessing 900 to 1,000 and I didn't have enough money to buy the whole collection at once. After settling on a per issue price I went back to stack up the ones that were the most important to me.

That day I believe I walked away with the following: A complete *Planet Stories*, about 100 *Shadow* pulps, all the weird tales, which wasn't a lot, and then I cover picked the rest of the titles. There were some *Dime Mystery* and a few *Horror or Terror Tales* though at this point I don't remember how many. I basically spent every last dime I had on these with the hopes of coming back for the rest; which I did.

I really wished I had kept better records so I could give you "the facts" but we will have to settle for my best guesstimate at this point. There were a lot of science fiction titles, in fact I would say that it was probably close to 75% sf. The collection of the high grade pulps started around 1939, just in time for him to pick up a stellar copy of *Planet Stories* #1. There were huge runs of *Thrilling Wonder Stories, Amazing Stories, Startling Stories, Famous Fantastic Mysteries, Fantastic Novels, Future, Marvel Stories, Science Fiction Quarterly, Unknown, Out Of This World* (both), *Comet, Cosmic Stories, Super Science Storie*s, and many others. The *Fantastic Adventures* started with #1. I would say that from 1939 to 1953 it was close to being the entire output of science fiction titles for that time period. Except there were no *Astounding Stories*. What happened there?

Well, they ended up with someone else in Yakima. After tracking them down I made yet another trip to Yakima and negotiated a different deal with this other person and bought all the *Astounding*'s he had.

When I bought it the condition was just so striking I knew I had something special and it needed to be treated as such. Creating a pedigree out of it made a lot of sense especially since it met the two major criteria's at the time. First it was bought by one person new off the racks as they came out and two, the condition needed to be exquisite. This collection met both with flying colors. I felt it vitally important to be able to prove the pedigree to future buyers so I came up with a "Certificate of Authenticity". I signed and dated each one with the name and date of the pulp. As long as this certificate is with the pulp it means it is from the Yakima pedigree collection and it was sold by me.

I sold the *Planet* run but did keep an issue or two, including my favorite cover of the run; the Summer 1948 issue of a girl in a test tube type contraption. I also kept a few of the really great (in my opinion) *Startling Stories* covers. For instance the spring 1945 issue of the robot from *Captain Future* battling a dragon with a space babe in the background. Another is the "flame girl" cover by Earl Bergey from September 1950. One of my all-time favorite science fiction pulp covers is another *Captain Future* cover from January 1950. It features the robot clutching a space babe in a protective stance with a ray gun blasting a foe off cover. To me it's very iconic of the science fiction pulps: robot, ray guy and space babe. The only thing missing is a rocket ship. By the way, this was later "swiped" for a Vampirella cover.

As soon as I made the Yakima's available they started to sell very briskly. Discerning collectors who had been buying pulps for a long time realized just how special they were. When I first started showing them around people were almost at a loss for words at first. Many had never seen anything like it before. One collector actually flew in from out of state to purchase some. Some went to a collector in Japan. The Shadows were also brisk sellers going to several people.

Dime Mystery 1944 May

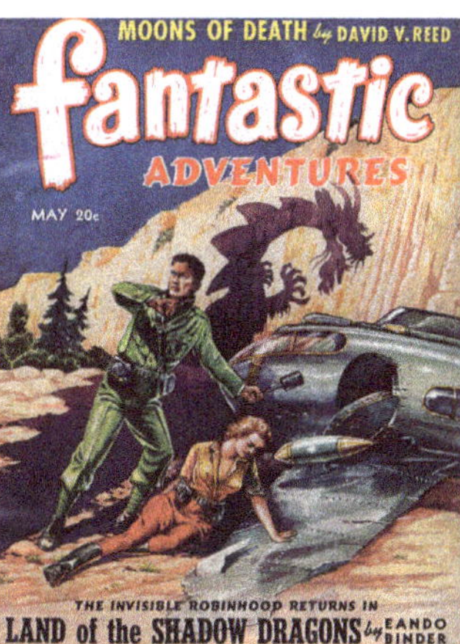

Fantastic Adventures 1941 May

Fantastic Adventures 1942 July

Horror 1937 Oct

The collection went way back before 1939. There were a lot of earlier issues in average condition prior to this. I think what happened here is that the original owner started buying them new in 1939, but also sought out back issues to fill in the runs that he liked and he bought those used. There were some earlier issues of *Astounding* and *Amazing Stories* I remember in particular. These would not have the "pedigree" clout as the others and when I included a certificate with them I would cross out the phrase "is deemed as one of the finest copies of this particular pulp in existence." Even without the high condition, many of these still had the nice paper due to how he stored them. There were a very few duplicates but not many. The collection came on the market as the result of his estate being settled. He passed away sometime in late 1990's I assume. I never knew his name.

Part of the collection was featured in the last print catalogue I did back in 1999. It was my 30th anniversary catalog of being in the business and was also my 30th catalogue. It featured a brief write up on the Yakima collection along with 24 b&w covers. Now we have come full circle to this 50th Anniversary catalogue. To celebrate I have pulled a few Yakima's out of the vault that I have been holding onto since I bought them together with a few I have re-bought along the way. Many of these have never been offered for sale or have been off the market for 20 years. All are with original certificate of authenticity issued when first sold with white paper and unread type condition.

Yakima Pedigree Pulps

Amazing Stories
1944 March . Yakima pedigree with certificate. Classic skull cover by J. Allen St. John. Small chip off crown of spine, mild wear
to extremities, large 210 page issue, FN.   750.00
1950 February. Yakima pedigree with certificate. GGA cover by Robert Gibson Jones. Mild fold to top left of back cover, slight loss
of paper at spine FN+.   450.00
1952 August. Yakima pedigree with certificate. Walter Popp cover art. Smudge and couple of small closed tears to bc, cover a bit
askew due to bindery flaw, not an after-market flaw. FN+.   450.00

Amazing Stories Quarterly
1948 Winter. Yakima pedigree with certificate Nude cover. Full spine with very small tear toward the back cover with the Yakima
white paper. There were very few of the quarterlies in the collection and this is the first one I have offered for sale in
twenty years. These are almost unheard of in high grade, FN/VF.   1250.00

Dime Mystery Magazine
1944 May. Yakima pedigree with certificate. Gloria Stoll cover art. VF-.   650.00

Mystery Magazine
1940 January. Yakima pedigree with certificate. Robert Stanley cover art. **Norgil the Magician** story by Walter Gibson. Small
smudge at the "s" in Mystery which could be a production flaw. VF-.   650.00

Famous Fantastic Mysteries
1939 Sept-Oct, #1. One of the few lesser graded Yakima's. Covers dingy, few small tears to over hangs, paper quality is cream but it
still has the Yakima scent and is guaranteed to have come from the collection, with "one of the finest known copies"
crossed off on certificate.   250.00

Fantastic Adventures
1941 May. Yakima pedigree with certificate Mild crease to top right corner which does not break color, FN.   400.00
1942 July. Yakima pedigree with certificate J. Allen St. John front cover and Frank R. Paul back cover art.
Store stamp to cover; FN.   450.00

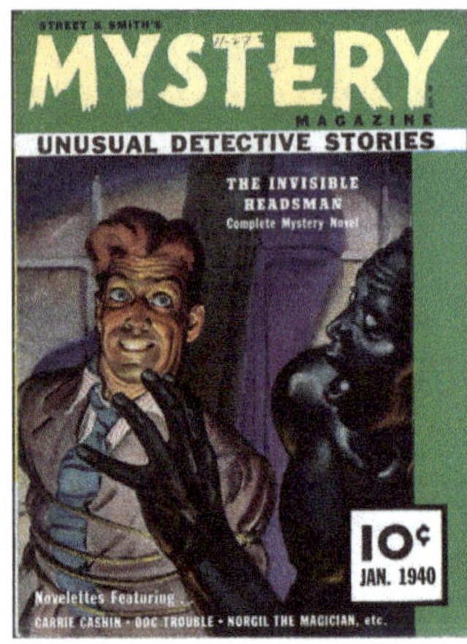
Mystery 1940 Jan

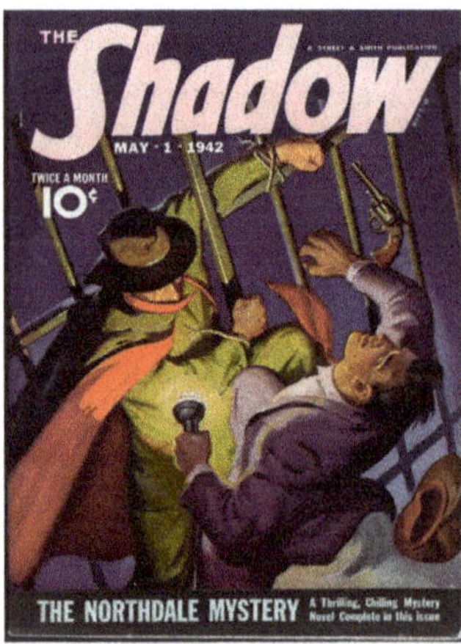
Shadow 1942 May 1

Shadow 1942 June 15

Startling 1951 Jan

Horror Stories
1937Oct/Nov. Yakima pedigree with certificate. Bondage torture cover. One of the very few of this title in the Yakima collection. A very few small tears and creases to overhangs, FN/VF.   1,500.00

Shadow
1942 May 1. Yakima pedigree with certificate Small crease to lower right corner does not break color, FN/VF with white paper.   500.00
1942 June 15. Yakima pedigree with certificate. Mild handling for FN/VF condition with white paper.   500.00
1943 October Yakima pedigree with certificate. White Paper. Mild handling for VF condition with white paper. With original certificate of authenticity issued when first sold. Name in pencil to upper back cover.   500.00

Startling Stories
1950 September. Yakima pedigree with certificate. Classic nude flame girl cover by Bergey. Very mild wear to extremities for VF condition. This is the very first time this particular issue has even been offered for sale.   2,500.00
1951 Jan. Yakima pedigree with certificate. Contains the Captain Future story *Moon of the Unforgotten* by Edmond Hamilton. Very light wear and mild surface crease to the right of the space man, FN+.   400.00

Thrilling Mystery Novel
1945 Nov. Yakima pedigree with certificate Few small tears mainly to over hangs, FN.   325.00

End of Yakima section

Sets and runs

All-American Fiction
The complete run including issues combined with Argosy

All-American Fiction Magazine was a publication of the Frank A. Munsey Company out of New York. This was a sister publication of their flag ship title Argosy Weekly. After the eight issue run Munsey folded it into Argosy Weekly with a "combined with the All-American Fiction Magazine" blurb under the Argosy logo on each cover beginning with the September 24 1938 issue.

The first issue of the "combo" had a huge banner across the cover art proclaiming "The Famous Writers and Best Features of All-American Fiction Now Combined with Argosy." This went on for 13 issues ending with the 9-17-38 release thus ending after three months. I don't think this changed up the offerings much, as All-American was basically the same general fiction magazine as Argosy. Munsey was probably just trying to grasp more retail rack space with the additional title.

Many famous collectible authors were represented here including Cornell Woolrich, H. Bedford-Jones, Max Brand, Richard Sale, Theodore Roscoe and others. The final issue contained part one of *Beat To Quarters* by C. S. Forester. At the end of part one there is a large blurb advertising the fact that succeeding chapters will appear weekly beginning with the September 24 issue of argosy. In order to entice readers to segue to Argosy this chapter was reprinted in the September 17, 1938 issue also and continued into the combo issues until the six part story was completed. A bit of unusual promotion I would say. $1,495.00

All-American Fiction Magazine
Nov 1937 #1 (FN), Dec 1937 #2 (VG-), Jan 1938 #3 (FN), Feb 1938 (FN), Mar-Apr 1938 (FN-),
May-Jun (int. tp. G/VG), July-Aug (G/VG), Sept-Oct (VG-),

Argosy
9-24-38(G/VG), 10-1-38 (G),10-8-38 (VG-), 10-15-38 (FN), 10-22-38 (large tear G), 10-29-38 (G+), 11-5-38 (G), 11-12-38 (G/VG), 11-19-38 (VG-), 11-26-38 (VG), 12-3-38 (VG+), 12-10-38 (G), 12-17-38 (FN),

Dusty Ayres 1934 Nov

Dusty Ayres 1934 Dec

Jungle 1944 Sum

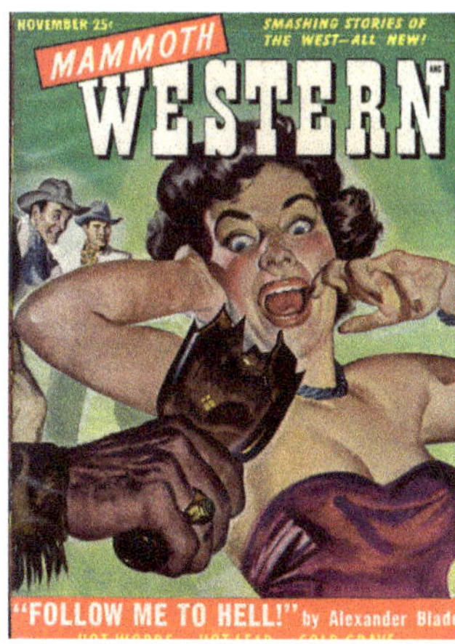

Mammoth Western 1949 Nov

Dusty Ayres and his Battle Birds - The complete twelve issue run

Popular publications started publishing the title Battle Birds with the December 1932 issue. After 19 issues the title changed to Dusty Ayres and His Battle Birds for twelve issues. Once this was done and after a gap of about four and a half years Battle Birds started back up again with a new #1 issue in 1940. The second run lasted 26 issues. One of the interesting concepts with the short twelve issue run is that the covers segued from aviation to that of science fiction for several of its issues. The classic cover of a rocket ship crashing through skyscrapers is the Dec 1934 issue.

$3,500.00

1934 July (VG+), 1934 Aug. (VG), 1934 Sept. (VG), 1934 Oct. (FN-), 1934 Nov (FN.), 1934 Dec. (VG), 1935 Jan. (VG), 1935 Feb. (VG-), 1935 Mar. (VG+), 1935 Apr. (FN), 1935 May/Jun. (FN-), 1935 Jul/Aug. (VG/FN)

Jungle Stories
A complete run of this high demand Fiction House title.

Jungle Stories featured a Tarzan type character named Ki-Gor Jungle Lord, who appeared in all 59 issues. Because of this the title was listed in the Hero Pulp Index by Robert Weinberg. The vast majority of the cover art was by Fiction House artist George Gross. George created possibly hundreds of covers for Fiction House and along with Allen Anderson helped create the "good girl art" persona that the publisher was known for. Gross was responsible for putting Ki-Gor's girlfriend Helena (they married in the sixth issue) into many vulnerable situations depicted on the covers in a mostly sexy fashion which appealed to "good girl art" collectors. Average condition is VG/FN. $4,995.00

Winter 1938 #1 (VG/FN), Summer 1939 #2 (VG), Fall 1939 #3 (VG/FN), Winter 1939 (VG), Spr 1940 (VG),Summer 1940 (VG), Fall 1940 (FR loose fc), Winter 1940 (FN-), Spring 1941 (VG/FN), Summer 1941 (VG+), Fall 1941 (VG), Winter 1941 (FN), Spring 1942 (VG), Summer 1942 (FN+), Fall 1942 (FN+), Winter 1942 (FN-), Feb 1943 (FN), April 1943 (sm tos, VG), Summer 1943 (VG-), Fall 1943 (VG/FN), Winter 1943**** , Spring 1944 (FN), Summer 1944 (FN), Fall 1944 (G/VG), Winter 1944 (FN-), Spring 1945 (FN), Summer 1945 (VG), Fall 1945 (VG/FN), Winter 1945(VG/FN), Spring 1946 (FN), Summer 1946 (VG/FN), Fall 1946 (FN), Winter 1946 (FN-), Spring 1947 (VG), Summer 1947 (SM tos, VG+), Fall 1947 (VG+), Winter 1947/48 (VG-), Spring 1948 (VG/FN), Summer 1948 (VG), Fall 1948 (FN-), Winter 1948/49 (VG/FN), Spring 1949 (FN), Summer 1949 (VG), Fall 1949 (VG/FN), Winter 1949/50 (FN), Spring 1950 (VG-), Summer 1950 (VG/FN), Fall 1950 (FN), Winter 1950 (VG), Spring 1951 (sm int tp VG-), Fall 1951 (FN) , Winter 1951/52 (VG+), Spring 1952 (FN), Fall 1952 (VG), Winter 1952/53 (VG+), Spring 1953 (VG/FN), Fall 1953 (FN-) Winter 1953/54 (VG/FN), Spring 1954 (VG-), Sheena (Stories of) Spring 1951 (G/VG).

Mammoth Western - A near complete set.

Ziff-Davis Publishing Co. entered the pulp field when it bought Amazing Stories and started publishing it with the April 1938 issue. Its success prompted the addition of Fantastic Adventures as a second science fiction title. Both titles would last in the pulp format till March 1953. They were not a big pulp publisher as compared to the likes of Street & Smith or Popular Publications, only producing 11 titles with three of them being quarterlies which existed to try to sell remaindered issues. The three quarterly (Amazing Stories, Fantastic Adventures and Mammoth Western) published no new material. They also produced four of the" Mammoth" titles; Adventure, Detective, Mystery and Western, so called as they all started off as very thick magazines. Ziff-Davis published two western titles; Mammoth Western and Mammoth Western Quarterly. Mammoth Western ran 51 issues.

Presented here are 50 of the 51 issues of Mammoth Western. Authors included are Les Savage, Jr., Wayne D. Overholser, Emil Petaja, Frank Gruber and Robert Bloch among others. Artists included H. W. McCauley, Arnold Kohn, Robert W. Tillotson, Walter Haskell Hinton and J. Allen St John (interior.) Mammoth Western had a bit of an erratic publishing schedule in its early years. Just one issue was published in 1945 before beginning an almost bi-monthly schedule for 1946 and most of 1947. With the October 1947 issue it was finally put on a monthly schedule which it adhered to till the final issue was published in January 1951. Average condition is VG. $1,750.00

1945 Sept #1 (VG-), 1946 Jan #2 (VG+), 1946 April #3 (VG-), 1946 June (VG-), 1946 August (G/VG), 1946 Oct (VG+), 1946 Dec (VG), 1947 Feb (FN), 1957 April (G), 1947 June (VG/FN), 1947 Aug (VG-) 1947 Oct (G/VG), 1947 Nov (G/VG), 1947 Dec. (sm int. Tp, G+), 1948 Jan (VG), 1948 Feb (VG-)1948 Mar (VG), 1948 Apr (VG-), 1948 May (VG), 1948 June (FN-), 1948 July (G/VG), 1948 Aug (FN), 1948 Sep (VG), 1948 Oct (VG), 1948 Nov (G/VG), 1948 Dec (FN-), 1949 Jan (G), 1949 Feb (G/VG), 1949 Mar (G)1949 Apr (VG), 1949 May (G), 1949 July (G+), 1949 Aug (G/VG), 1949 Sep (G/VG) 1949 Oct (VG+)1949 Nov (FN-), 1949 Dec (VG/FN), 1950 Jan (VG-), 1950 Feb (G/VG), 1950 Mar (VG-), 1950 Apr (G+) 1950 May (FN), 1950 Jun (VG-), 1950 Jul (G/VG), 1950 Aug (G/VG), 1950 Sep (VG), 1950 Oct (G/VG) 1950 Nov (G/VG), 1950 Dec (G/VG), 1951 Jan (G/VG)

Pete Rice 1934 Oct

Pete Rice 1936 May

Planet 1939 Win

Planet 1942 Spr

Pete Rice Magazine
A very scarce and desirable western title.

Pete Rice Magazine was one of several single character hero pulp titles published by Street & Smith. With a cover date of November 1933 for the first issue, he appeared just eight months after *Doc Savage* appeared on the stands and nine months after *Nick Carter*. The title changed to Pete Rice Western Adventures with the September 1935 issue and continued as such until the end of the run. Austin Gridley was the Street & Smith house author that the *Pete Rice* stories appeared under however most were written by a pulp author named of Ben Conlon.

In "*Cheap Thrills*", Ron Goulart describes the Pete Rice realm as "built around a cowboy with a coterie of distinctive sidekicks." In his book "*The Pulp Western,*" John Dinan considered Pete Rice more a modern detective than your typical pulp fiction cowboy, "as the crimes and circumstances surrounding them were modern and not particularly western (e.g., counterfeiting)." Nick Carr cites Link Huller as referencing telephones and cars popping up in the stories occasionally. Pete seemed to be stuck somewhere between the old west and the early 20th century.

The first 26 issues had nice striking cover art by Walter Baumhofer. Starting with the January 1936 issue, R.G. Harris took over and continued until the end of the run with the June 1936 issue. Pete Rice has traditionally been a very difficult run to put together and to obtain all 32 issues can be quite a daunting task. Average condition is about VG/FN with many high grade.

$8,500.00

Nov 1933 #1 (VG), Dec 1933 #2 (VG sm int tp), Jan 1934 #3 (VG+), Feb 1934 (FR/G), Mar 1934 (G, int tp), April 1934 (G), May 1934 (int. tp. G), June 1934 (FN/VF), July 1934 (FN), Aug 1934 (FN/VF), Sept 1934 (FN-), Oct 1934 (FN-), Nov 1934 (int. tp. G/VG), Dec 1934 (FN/VF), Jan 1935 (FN/VF), Feb 1935 (FN/VF), Mar 1935 (FN/VF), April 1935 (VG), May 1935 (G/VG), June 1935 (VG-), July 1935 (int. tp. G), Aug 1935 (VG), Sept 1935 (FN/VF), Oct 1935 (2" tear, VG), Nov 1935 (FR/G), Dec 1935 (FR/G), Jan 1936 (FN/VF), Feb 1936 (VG), Mar 1936 (FN), April 1936 (VG/FN), May 1936 (FN-), Jun 1936 (FN-)

Planet Stories
A complete run of this highly popular science fiction title.

Planet Stories have always been a perennial seller touting tremendous cover art by the likes of Allen Anderson, Kelly Freas, Virgil Finlay, Frank R. Paul, Gram Ingles and Hannes Bok among others. Although on one hand this title is graphic drive due to the cover art, it also contained a very impressive line-up of authors. Leigh Brackett, Edmond Hamilton, Fredric Brown, Theodore Sturgeon, Jack Vance and especially Ray Bradbury are all represented here. You will find such classic Bradbury titles as *The Million Year Picnic, The Golden Apples of the Sun* and *A Sound of Thunder*. In addition, there are five appearances by Philip K. Dick including his first published appearance with the classic *Beyond Lies the Wub* in the July 1952 issue.

We have sold several complete sets in the past, and single issues remain solid sellers for us. This 71 issue medium size run makes it a much more affordable option to own when compared to how much it would cost to put together runs of say Amazing Stories or Astounding Science Fiction. Average condition is about VG/FN.

$5,500.00

Winter 1939 #1 (FN-), Spring 1940 #2 (VG), Summer 1940 (#3 G/VG), Fall 1940 (VG), Winter 1940 (FN), Spring 1941 (G+), Summer 1941 (FN), Fall 1941 (VG-), Winter 1941/42 (sm tos, VG+), Spring 1942 (FN+), Summer 1942 (FN), Fall 1942 (FN+), Winter 1942 (FN-), March 1943(FN-), May 1943 (sm tos, VG+), Fall 1943 (FN), Winter 1943 (FN), Spring 1944 (sm tos, VG+) Summer 1944 (int tp, VG) Fall 1944 (FN-), Winter 1944 (sm tos, VG+), Spring 1945 (sm tos, VG+), Summer 1945 (FN) Winter 1945 (FN), Spring 1946 (VG), Summer 1946 (sm tos, VG+), Fall 1946 (FN-), Winter 1946 (FN-), Spring 1946/47 (VG/FN), Summer 1947 (VG) Fall 1947 (VG+), Winter 1947 (G+) Spring 1947/48 (G/VG), Summer 1948 (sm tos, VG+), Fall 1948 (VG/FN), Winter 1948 (VG-) Spring 1949 (VG/FN), Summer 1949 (VG+), Fall 1949 (VG), Winter 1949 (VG+), Spring 1950 (FN-), Summer 1950 (VG/FN), Fall 1950 (VG+), Nov 1950 (VG+), Jan 1951 (VG), March 1951 (VG), May 1951 (VG+) July 1951 (VG), Sept 1951 (VG), Nov 1951 (VG), Jan 1952 (VG), Mar 1952 (VG+), May 1952 (VG), July 1952 (VG-) Sept 1952 (G) Nov 1952 (VG+) Jan 1953 (VG), March 1953 (VG), May 1953 (G/VG), July 1953 (G) Sept 1953 (G/VG), Nov 1953 (VG) Jan 1954 (VG+) March 1954 (VG+), May 1954 (VG), Sum 1954 (VG+), Fall 1954 (VG), Winter 1954/55 (VG+), Spring 1955 (VG+), Summer 1955 (VG/FN)

Uncanny Tales 1939 Aug

Uncanny Tales 1939 Nov

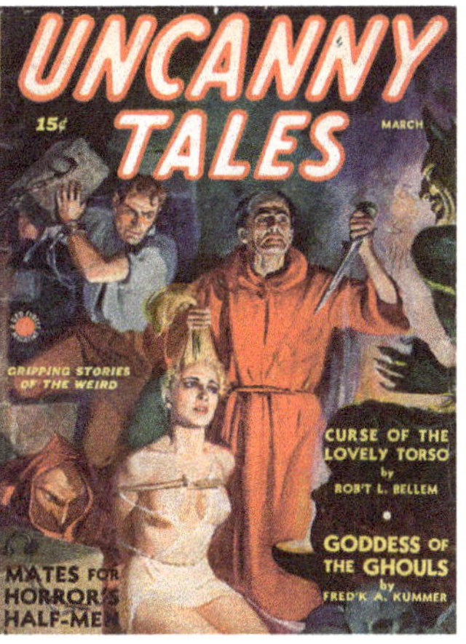
Uncanny Tales 1940 Mar

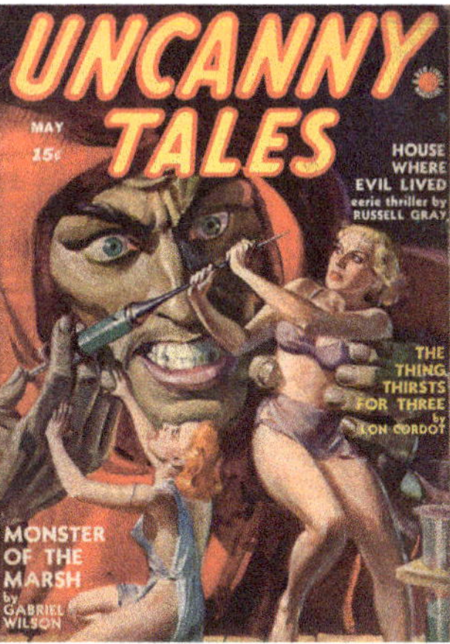
Uncanny Tales 1940 May

Uncanny Tales
A complete run of this classic weird menace title

Each cover of this short run Red Circle (Marvel/Timely) title is packed with what is the epitome of the weird menace pulp genre. Almost all covers are bondage/torture centric with more than just a little flesh showing. "There were only five issues of Uncanny Tales, but put together they offered an encyclopedia's worth of aberrant sexual behavior and assorted depravities." (Ed Hulse, The Art Of The Pulps.) This is a very high demand title and though just five issues long is still a very difficult run to put together. $2,950.00

1939 April-May. First issue. (FN-), 1939 August. (FN.), 1939 Nov. (VG/FN) 1940 March. (VG/FN) 1940 May. Mild trim, (VG/FN.)

Rangers (Of Freedom) Comics
An unbroken run issues #1 through #57

Rangers Comics was published by Fiction House Magazines and began in1941 clearly positioning itself firmly into the early days of the golden age of comics. There are many WWII covers here featuring Nazis and Japanese soldiers battling it out with Uncle Sam. In addition, bondage and torture covers were plentiful on this comic book as were on many of the Fiction House titles. The first seven issues was titled Rangers of Freedom Comics before shortening to just Ranger Comics. "It was one of the more intriguing anthologies in the Fiction House line [with a] fun, eclectic mix of high adventure features that spanned nearly every genre from war, to western, horror, jungle adventure, and some exceptionally well done humor." (Mitch Maglio, *Fiction House From Pulps to Panels, From Jungles To Space.*)

This set lacks only the final ten issues to be a complete run. All the early difficult issues are present, many in exceptional condition. Cover re-flectively is quite high on most issues. This is a title which could take many years to complete. Here you're almost done in one fell swoop.

$22,500.00

#1 Sm tp top of spine FN- 5.5, #2 FN/VF 7.0, #3 FN 6.0, #4 FN 6.0, #5 VG 4.0, #6 Sm tp VG+ 4.5, #7. FN 6.0, #8. FN+ 6.5, #9. FN- 5.5, #10. VG/FN 5.0, #11. VG+ 4.5, #12. FN/VF 7.0, #13. VG/FN 5.0,#14 VG+ 4.5, #15 VG/FN 5.0, #16 VF 8.0, #17 VG+ 4.5, #18 FN/VF 7.0, #19 FN 6.0 #20 FN 6.0, #21 VF 8.0, #22 VG+ 4.5, #23 FN 6.0, #24 VF 8.0 #25 VG 4.0, #26 VG 4.0, #27 FN 6.0, #28 FN/VF 7.0, #29 FN- 5.5, #30 VG- 3.5, #31 FN 6.0, #32 FN 6.0, #33 FN 6.0, #34 FN/VF 7.0, #35 FN/VF 7.0, #36 VG+ 4.5, #37 VG/FN 5.0, #38 VG/FN 5.0, #39 VG 4.0, #40 FN 6.0, #41 VF 8.0, #42 VG 4.0, #43 FN+ 6.5, #44 FN/VF 7.0, #45 FN 6.0, #46 VG+ 4.5, #47 VG 4.0, #48 VG+ 4.5, #49 VG 4.0, #50 G/VG 3.0 #51 VF- 7.5, #52 G/VG 3.0, #53 VG- 3.5, #54 VF 8.0, #55 FN 6.0, #56 VF 8.0, #57 G/VG 3.0.

Rangers #1

Rangers #3

Rangers #14

Rangers #25

10 Story Mystery 1942 Feb

15 Mystery 1950 April

Ace G-Man 1938 May

Ace-High 1936 Dec

5 Detective Novels
1950 Winter, #2. Bondage cover. Green Ghost reprint. Int. tp to covers, shows well, VG-.	85.00
1950 Spring, #3. Mild edge wear, NF.	40.00
1950 Fall. Lite surface creasing, VG/FN.	30.00
1950 Summer. Contains The Reptile Murders by Richard B. Sale, The Shipwreck Murders by Norman A. Daniels, VG+.	55.00
1951 Fall. Two moderate chips off extremities, G/VG.	15.00
1952 Winter. Contains Compliments Of A Fiend by Fredric Brown. General wear one three inch tear to back cover with chip missing for about very good condition with cream supple paper.	35.00
1953 Summer. Contains Death All Around Me by Norman Daniels, Murder In Florida by E. Hoffman Price. General wear and handling some small tears, VG with cream supple paper.	40.00
1953 Win. Contains *Once Upon A Train* by Craig Rice and Stuart Palmer, *Stop The Presses* by Frederick C. Davis. VG+	55.00

5-Detective Mysteries
1942 Oct/Nov, #1. General lite wear, some creasing, FN-.	200.00

10 Short Novels Magazine
1938 October, #1. Norman Saunders cover art. Beautiful condition, FN/VF.	250.00

10 Story Mystery
1943 April. Skeleton cover. Small lower left corner off, else very nice, VG/FN.	75.00
1942 February. Great skull cover, mod wear, chipping and some tears G+.	50.00
1943 March. Great atmospheric cover, VG+, Canadian printing.	50.00

10-Story Detective
1939 July. Norman Saunders cover art. General lite wear and some surface creasing, VG.	45.00
1941 May. Moderate wear and creasing, G/VG.	30.00
1943 Sept. Spine lean, mild wear to extremities, VG-.	35.00

15 Mystery Stories (Continuation of Dime Mystery)
1950 April. Great skull cover. Moderate chipping, G+.	45.00
1950 February. General lite wear, readers crease, VG.	50.00

15 Story Detective (continued from All-Story Detective)
1950 February, #1. Lite wear and creasing, FN.	95.00
1950 October. General wear and creasing, VG.	40.00

20 Million Miles to Earth by Henry Slesar.
New York: Ziff-Davis Publishing Company. Amazing Stories Science Fiction Novel 1st Edition, 1957. First Edition. The only Amazing Science Fiction Novel, A movie tie-in to the 1957 film 20 Million Miles to Earth. General creasing to cover, VG. Seller Inventory 4477.	50.00

Ace G-Man Stories
1937 Sept/Oct. Some surface creasing, edge wear, VG.	110.00
1938 July/August. Publishers file copy stamped "Not Made Ready" to first page. VF.	450.00
1938 May/June. Publishers file copy stamped "Not Made Ready" to first page. VF.	450.00

Ace-High Detective
1936 December. Keyhole Kerry story by Frederick C. Davis. Moderate wear, creasing, some chipping, G/VG.	125.00

Ace-High Magazine
1931 December 1. General lite wear and creasing, some interior tape, VG-.	40.00
1931 November 1.. Tape on spine, interior tape stains, damp staining, G/VG	40.00
1932 February 19. Story by Johnston McCulley. Mod wear, tos, G+.	35.00

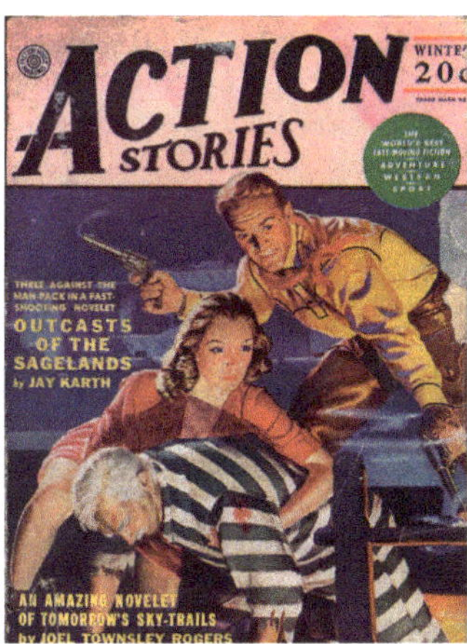

| **Action 1942 Win** | **Adventure 1922 Oct 30** | **Adventure 1926 Mar 30** | **Adventure 1935 Feb 1** |

Aces Sports
1938 August. Moderate wear, creasing and some tears with tanning paper. G+   25.00

Action Packed Western
1956 September. General wear, some scuffing to cover, VG-.   20.00

Action Stories
1939 December. Color copy front cover, no back cover. FR.   25.00
1942 June. Allen Anderson cover art. Large tear thru cover at spine repaired on verso by tape.
    From the Glenn Lord collection with certificate. G+.   25.00
1943 Winter. George Gross cover art. Mild trim, general wear and creasing to cover, VG-.   25.00

Adventure
1922 October 30. Contains part two of *The Sea Hawk.* by Rafeal Sabatini. General wear and handling, VG
    with just a hint of mild flaking. A very scarce issue.   100.00
1924 September 30. General wear and handling, for above average VG.   40.00
1925 September 1925. Contains *Days of '49* by Gordon Young. General moderate wear, G/VG.   30.00
1926 March 30. General wear and handling, VG with Lite tanning and very mild flaking paper.   40.00
1927 June. Cover art by Rockwell Kent. 2" split at foot of spine, NF with totally white supple paper.   150.00
1927 September 15. Slight spine lean and general wear and handling , VG.   30.00
1927 November 1. Contains *Shotgun Gold* by W. C. Tuttle. General moderate wear, some flaking , G+.   20.00
1928 June 1. General wear, slight spine lean, VG-.   25.00
1929 April 15. General wear, handling for about very good condition with decent supple paper.   25.00
1929 May 1. General wear, handling for about very good condition with decent supple paper.   25.00
1929 Aug 15. Contains *Boots* by Murray Leinster. General wear, handling VG.   35.00
1935 February 1. Contains *Pecos Bill Goes Hunting* by Tex O'Reilly and a great cover of Pecos Bill by Walter
    Baumhoffer. General Lite wear and handling for near fine condition with decent supple paper.   5.00
1935 March 15 Baumhofer cover art. *Hard Range* by S. Omar Barker. Mild Damp stain mainly to bc, VG.   25.00
1935 April 1 Baumhofer cover art. *Fools for Glory* by Georges Surdez. Some paper perished to top 3" of fore edge.   25.00
1936 May. Great atmospheric cover by Walter Baumhofer. General light wear, VG+.   40.00
1936 December. Contains *The Hawk Of Zaguamon* by Arthur O. Friel. Lite surface creasing, VG.   25.00
1937 February. Contains *The Devil Is Dead* by H. Bedford-Jones. Lite surface creasing, VG   25.00
1937 July 1937. Contains *West Point Gray* by H. Bedford-Jones. General Lite wear, FN.   40.00
1938 February. General light wear, FN-.   30.00
1938 August. General Lite wear, some creasing, 1.5" tear to top left corner, off white supple paper interior.   5.00
1939 May. Small chipping to lower edge, VG.   25.00
1939 August. Contains *The Dark Trail.* an RCMP Story by Allan Vaughan Elston. Some chipping VG-.   30.00
1940 April. *Low And Inside* by W. C. Tuttle, *Quantrell's Flag* pt 3 by Frank Gruber. Lite wear, handling, sl chip off l.l. corner , FN-.   30.00
1940 July. General Lite wear, some creasing, cream supple paper interior.   25.00
1941 February. General Lite wear, some creasing, few small tears, lower left corner off back cover.   25.00
1941 June. General Lite wear, some creasing, few small tears, cream supple paper interior.   25.00
1941 August. *Wagons Away.* by H. Bedford-Jones. General Lite wear, some creasing, few small tears,   35.00
1944 June. General Lite wear, some creasing, few small tears, VG.   25.00
1945 February. General Lite wear, some creasing, few small tears, Lite tan supple paper interior.   25.00
1945 April. General light wear, some creasing, few small tears, VG.   25.00
1945 May. General Lite wear, some creasing, few small tears, Lite tan supple paper interior. VG.   25.00
1945 June. General Lite wear, some creasing, few small tears, Lite tan supple paper interior. VG.   25.00
1945 Sept. General Lite wear, some creasing, few small tears, Lite tan supple paper interior. VG   25.00
1945 Nov. General Lite wear, some creasing, few small tears, cream supple paper interior. VG   25.00
1946 February. some creasing, few small tears and one 2" tear, cream supple paper interior. VG-   20.00
1946 March. Contains *Obrien and Oberov* first published work of Philip Jose Farmer. Lite wear and mild trim, FN-   300.00
1946 June. General Lite wear, some creasing, few small tears, cream supple paper interior.   30.00
1946 July. General Lite wear, some creasing, few small tears, cream supple paper interior.   25.00

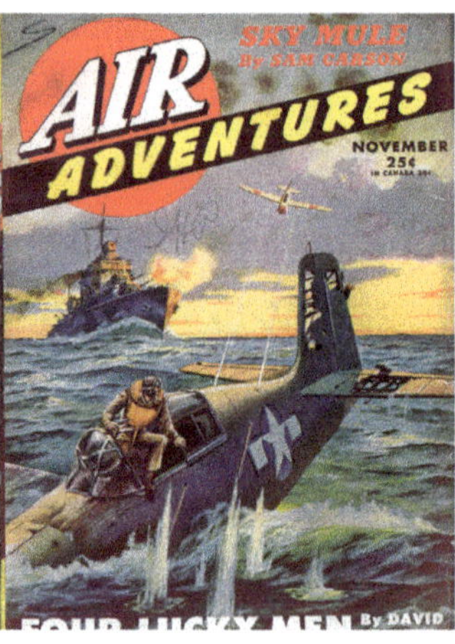

Air Action 1938 Dec   **Air Action 1940 Apr**   **Air Adventure 1945 Nov**   **Air War 1941 Win**

1947 March. General wear, damp staining to cover with Tanning supple paper. VG-	18.00
1947 October. General Lite wear, some creasing, few small tears, cream supple paper interior.	25.00
1947 November. Cover by Rafael de Soto. Contains *Border Incident* by E. Hoffmann Price. Lite wear, FN-.	30.00
1948 February. General Lite wear, some creasing, few small tears, cream supple paper interior.	25.00
1948 June. Some creasing, few small tears, cream supple paper interior.	35.00
1949 February. Contains *Red Roundup* by R. G. Emery. General wear, some creasing, VG.	20.00
1949 July. *Death is a Lap Ahead* by John D. MacDonald. General Lite wear, some creasing, small tears, VG+.	50.00
1949 August. General Lite wear, some creasing, few small tears, no back cover, G.	12.00
1951 September. General Lite wear, some creasing, few small tears, cream supple paper interior.	20.00

Air Action

1938 December, #1. General lite wear and handling with nice paper, FN.	200.00
1939 April. Bi-plane vs. machine-gun nest. Moderate creasing, some chipping, G/VG.	95.00
1940 April, #1. FN, sm tear to right edge.	150.00
1940 September, #2. Second of two issue run. Slight lean to spine, mild surface creasing, VG.	60.00

Air Adventures

1945 November. General Lite wear with tanning supple paper. Scarce later issue not listed in guide.	100.00

Air Stories

1927 August, #1 Water damage, cover loose. G.	125.00

Air Wonder Stories

1929 November, #5. Wear hole at spine, lite overall wear, VG.	125.00

Air War

1940 Fall (#1). Small tp to spine, general wear, creasing and piece of paper stuck to middle of cover. G/VG.	65.00
1941 Winter, #2. Few small Tears at lower edge of cover, FN-.	85.00
1941 Spring, #3. Contains *The Tolkien of Glory* by David Goodis. Moderate chipping, G+.	45.00
1941 Summer. Mild trim, FN-.	60.00
1941 Fall. 5" spine split, slight spine lean, G/VG.	35.00
1941 Winter (Dec) 1st page glued to front cover, G.	20.00
1942 March. Belarski cover art. Contains *Fiats Over Albania* by David Goodis. General wear, VG.	95.00
1942 March. Contains *Fiats Over Albania* by David Goodis. Some chipping, mild flaking, VG-.	75.00
1942 Summer. Contains *The Man Who Hated* by Norman Daniels. Some loss of paper to lower right corner, G/VG.	28.00
1942 Fall. General wear, some chipping, large tear to bc, G/VG.	30.00
1943 Winter (February.) Some surface creasing, some chipping, VG.	45.00
1943 Fall. Contains *The Captain's Birthday Present* by Norman A. Daniels, *Guns on Guadalcanal* by Clifford Simak. General wear, some creasing , 1.5" tear to back cover, VG.	60.00
1943 Spring. General Lite wear, some creasing ,VG+.	50.00
1943 Summer. Contains *The Fight Over The Solomons* by Lieut. Hubert Burroughs, ERB's son. FN.	100.00

All Aces Magazine

1936 April, #1. Sm tos, general creasing, sm chip of edge, G/VG.	110.00

All American Fiction

1937 Nov, #1.Contains stories by Cornell Woolrich, H. Bedford-Joes, Max Brand, others. Lite wear, FN.	175.00
1938 January, #3. String indentations to top of pulp, nice paper, VG.	75.00

All Detective

1932 November. #1. Contains *Black Brotherhood* by Hugh B. Cave. General wear, some creasing and paper perished from over hangs, scarce, VG.	200.00

Amazing Stories 1927 Nov

Amazing Stories 1928 Aug

Amazing Stories 1928 Oct

Amazing Stories 1929 Mar

All Novels Magazine
1938 Aug, #1. Saunders cover art. Beautiful looking pulp, FN/VF.   250.00

All -Story Detective
1949 October. Chips off cover edge, 10% of bc gone, G/VG.   65.00

All-Story Weekly
1915 July 17. General wear, few small tears to extremities, VG.   85.00
1920 January 24. Contains *The People of the Atom* by Ray Cummings part one. General wear and small piece off
   lower left corner, shows well with decent paper, VG.   350.00
1920 January 31. Contains *The Eye of Balamok* pt 3 by Victor Rousseau, and *The People of the Golden
   Atom* pt 2 by Ray Cummings. 3" spine split, 1" off spine, general wear, G/VG.   140.00

All Western Magazine
1933 November. Nbc, moderate wear and creasing, G.   15.00
1937 June. Norman Saunders cover art. Some surface creasing, edge wear, VG.   35.00
1937 August. Some creasing to cover and edge wear, VG.   35.00
1938 May. Some creasing to cover and mild edge trim, VG.   35.00
1943 April-June, final issue. Cream paper, FN/VF.   100.00

All-Star Love Magazine
1942 April. Faye Emerson (Warner Bros.) photo cover. Scarce. Rusty staples, center fold. Loose. G/VG   65.00

Amazing Stories
1927 November. Excess glue to inside fc, lite wear, VG.   125.00
1928 August. First appearance of space man **Buck Rogers** predating his appearances in comic strips,
   movies and TV to become an important part of American popular culture. Also the iconic jet pack cover.
   General mild wear and crease, 1" sealed tear at spine, VG+. A very scarce and high demand pulp.   1,750.00
1928 October. Classic Robot Vs. Lion Cover. General wear, store stamp, name written on cover,
   some interior tape and excess glue, G/VG.   85.00
1929 January. New York buildings being destroyed. Minor spine damage, some creasing to cover, VG.   95.00
1929 March. Second appearance of **Buck Rogers** and only cover appearance in Amazing Stories.
   Mild creasing and handling, sm tp stains to spine ends, a sound copy, VG+.   400.00
1929 July. Small label pasted above logo, else nice, lite wear, VG+.   75.00
1929 November. General wear, creasing, store stamp, G/VG.   40.00
1929 December. Top right corner off, ½" off crown of spine, general wear, G/VG.   40.00
1930 January. Moderate creasing, store stamp, VG-.   65.00
1930 February. Small label pasted above logo, general wear, VG.   65.00
1930 March. Pt. 1 of *The Green Girl* by Williamson. Scribble marks in pencil at logo, general wear, VG.   95.00
1930 April. *The Green Girl* by Williamson. Small label pasted above logo, some surface creasing, VG.   80.00
1930 May. Store stamp to cover, moderate creasing, name in ink on spacecraft, G/VG.   75.00
1930 June. General wear, some creasing, nice looking, VG+.   75.00
1930 July. Store stamp, moderate readers creasing, VG-.   55.00
1930 August. Contains Pt. 1 of *Skylark Three*. Store stamp, piece off right edge, moderate creasing, G/VG.   40.00
1930 September . Empire State Building Cover. General Lite wear and handling, VG.   95.00
1930 October. Aggressive creasing, name on cover, G.   30.00
1930 November. Brown tape to crown and foot of spine, aggressive creasing, excess glue to interior, G.   30.00
1931 January. Contains The Prince of Space by Williamson. Gorilla cover. Average wear, VG-.   45.00
1931 March. Piece off bottom edge and lower left corner (small) VG-.   45.00
1931 May. Moderate creasing, sm interior brown tape, G/VG.   45.00
1931 June. Store stamp, some creasing, sm interior brown tape, G/VG.   45.00
1931 July. Moderate creasing, interior brown tape, G/VG.   45.00
1931 August. Tos, general wear, G/VG.   40.00
1931 September. Tos, general wear, G/VG.   40.00
1931 October. General wear and handling, small brown interior tape, G/VG.   45.00

Amazing Stories 1933 Dec

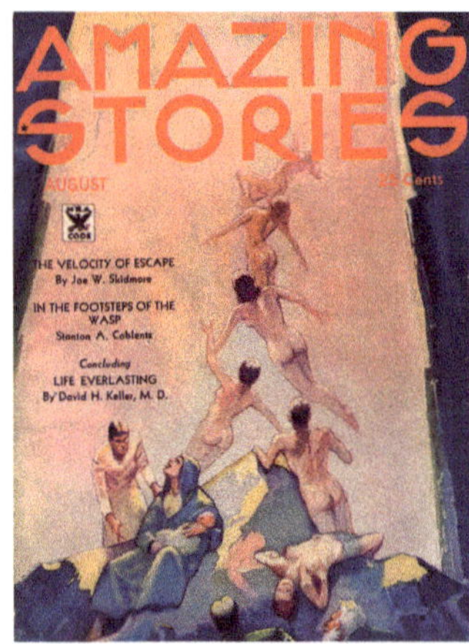

Amazing Stories 1934 Aug

Amazing Stories 1935 Apr

Amazing Stories 1936 Apr

1931 December. General moderate wear and handling, store stamp, VG-.	45.00
1932 January. Store stamp to logo, moderate surface creasing, VG-.	45.00
1932 February. Store stamp to logo, moderate surface creasing, VG-.	45.00
1932 March. Moderate wear and creasing, store stamp, G/VG.	45.00
1932 April. General wear and handling, creasing to lower right corner area, VG.	50.00
1932 May. General wear surface creasing, VG-.	45.00
1932 July. General wear, some spine damage, G/VG.	45.00
1932 August. Some loss of paper to spine, aggressive creasing to cover, G+.	30.00
1932 September. Some clear glue substance to cover, store stamp, G/VG.	40.00
1932 October. Contains *The First Martian* which is the first published appearance of Eando Binder. General Lite wear and handling and some creasing to cover, VG+.	70.00
1932 October. Contains *The First Martian* which is the first published appearance of Eando Binder. Top right corner off, VG-.	50.00
1932 November. Light wear, some creasing, cream supple paper, VG+.	60.00
1932 December. General wear, some creasing, store stamp, sm paper pull, VG-.	45.00
1933 March. Surface creasing, store stamp, VG-.	45.00
1933 April. General Lite wear and handling, VG+.	50.00
1933 April. Moderate surface creasing, VG.	40.00
1933 May. Store stamp, general wear, VG.	50.00
1933 July. Store stamp, slight loss of paper to spine tips, general wear, VG-.	50.00
1933 Aug-Sept. Store stamp, small tos, slight loss of paper to spine, creasing, top right corner chewed, G/VG.	30.00
1933 November. Amazing Stories 1933 November. Front cover has chipping and is loose, G.	15.00
1933 December. General lite wear and handling, VG+.	60.00
1934 January. *Triplanetary* by E.E. Smith pt one. Small loss of paper at foot of spine, sm tos,VG+.	65.00
1934 February. Mild loss of paper to spine, some chipping, VG-.	40.00
1934 March. Contains a reprint of *Ms. Found In A Bottle* by Edgar Allan Poe. 1.5 inch tear, VG.	75.00
1934 March. General wear and handling, 1st page stuck to fc, VG-.	40.00
1934 April. *The Gold Bug* by Edgar Allen Poe. Few small tears and creasing, VG.	50.00
1934 May. Jules Verne monument cover. 2" tear near lower right corner, VG.	50.00
1934 June. Lite wear, VG/FN.	75.00
1934 July. Small tape to foot of spine, slight lean, some chipping to extremities, VG-.	40.00
1934 July. Two small pieces of tape to spine, pulp trimmed on three sides, G+.	20.00
1934 July. Mild staining to edge of cover and few pages, shows well, VG+.	50.00
1934 August. Nude cover. Mild wear few small tears, NF.	85.00
1934 September. Lite wear, name in pencil on cover, VG+.	50.00
1934 October. Skeleton cover, General lite wear, mild surface creasing, VG.	50.00
1934 November. Dinosaur cover. Lower right corner off, VG-.	45.00
1934 December. General wear, some chipping and small tears to extremities, mild flaking, G/VG.	40.00
1935 February. Mild chipping to edge, VG+.	50.00
1935 March. General wear and handling mainly to extremities, VG+	50.00
1935 April. Zeppelin cover. General wear, some surface creasing, VG.	60.00
1935 May. General wear, surface creasing, small tip off foot of spine, VG.	40.00
1935 June. Zeppelin cover. Small tape to spine ends, VG.	50.00
1935 July. 1" tear at logo, else excellent condition, VG+.	50.00
1935 August. General lite wear, creasing mainly at extremities, VG.	40.00
1935 October. Mild surface creasing, mild wear, VG+.	50.00
1935 January. General lite wear, FN.	85.00
1935 July. General surface creasing, edge wear and small tears, G/VG.	40.00
1935 March. Moderate cover trim to three sides, G+.	20.00
1935 May. General lite wear and handling, VG+.	50.00
1935 December. ¼" by 2" off overhangs, 1" off crown of spine, G/VG.	25.00
1936 February. Small tp to crown of spine, lite wear, nice, VG+.	50.00
1936 April. Small chip off right edge, lite wear, VG.	40.00
1936 April. Small loss at foot of spine, general lite wear, VG+.	50.00
1936 June. Small chip off right edge, moderate wear, small tape to crown of spine, VG-.	35.00

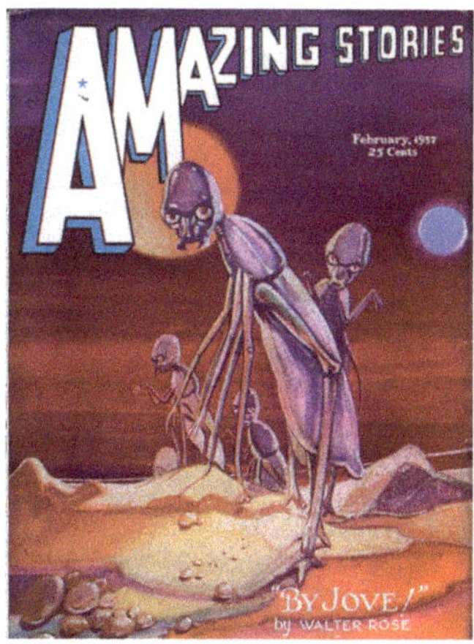

Amazing Stories 1937 Feb

Amazing Stories 1938 Feb

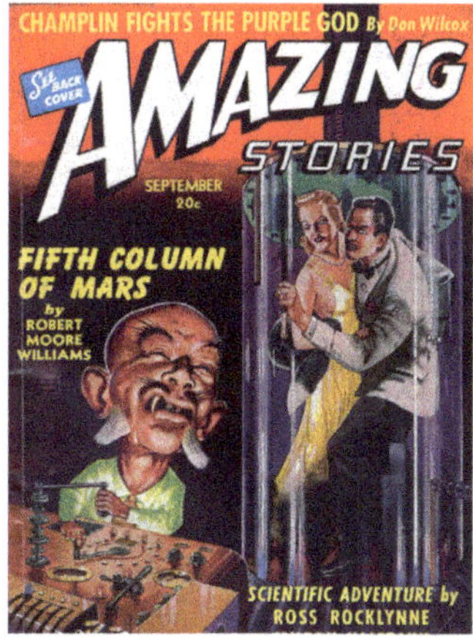

Amazing Stories 1940 Sep

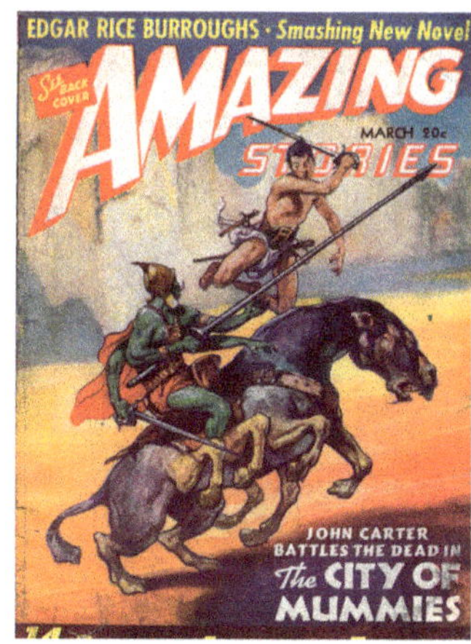

Amazing Stories 1941 Mar

1936 October. Small tape repair to right edge to cover a medium chip out, sm tape to spine tips, G/VG.	30.00
1936 August. Lite wear, FN.	85.00
1936 August. General wear, some chipping and small tears, 1.5" tear at lower spine, G/VG.	40.00
1936 December. General lite wear, FN.	85.00
1936 December. General lite wear, 3/4" closed tear at logo, Some creasing VG-.	50.00
1936 June. General lite wear and handling, VG+.	50.00
1937 April. *Shifting Seas* by Stanley Weinbaum, *The Chemical Murder* by Eando Binder. VG+.	75.00
1937 February. Very lite wear, FN/VF.	95.00
1937 February. Two pieces of brown tape to spine ends, aggressive interior tape, G+.	25.00
1937 April. Stanley Weinbaum. Moderate wear, tape on spine, small tears, G/VG.	40.00
1937 June. General wear, VG+.	75.00
1937 June. Very lite wear, FN.	85.00
1937 June. Two 1" tears at over hangs, moderate creasing, G/VG.	40.00
1937 August. General lite wear and handling, VG/FN.	65.00
1937 August. Store stamp and sticker at top right, general wear, G/VG.	40.00
1937 December. Moderate chip off lower left corner, small tears to overhangs, G/VG.	40.00
1937 October. General lite wear and very mild surface creasing, VG/FN.	75.00
1938 Feb. Lite wear, FN/VF.	85.00
1938 April. Robot cover. General wear, store stamp to cover, small lower left corner off, G/VG.	30.00
1938 April. Sm l.l. corner off, mild chipping to bottom edge, FN-.	85.00
1938 August. Contains *Secret of the Observatory* by Robert Bloch. Bondage torture photo cover. Small piece off lower left corner, surface creasing, G/VG.	50.00
1938 August. Contains *Secret of the Observatory* by Robert Bloch. Bondage torture photo cover. Moderate surface and readers creasing, G+.	30.00
1938 February. General lite wear, name stamp to back cover, VG/FN.	75.00
1938 June. One of the few photo covers of the run. General wear, surface and slight slant to spine, VG-.	35.00
1938 October. Contains *Revolution of 1950* by Stanley G Weinbaum. General wear, surface & readers crease, VG-.	45.00
1938 December. Mild chipping on bottom edge, FN-.	85.00
1939 January. 1st Adam Link. Chipping on bottom edge, 1" tape repair on bottom cvr, VG.	75.00
1939 February. Store stamp to logo, fold on upper right corner cvr, general lite wear, VG-.	35.00
1939 March. Contains the first published sf by Isaac Asimov and *The Strange Life of Richard Clayton* by Robert Bloch. Sm tear on fc, mild center crease, VG.	100.00
1939 April. Lite price marking on cvr, ding on spine, VG-.	35.00
1939 June. Contains *Microbes From Space* by Thornton Ayre and *The Radio Man Returns* by Ralph Milne Farley. General Lite wear and creasing and mild trim , VG.	40.00
1939 August. Contains *The Man Who Walked Through Mirrors* by Bloch, writing on cvr, store stamp on inside cvr, 1" tear, G/VG.	35.00
1939 September. General Lite wear and mild trim to right edge for VG+.	45.00
1939 October. Mild center crease, minor chipping on bottom edge, indentation on bottom left cvr, VG/FN.	60.00
1939 November. Dime sized paper pull at logo, writing indentations at logo, VG/FN.	60.00
1939 December. Writing indentations on upper front cover, bottom edge wear, VG/FN.	60.00
1940 January. Stain to cover, water stain back cover, top edge wear, VG.	40.00
1940 April. Small name stamp on cover, VF.	70.00
1940 June. Minor wear on top cover, mild damp staining to cover, VG+.	45.00
1940 July. Slight edge wear on cover, 2" cover split on bottom front cover, VG.	40.00
1940 August. Contains *Lost Treasure Of Mars* by Eando Binder. General Lite wear and handling , VG.	25.00
1940 September. Contains *Fifth Column Of Mars* by Robert Moore Williams. General Lite wear, VG+.	25.00
1940 October. *Raiders Out Of Space* by Robert Moore Williams. General wear, creasing and store stamp to cover, G/VG. Robot cover.	20.00
1940 November. *Revolt On The Tenth World* by Edmond Hamilton and West Point 3000 A. D. by Manly Wade Wellman. General Lite wear and handling VG+.	25.00
1940 November. Damage to upper right corner, back cover corner tear, overall general minor wear, G+.	15.00
1940 December. Adam Link. Edge wear on cover, folded tear on back cover, small piece off lower spine, VG.	60.00
1941 January. Contains *John Carter and the Giant of Mars* by Edgar Rice Burroughs. Chipping on edges, paper pull lower right corner, 1" tear on back cover, spine split on top back cover, G.	50.00

Amazing Stories 1948 May

Amazing Stories 1948 Aug

Amazing Stories 1949 Jan

Amazing Stories 1953 Aug

1941 March. Contains the John Carter story *City of the Mummies* by Edgar Rice Burroughs. Edge wear, General surface wear, VG-	115.00
1941 March. Contains *The City Of Mummies* by Edgar Rice Burroughs. General wear, surface creasing, mild trim, VG.	120.00
1941 May. Edge wear, 1" rip bottom & creases to front cover, VG	
1941 June. Contains *Black Pirates of Barsoom* by Edgar Rice Burroughs. Illustrations by Allen St. John. Damp stain at logo, slight even wear, G/VG.	75.00
1941 July. Slight edge wear, ½" tear on lower left cover, price on cover, VG.	40.00
1941 Aug. Contains *Yellow Men of Mars* by Edgar Rice Burroughs. Moderate surface creasing, in tare to right edge, slight spine lean, G/VG	75.00
1942 Jan. General wear, small lower right corner off, readers crease, VG-	30.00
1942 Feb. Contains *The Return to Pellucidar* by Edgar Rice Burroughs, moderate surface creasing, 5" spine split, small t.r. corner off. G+	40.00
1942 March. Moderate surface creasing, small tape to spline and f.c., name stamp to toc. G+	20.00
1942 May. General light wear, some chipping, VG	30.00
1942 Sept. Small spine damage, 1" ss, general wear. VG	30.00
1942 Dec. Light wear, FN-.	35.00
1943 Jan. Dinosaur cover, ½" off at foot of spine, mild chipping, VG	35.00
1943 Feb. Contains *Skeleton Men of Jupiter* by Edgar Rice Burroughs. Sm tp at logo and int., slight loss near spine, G/VG.	40.00
1943 April. Contains *Never Trust a Demon* by Robert Bloch. Light wear, some chipping to extremities, VG.	40.00
1943 June. Contains *Me the People* by Emil Petaja. General wear, some creasing, VG.	25.00
1944 Dec. Contains *Undersea Guardians* by Ray Bradburry. Light wear. VG/F	50.00
1945 Mar. Richard S. Shaver story, mild readers crease, general light wear, VG	30.00
1946 Nov. Contains *The Return Of Sathanas* by Richard S. Shaver and Bob McKenna. General wear, mild trim , VG.	20.00
1946 Sept. Richard S. Shaver story, moderate creasing, ½" tear, VG	30.00
1946 Dec. Richard S. Shaver story. Classic cover, moderate creasing, VG-	30.00
1948 August. General wear, some tape to inside f.c., G/VG.	20.00
1948 July. General wear and handling, VG.	20.00
1948 May. Contains *The Proof of the Shaver Mystery* by Ray Palmer. General wear, VG.	30.00
1948 November. Contains *Daughter Of The Night* by Richard S. Shaver. General wear, tears, creasing, G+.	15.00
1949 June.. Some creasing and few edge tears, VG-.	25.00
1949 March. Contains *The Chemical Vampire* by Lee Frances. General wear, some creasing, few edge tears, VG-.	25.00
1950 August. Contains *From These Ashes* by Fredric Brown. FN with great colors to cover.	40.00
1951 February. Chip off lower left corner, VG.	20.00
1951 July. Contains *Good Luck, Columbus* by Frank Robinson (Towering Inferno) We, *The Machine* by Gerald Vance. General wear with some chipping, VG-.	25.00
1951 May. *Planet of No Return.* by Lawrence Chandler. Loss of paper to t.r. of b.c. & many pages. Not affecting text, G+.	15.00
1952 July. General creasing, some chipping with 4" split to back cover and spine, G.	12.00
1953 August-September. Contains the Philip K. Dick story *The Commuter*. Lite wear, readers crease, VG/FN.	27.00
1953 August-September. Contains the Philip K. Dick story *The Commuter*. General wear, readers crease at spine, number 15 written in grease pen to front cover, small chip off foot of spine, VG-.	18.00
1953/1954 December-January. Contains the Philip K. Dick story *The Builder*. Moderate surface creasing and wear to cover, G/VG.	10.00
1953/1954 December-January. Contains the Philip K. Dick story *The Builder*. Lite surface creasing to cover, small piece off spine, VG.	18.00
1954 May. Contains Small Town Amazing Stories 1954 May. Contains *Small Town* by Philip K. Dick. Moderate surface creasing and wear to cover, G/VG.	10.00
1963 October. Contains the first appearance of Stand-By by Philip K. Dick.	20.00
1963 November. Contains *What'll we do with Ragland Park?* By Philip K. Dick. Moderate mild wear readers creasing with small piece off back cover, G/VG.	10.00
1966 August. Contains the first appearance of *Your Appointment Will Be Yesterday* by Philip K. Dick. Lite wear and readers crease at spine, VG+.	20.00
1966 August. *Your Appointment Will Be Yesterday* by Philip K. Dick. General Wear, readers crease and writing to cover, VG-.	10.00

Amazing Stories Q 1928 Fall

Amazing Stories Q 1929 Fall

Amazing Stories Q 1930 Win

Amazing Stories Q 1947 Win

1967 April. Contains *Small Town* by Philip K. Dick. Lite surface wear, FN-.	14.00
1967 June. Contains *The Builder* by Philip K. Dick. Lite surface wear, grease pencil mark, VG.	10.00
1967 June. Contains *The Builder* by Philip K. Dick. Moderate wear and handling, creasing, G.	5.00
1969 November. Contains *A. Lincoln, Simulacrum* part one by Philip K. Dick. Lite handling & creasing, VG/FN.	20.00
1969 November. Contains *A. Lincoln, Simulacrum* part one by Philip K. Dick. Lite handling and surface creasing, lite readers crease and two "R's" in ink near the word New, VG+.	15.00

Amazing Stories Quarterly (Series 1)

1928 Winter, #1. Fc almost off and bc off, moderate wear, chipping and tears, FR.	75.00
1928 Spring. Nbc, spine damage, lower right corner off, FR.	35.00
1928 Summer. Moderate wear, creasing some paper perished from spine and bc, G.	75.00
1928 Fall. Classic giant ant cover. Nbc, general wear, G.	95.00
1929 Winter. Tears, tos, partial spine paper perished, G.	60.00
1929 Spring. Tears, chipping to bc, partial spine paper perished, G.	60.00
1929 Summer. Moderate wear, tos, store stamp, FR.	35.00
1929 Fall. General wear mainly at extremities, some creasing, VG-.	95.00
1930 Winter. Contains *White Lilly* by John Taine. General lite wear some creasing, VG-.	95.00
1930 Spring. General mild wear 1" ss, VG.	125.00
1930 Summer. Contains *The Voice of the Void* by John Campbell, Jr. Bc loose, general wear, creasing, G.	50.00
1930 Fall. Contains *The Black Star Passes* by John Campbell, Jr. Moderate wear, chipping and creasing, G.	50.00
1931 Winter. Damp staining to book, int. tp, armature repair to right edges of covers, G.	35.00
1931 Spring. Contains *Islands of Space* by John Campbell, Jr. Moderate wear, creasing, chipping, G.	50.00
1931 Summer. Moderate wear, creasing some chipping, G.	35.00
1931 Fall. General wear, some chipping and creasing, G/VG.	60.00
1932 Spring/Summer. Lg pobc, moderate wear, FR.	25.00
1932 Fall/Winter. Moderate wear, creasing, tears, int tp, FR.	25.00
1933 Spr/Sum. General wear, writing to toc page, G/VG.	65.00
1933 Winter. General wear, store stamp, G/VG.	65.00
1934 Fall. Final issue. General wear, surface creasing, some tears, G+ .	50.00

Amazing Stories Quarterly (Series 2)

(Note: Due to the size these are rarely encountered in higher then low grade condition. See the Yakima Section for a Steller copy.)

1941 Sum, #3. Tape on spine, no back cover, g.	30.00
1941 Win. No back cover, chipping, G.	30.00
1941 Spr. Moderate wear and creasing, G/VG.	45.00
1941 Spr. Fc almost loose and bc is loose, G.	30.00
1942 Sum. Moderate wear, creasing, G/VG.	45.00
1943 Spring. 720 pages! General wear, chipping, G/VG.	55.00
1943 Spring. 720 pages! Fc loose, no back cover, moderate chipping, G.	35.00
1947 Win. 528 pages. The Shaver Mystery. General wear, creasing, VG-.	50.00
1948 Spring. 528 pages. General wear and creasing mainly to extremities, VG.	60.00
1948 Spring. 528 pages. General wear, moderate chipping, G/VG.	45.00
1948 Spring. 528 pages. Aggressive pieces missing form cover, FR.	20.00
1948 Sum. 528 pages. Tos and fc edge, moderate chipping, G.	30.00
1948 Win. 496 pages. Nude cover. Tos, moderate interior tp, G+.	35.00
1949 Spr. 456 pages. 3" tear to cover, aggressive chipping to edges, G.	30.00
1949 Spr. 456 pages. Large tear and hole to cover, FR.	20.00
1949 Sum. 456 pages. Dinosaur cover. No back cover, 3" tear to right edge, G.	30.00
1949 Win. 432 pages. Top right and left corners off, G.	30.00
1950 Spr. 480 pages. Damp staining to back cover, 3" closed tear to fc, shows exceptionally well, VG.	60.00
1950 Fall. General wear and creasing, G/VG.	45.00
1950 Sum. Piece off spine, general wear, some chipping, G/VG.	45.00

American Eagle 1942 Sum

American Eagle 1942 Fall

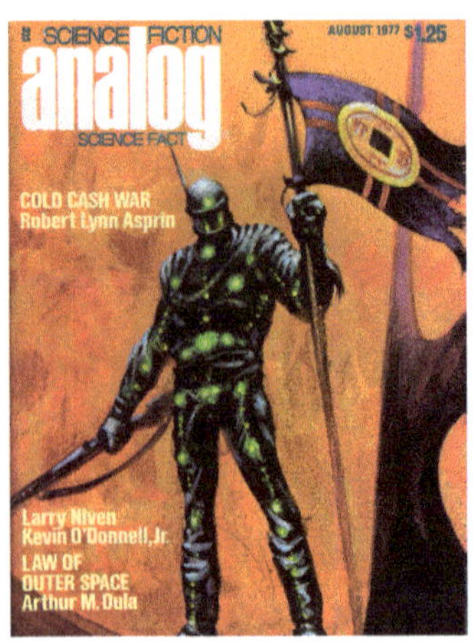

Analog 1977 Aug

Argosy 1895 Oct

American Eagle (Formally The Lone Eagle)

1941 August. 1st issue under this title. Moderate surface creasing, some chipping to edges, G/VG.	55.00
1942 April. F.c almost detached, trim, G.	20.00
1942 Summer. Mild readers creases, near white paper, VG/FN.	65.00
1942 Fall. General wear, surface creasing, VG-.	40.00
1949 Spring. British edition. Lite wear, mild readers crease, VG+.	40.00

Analog

August 1977. Contains the 1st publication of Orson Scott Card's novelette Ender's Game. VF.	200.00
August 1977. Contains the 1st publication of Orson Scott Card's novelette Ender's Game. General lite wear, mild readers crease at spine, VG.	60.00

Argosy (Argosy All-Story Weekly, Argosy Weekly)

1889 Apr 20. VG/FN	85.00
1890 Dec 6. FN-	95.00
1890 Dec 6. Staining to cover. VG	65.00
1890 Dec 13. VG/F	95.00
1891 Jan 10. Tape to cover, VG-	75.00
1891 Jan 17. Chipping to edges, VG	75.00
1891 Jan 24. VG/F	95.00
1891 Jan 31. VG/F	85.00
1891 Feb 7. Tos, VG-	75.00
1891 Feb 21. VG/F	95.00
1891 Feb 28. Spine split, VG-	75.00
1891 Mar 14. VG/F	95.00
1891 Mar 21. VG/F	95.00
1891 Apr 18. Spine re-glued, VG-.	65.00
1891 May 2. VG+.	85.00
1891 May 30. Staining to cover, VG.	75.00
1891 May 8. Small tos, VG.	75.00
1895 Feb. General wear, some loss at spine and nbc with exceptional off-white supple paper.	75.00
1895 Oct. Loss of paper at spine, bc loose, fc almost loose, exceptional off-white supple paper.	75.00
1894 Oct. Top right corner off, small tape to edge, VG-.	75.00
1894 Nov. Large top right corner off, some spine damage, chipping, G+.	60.00
1895 June. General light wear, VG.	85.00
1895 Nov. Moderate wear, some staining to cover, 1" paper perish from spine tips, G.	35.00
1896 Mar. General wear, some spine damage, G/VG.	55.00
1896 April. General wear, some loss of paper at spine, VG with exceptional off-white supple paper.	75.00
1896 April. General light wear, ½" off crown of spine, VG.	75.00
1896 May. Moderate chipping, G/VG.	55.00
1896 June. General wear, some loss of paper at spine, and nbc , G/VG with exceptional off-white supple paper.	75.00
1896 Aug. General wear, some loss of paper at spine, with back cover coming loose, G/VG with exceptional off-white supple paper.	75.00
1896 June. Small paper perish from tips of spine, VG-.	75.00
1896 June. Spine damage, some chipping, G/VG.	50.00
1898 Dec. General wear, some loss of paper to lower right corner of cover and first few pages not effecting type, VG with decent supple paper.	75.00
1896 Dec. Spine damage, moderate wear, G/VG.	50.00
1901 Oct. Large tear repaired on verso with tape, G/VG.	50.00
1901 Nov. 3" ss, staining to cover and first few pages, G/VG.	50.00
1901 Jul. Aggressive wear and damage to spine, FR.	20.00
1901 Aug. Some spine damage, light dust shadow, VG.	75.00
1901 Sept. Staining to bottom of cover, general wear, VG-.	65.00
1901 Nov. Contains *At Land's End* pt 7 by Jared L. Fuller. General wear, spine split & mild loss of paper to tl corner, G+.	125.00
1902 Apr. Professional cover recreation. Whoever did this facsimile did a great job, NG.	75.00
1902 Sept. Light wear, small stain, VG.	75.00

Argosy 1907 Apr

Argosy 1907 Jul

Argosy 1913 Sep

Argosy 1918 Oct 5

1903 Aug. 2" paper perish from spine, pencil marks to cover, G/VG.   45.00
1903 Sept. Contains *A Round Trip to the Year 2000.* part 3 by William Wallace Cook. General wear,
    spine split and large cover tear mended with tape and back cover perished, FR.   60.00
1903, Sept. Contains *A Round Trip to the Year 2000.* part 3 by William Wallace Cook. 2" paper perish
    from spine, staining to cover, G/VG   125.00
1904 June. General Lite wear, small split at foot of spine, FN-.   85.00
1904 July. General Lite wear, small split at foot of spine, VG+ with wonderful off-white supple paper.   95.00
1904 Aug. 2" paper perish from spine, grease pencil marks to cover, G/VG.   45.00
1905 Feb. Contains *The Misadventures of a Pearl Necklace* by Mary Roberts Rinehart. General Lite
    wear and handling, some paper perished from spine and no back cover, G/VG.   100.00
1905 Feb. Contains *The Misadventures of a Pearl Necklace* by Mary Roberts Rinehart. Some spine
    damage, paper perish from spine, VG.   125.00
1905 Mar.   Aggressive spine damage, 3" tear to cover, G.   30.00
1905 Apr. 1" paper perish from foot of spine, general light wear, pencil marks to cover, G/VG.   45.00
1905 April. General Lite wear and handling very good condition with Lite tan supple paper.   75.00
1905 May. Some staining to cover and lower spine, VG.   75.00
1905 July. General light wear, dust shadow to right edge, VG.   75.00
1905 August. Contains *The Fugitive* Pt 1 by Albert Payson Terhune. General wear, most of spine perished, some tape, G.   50.00
1905 Sept. General wear, 1" paper perish from foot of spine, slight lean, VG-.
1905 Dec. 3rd Pictorial cover, light wear, F-   100.00
1906 Jan. Small piece off crown of spine, dust shadow to cover, VG.   65.00
1906 January. General wear, some spine damage, triangle shaped piece of paper stuck to lower cover,
    tanning flaking paper. G+.   30.00
1906 Feb. Contains *In the Lions Mouth* Pt. 1, by Albert Payson Terhune, Sm hole in cover, general wear, VG-   50.00
1906 Apr. Moderate paper perish to spine, general wear, G+.   30.00
1906 Aug, Spine lean, small paper perish to crown of spine, pencil writing on cover, G/VG .   45.00
1907 February. Hot Air Balloon cover art. General wear, handling and some tape to spine, VG.   60.00
1907 April. Contains *Their Last Hope* part two by Albert Payson Terhune and *After the Play* by
    Mary Roberts Rinehart. General wear, tanning supple paper, VG.   95.00
1907 July. General Lite wear and handling and top 1.5" perished from spine, VG-.   60.00
1907 Aug. Small paper perish from tips of spine, light wear, VG.   65.00
1908 Feb. Some spine damage, general wear, VG-.   55.00
1908 Mar. 1" paper perish from foot of spine, crease in cover, store stamp, G/VG.   45.00
1908 June. Contains *With Sealed Lips* part four by Albert Payson Terhune. General Lite wear, top 1" perished from spine VG-.   60.00
1908 Aug. Stain to spine, general wear, VG.   65.00
1908 Oct. General wear, light staining to cover, VG.   65.00
1908 Oct. Some paper perished from spine tips, shows well, VG.   65.00
1908 Oct. Loss of entire corner of top left, spine damage, F.   90.00
1909 May. Contains *Drunk or Crazy?* by Albert Payson Terhune. General wear, v shaped hole in logo, G+.   60.00
1909 Aug. Light wear, dust shadow, VG.   65.00
1909 Oct. Moderate spine damage, lower left corner off, G/VG.   45.00
1909 Nov. Spine damage, damp staining to cover, some edge wear, G/VG.   45.00
1910 May. General wear, some paper perished from spine, G/VG.   45.00
1910 June. Some spine damage, foxing to cover, railway edition sticker, G/VG.   45.00
1912 September. Cover art by Tarzan artist Clinton Pettee. General wear, VG-.   75.00
1912 October. Contains *Castaways of the Year 2000* part one by William Wallace Cook. General wear 3"
    spine split and some tape to inside front cover, G/VG.   175.00
1913 August. Staining to cover and first few pages, VG-.   75.00
1913 Sept. Contains a long letter to the editor from **H. P. Lovecraft**. Also "Out of Algiers" part one by H. Bedford-Jones.
    Mild wear few small tears and supple tanning paper. Exceptional condition for its age. VG+.   400.00
1918 February 23. General wear with cover split in two at spine, G.   35.00
1918 May 4. Contains *Daughter of the Sun* part one (and cover subject) by Johnston McCulley and
    In Cold Blood by Murray Leinster. General wear, minor bug damage at margin.   60.00
1918 October 5. 1st appearance of Peter the Brazen. ½" off crown of spine, mild wear, nice looking pulp
    with nice paper. Very scarce especially in condition, VG.   300.00

| Argosy 1920 Aug 7 | Argosy 1922 May 6 | Argosy 1924 Aug 16 | Argosy 1927 Mar 19 |

1919 June 21. General wear, some damage and splits at spine, G+. 35.00

1920 May 1. Sm paper perished from foot of spine, some wear to extremities, VG. 85.00

1920 August 17. Contains **The Metal Monster** part one and cover by A. Merritt. General wear, some tape to inside front cove, shows well, VG. 300.00

1921 August 20. *The Guide to Happiness* part 2 by Max Brand. General wear, some loss at extremities, Lite tan supple paper, VG-. 25.00

1921 February 19. *Tarzan the Terrible* by Edgar Rice Burroughs. Moderate wear, trimming to covers, G/VG. 75.00

1922 February 11. Contains *The Bandit of Batakaland* part 3 by Victor Rousseau. Moderate tos, chipping, G/VG. 15.00

1922 April 8. 1" paper perished form crown of spine, creasing, VG-. 75.00

1922 May 6 . Part one of the second Zorro story, *The Further Adventures of Zorro*. Also only the second cover appearance. This is the one where the publisher misspelled Zorro as Zoro on the cover! Lite to moderate wear, some creasing & chipping, some tape to foot of spine, VG-. 400.00

1922 May 13. Part two of *The Further Adventures of Zorro* by Johnston McCulley. Fc almost separated from pulp, moderate creasing, G. 55.00

1922 May 20 1922. Part three of the second Zorro story, *The Further Adventures of Zorro* pt 3. General moderate wear, creasing and some chipping to extremities, G/VG. 85.00

1922 May 20. *The Further Adventures of Zorro* pt. 3. Lite wear, mild creasing, small piece off top of spine with tanning interior. VG. A scarce and high demand pulp. 150.00

1922 May 27. *The Further Adventures of Zorro* pt. 4. 5" paper perished from crown of spine and 1" at foot, G. 75.00

1924 August 16. Contains the Semi Duel story *Poor Little Pigeon* part three. General wear, some loss at over hangs and small chip to lower left corner, VG. 75.00

1924 February 23. *Tarzan and the Ant Men* part four By Edgar Rice Burroughs. General wear, moderate trim to right edge of cover, few small tears to extremities, G/VG. 65.00

1924 March 1. *Tarzan and the Ant Men* part five By Edgar Rice Burroughs. Moderate trim to right edge of cover, few small tears to extremities, G/VG. 65.00

1924 April 26. Lite wear, VG+. 60.00

1924 May 3. Contains *A Stranger In Town* part 2 by J. U. Giesy and Junius B. Smith. Mild flaking to paper, shows very well, VG+. 30.00

1924 July 12 . Contains *The Man Who Mastered Time* pt 1 by Ray Cummings and *The Radio Man* pt 3 by Ralph Milne Farley. General wear, creasing, small tears to cover edge & back cover loose, G+. 80.00

1924 August 16. Contains *Poor Little Pigeon* part two a Semi Dual story. General wear, VG. 95.00

1925 February 28. Contains *The Moon Men* part 2 by Edgar Rice Burroughs. Some tape to cover, wear, creasing, G/VG 45.00

1926 March 27. General wear, tape to front cover and trimmed, G/VG. 35.00

1927 March 19. General Lite wear and handling, VG. 65.00

1928 March. Spine lean with mild damage to spine, VG. 65.00

1929 April 27 1929. *By Allah Who Made Tigers*. General wear, some paper perished from spine, VG. 40.00

1929 June 15. Contains *The Big Shot* part 5 by Frank L. Packerd. General wear and handling, VG. 25.00

1929 June 29. Contains *The Shadow Girl* part two by Ray Cummings. General Lite wear, VG/FN. 75.00

1929 August 17. Contains *The Planet of Peril* part five by Otis Adelbert Kline. Corner off top right cover, G. 15.00

1930 January 4. Contains *Maza of the Moon* part three by Otis Adelbert Kline, *Blue for Blooey* by Erle Stanley Gardner. General wear half inch off foot of spine, VG-. 40.00

1930 January 18. Contains *The Red Owl* by Rafael Sabitini. Tape to spine, G+. 40.00

1930 February 1 1930. Cover coming loose and most of spine perished , G-. 15.00

1930 February 8. Contains *The Man Who Was Two Men* part one by Ray Cummings and *The Sapphire Smile* a Peter The Brazen story by Loring Brent. Some creasing, few tears to extremities, VG-. 35.00

1930 April 5. Contains *Alexander the Red* part one by Don McGrew. General Lite wear , FN-. 35.00

1930 April 12. Contains *Alexander the Red* part two by Don McGrew. General wear, creasing and splitting to spine , VG-. 20.00

1930 April 19. Contains *Alexander the Red* part three by Don McGrew and *Romance and Man-Root* by H. Bedford-Jones. General Lite wear, VG. 35.00

1930 April 26. Contains the Peter the Brazen story *The Man in the Jade Mask* by Loring Brent . General Lite wear and handling, VG+. 40.00

1930 May 24. Contains *Voodoo'd* part 3 by Kenneth Perkins and *The Affair at Kaligaon* by Talbot Mundy. Creasing, 40% of spine perished, G+. 20.00

Argosy 1930 Aug 2	**Argosy 1930 Dec 13**	**Argosy 1931 Jan 17**	**Argosy 1931 Aug 1**

1930 June 21. Contains *The Radio Menace* part three by Ralph Milne Farley, and *That Cargo of Opium* a Peter Brazen story by Loring Brent. General wear, small chipping G/VG.   40.00

1930 June 28. Contains *The Radio Menace* part four by Ralph Milne Farley, and *That Cargo of Opium* part two a Peter Brazen story by Loring Brent. General wear, 30% of spine perished for G+.   35.00

1930 July 5. Contains *The Radio Menace* part five by Ralph Milne Farley. General Lite wear, FN-.   45.00

1930 July 12. Contains *The Radio Menace* part six by Ralph Milne Farley. General wear, handling, some tape to spine and surface creasing G/VG.   30.00

1930 July 19. Contains *A Year in a Day* by Erle Stanley Gardner. General wear, handling VG.   45.00

1930 July 26. Contains *The Czarina's Pearls* part two by Malcolm Wheeler-Nicholson, and *First Law* by Jack Woodford. Tips off spine ends, otherwise a nice looking FN.   35.00

1930 August 2. Contains *The Prince of Peril* part one by Otis Adelbert Kline, *Pegleg Baron in Hollywood* by H. Bedford-Jones. General wear, chipping, creasing to extremities, VG-.   85.00

1930 August 9. Contains *The Prince of Peril* part two by Otis Adelbert Kline. General Lite wear, VG.   40.00

1930 August 16. Contains *The Prince of Peril* part three by Otis Adelbert Kline, *The Emergency Mate* by H. Bedford-Jones. General wear, some paper perished from spine, VG-.   35.00

1930 August 30. Contains *The Prince of Peril* part five by Otis Adelbert Kline. General Lite, FN-.   35.00

1930 September 6. Contains *The Prince of Peril* part six and final by Otis Adelbert Kline. General wear, chipping and back cover perished, G+.   20.00

1930 September 13. Contains *The Valley of Little Fears* by Erle Stanley Gardner. FN.   40.00

1930 September 27. Contains *Spawn of the Comet* by Otis Adelbert Kline. Two inch split at foot of spine, VG.   75.00

1930 October 4. Two inch split at foot of spine else, VG.   25.00

1930 October 18. Lite wear and handling and slight loss of paper to right edge, VG+.   25.00

1930 December 13. Contains *The Elephant Sahib* part two by Talbot Mundy, and *Tama of the Lite Country* by Ray Cummings. General wear and handling, no back cover, G.   35.00

1931 January 10. Contains *The Elephant Sahib* part six by Talbot Mundy, and *The Man with Pin-Point Eyes* by Erle Stanley Gardner. No back cover and front cover loose, G.   15.00

1931 January 17. Contains *Caves of Ocean* part one by Ralph Milne Farley. General Lite wear, some creasing to lower right corner area, VG+.   85.00

1931 January 24. Contains *Caves of Ocean* part two by Ralph Milne Farley. General Lite wear, some creasing to extremities and small piece off lower left corner, VG.   40.00

1931 March 14. General Lite wear, small split to foot of spine, FN-.   25.00

1931 March 21. General Lite wear and handling, FN-.   25.00

1931 March 28. General Lite wear and handling, FN-.   25.00

1931 April 4. General Lite wear and handling, FN-.   25.00

1931 April 11. General wear, spine split, some paper perished from spine, G+.   15.00

1931 May 9. Contains *The Coral of Idris* by H. Bedford-Jones and *Jan of the Jungle* part four by Otis Adelbert Kline. General wear, small piece off foot of spine, VG.   35.00

1931 May 16. Contains *Jan of the Jungle* part five by Otis Adelbert Kline. General wear, back cover has 2/3rd spine split, G+.   15.00

1931 June 6. Front and back covers in two and loose from text block, FR.   10.00

1931 June 20. General Lite 3" tear at top of spine, VG-.   20.00

1931 July 4. Contains *Tama, Princess of Mercury* part two by Ray Cummings and *House of Missing Men* by H. Bedford-Jones. General Lite wear, some creasing, VG.   30.00

1931 July 11. Contains *Tama, Princess of Mercury* part three by Ray Cummings and *Blood of the Scanderoon* by H. Bedford-Jones. General Lite wear , wrap around loose, VG.   20.00

1931 July 18. Contains *Tama, Princess of Mercury* part four (final) by Ray Cummings and *Steal a Dog's Bone* by Hugh B. Cave. General Lite wear, some creasing VG+.   30.00

1931 July 25. General wear, some creasing, VG-.   20.00

1931 August 1. Contains *The Radio Pirates* part one by Ralph Milne Farley. Chip off right edge, VG.   50.00

1931 August 8. Contains *The Radio Pirates* part two by Ralph Milne Farley. General wear, creasing, VG-.   25.00

1931 September 12. General wear, some creasing, VG.   25.00

1931 September 19. General wear, some creasing, VG.   25.00

1931 September 26 . General wear, chip off bottom edge of cover, VG-.   20.00

1931 November 14. Contains *The jungle Rebellion* part three by Ray Cummings. Lite wear, VG.   25.00

Argosy 1936 Oct 31

Argosy 1937 Jan 23

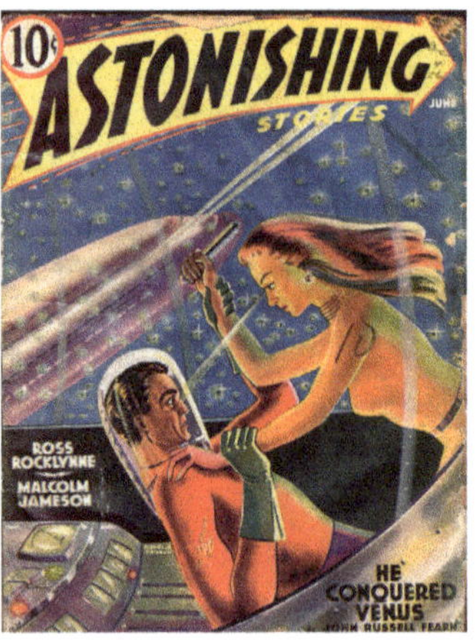

Astonishing 1940 Jun

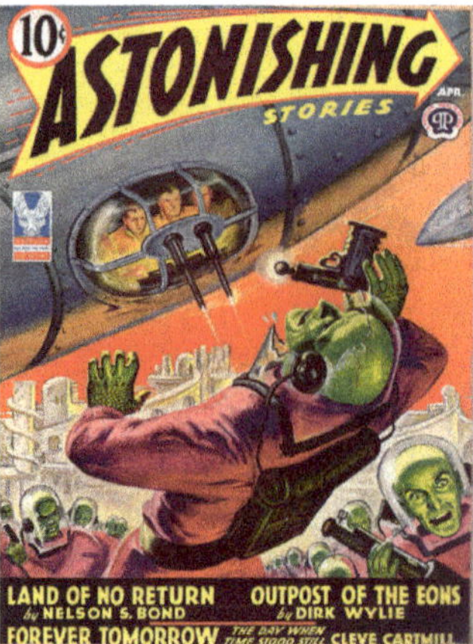

Astonishing 1943 Apr

1931 November 7. Contains *Singing Sand* by Erle Stanley Gardner and *The jungle Rebellion* part two by
Ray Cummings. General Lite wear, VG. — 30.00

1931 December 19. Contains *The Human Zero* by Erle Stanley Gardner and *Connor Takes Charge* by
H. Bedford-Jones. General Lite wear, 3" split at top of spine, vg-. — 25.00

1931 December 26. General Lite wear 3" split at bottom of spine, Vg-. — 20.00

1932 April 2. T*arzan and the City of Gold* part four by Edgar Rice Burroughs. Mild damp stain mainly to
back cover, 1" tear to right edge of front cover, VG. — 50.00

1932 April 9. *Tarzan and the City of Gold* part five by Edgar Rice Burroughs. General moderate wear,
some paper off tips of spine, few small tears to extremities, G/VG. — 50.00

1932 March 19. *Tarzan and the City of Gold* part two by Edgar Rice Burroughs. General wear, creasing, first
page glued to inside front cover, G+. — 30.00

1934 September 22 Contains *No Quarter* by Erle Stanley Gardner and *Creep Shadow!* By A. Merritt, VG. — 75.00

1936 February 15. Contains *Madison Square Garden* by Judson P. Philips, *The Streak* by Max Brand. Few tears, mild trim, VG. — 20.00

1936 Oct 24. Contains *Deep-Sea Diver* by L. Ron Hubbard, VG+. — 95.00

1936 Oct 31. Contains *The Riot At Bucksnort* by Robert E. Howard & *The Big Cats* by L. Ron Hubbard, VG. — 150.00

1937 January 16. *Seven Worlds to Conquer* by Edgar Rice Burroughs. Top corner off, general wear, VG-. — 40.00

1937 January 23, *Seven Worlds to Conquer* part three by Edgar Rice Burroughs. *Flying Trapeze* by
L. Ron Hubbard. General wear and creasing, few small tears to extremities, VG. — 95.00

1937 January 30, *Seven Worlds to Conquer* part four by Edgar Rice Burroughs. Some creasing, few small tears to extremities, VG. — 65.00

1937 January 30, *Seven Worlds to Conquer* part four by Edgar Rice Burroughs. Sm tp at spine ends, VG-. — 50.00

1937 February 13. *Seven Worlds To Conquer* by Edgar Rice Burroughs. Small tears to right extremity, 1.5"
tear to left edge and some pages, G+. — 45.00

1937 February 20. *The Resurrection of Jimber Jaw* by Edgar Rice Burroughs. Some spine damage, VG. — 60.00

1938 May 14. Contains *The Brand Of Eve* by C. S. Forester. Mild Surface creasing, VG+. — 25.00

1938 May 21 Clean, Green and Phony by Donald Barr Chidsey. General wear, mild trim, VG- — 20.00

1938 May 28. Contains *The Living Ghost* pt. 4 by Max Brand. Shrunken head cover. T. R corner off,
paper perished from fore edge, marks to back cover. G — 10.00

1938 May 7. *The Living Ghost* by Max Brand. Some loss of paper and flaking at lower left corner. VG- — 15.00

1938 January 15. *Carson of Venus* by Edgar Rice Burroughs. General wear, some creasing to cover, VG. — 50.00

1938 February 5. *Carson of Venus* by Edgar Rice Burroughs. Also *Wild Bill Hiccup* by Cornell Woolrich. 2"
tear on front cover with several interior tears some corresponding to front cover tear, G. — 25.00

1939 January 14. *The Synthetic Men of Mars* by Edgar Rice Burroughs. Moderate wear, surface creasing,
large chip off right edge of cover, G/VG. — 30.00

1939 January 21. *The Synthetic Men of Mars* by Edgar Rice Burroughs. Also *The Eye of Doom* by
Cornell Woolrich Lite wear, VG/FN. — 75.00

1939 February 11. *The Synthetic Men of Mars* by Edgar Rice Burroughs. General lite wear,
small piece off lower right corner, VG+. — 75.00

1939 February 4. *The Synthetic Men of Mars* by Edgar Rice Burroughs. General lite wear, small tears
to right extremity, small piece off lower right corner, VG-. — 65.00

1941 August 16. Virgil Finlay cover art. Contains *Town Marshal* by Walt Coburn. Small paper perished
from top left corner, VG. — 35.00

1941 July 26. Contains *Five Aces West* by Cliff Farrell. Paper pull near price,1" tear to right edge
repaired by tape, nice supple paper, VG. — 35.00

1941 November 29. H. J. Ward cover art. Contains *Seven Mile House* by Max Brand. Tr Corner & small lr corner off, VG — 40.00

1942 January 10. H. J. Ward cover art. Contains *Killer, What's Your Name?* By Frederick C. Davis, FN. — 60.00

Astonishing Stories

1940 June, #3. Damp staining to fc, moderate chipping, G/VG. — 20.00

1942 March. Stories by Neil R. Jones and Ray Cummings. 20% paper perished from lower fc, G. — 10.00

1943 February. Moderate surface creasing, some tears, G+. — 15.00

1943 April. Contains *Subterfuge* by Ray Bradbury. Moderate trim, nice paper, G/VG. — 50.00

Astounding Science Fiction

1932 February. General wear, readers crease, mild flaking, VG-. — 85.00

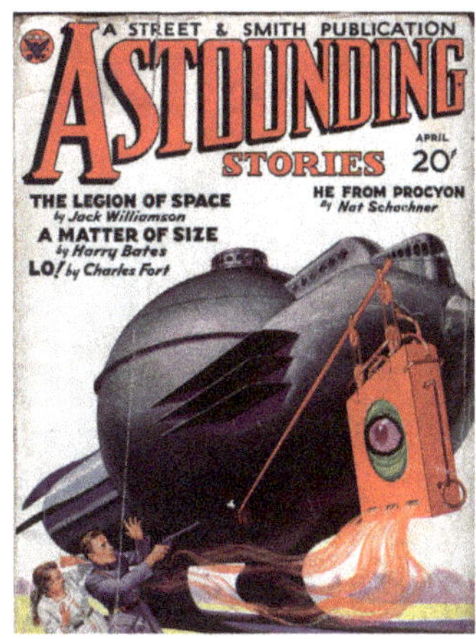

Astounding 1934 Apr

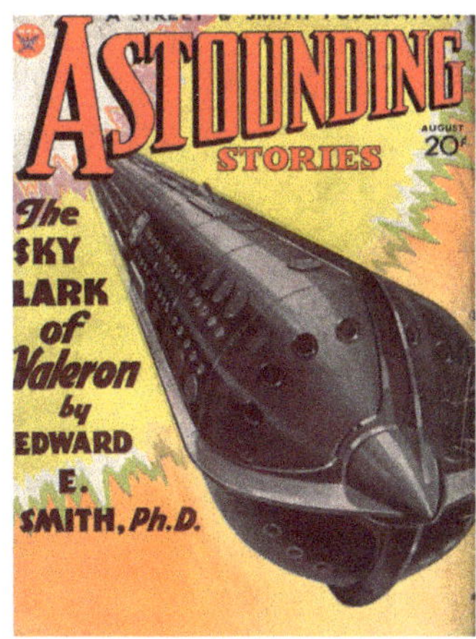

Astounding 1934 Aug

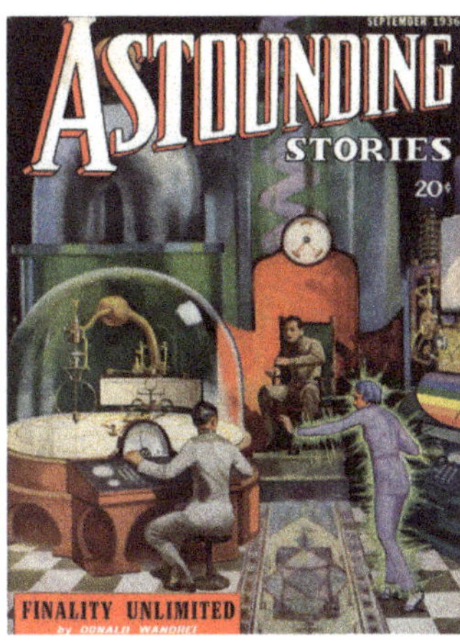

Astounding 1936 Sep

Astounding 1938 Mar

1934 April. *Legion of Space* by Jack Williamson. 1.5" tear at logo, general wear, some creasing, G.	50.00
1934 May. Large pieces off cover, G.	25.00
1934 July. Contains *Legion of Space* part 4 by Jack Williamson. Trim right & bottom edges of book, G/VG.	50.00
1934 July. Front cover loose, some chipping, ½" off top of spine, G.	25.00
1934 August. *Skylark of Valeron* Pt. one by E. E. Doc Smith. 2" split at foot of spine, lite wear, VG-.	95.00
1934 November. Front cover almost separated, spine damage, FR.	25.00
1935 February. Large piece off front cover chipping, tears, FR.	20.00
1935 May. Moderate chipping to right edge, some creasing, store stamp, G+.	30.00
1935 June. Aggressive chipping to extremities, general wear, G/VG.	50.00
1935 September. Jack Williamson sty. Slight spine lean, few small tears, mild flaking, VG.	85.00
1935 November. Lower right corner off, chipping, some tears, FR.	15.00
1936 May. Mild wear and some surface creasing, VG.	50.00
1936 July. Pencil marks to cover and rubber stamp, some creasing, G+.	30.00
1936 August. 1" off crown of spine, general wear, creasing and 1" tear to left cover, 2" spine split, G/VG.	40.00
1936 August. Lower right corner off, some paper perished form spine, G/VG	35.00
1936 September. Few small holes in back cover, shows well, VG/FN.	85.00
1936 October. Moderate surface creasing, 1" tear at spine, G/VG.	35.00
1936 November. Moderate surface creasing, VG-	45.00
1936 December. Hole punch cover, small spine split, writing, G/VG.	35.00
1937 January. 2.5" tear to front cover, G+.	25.00
1937 February. ½" off crown of spine, general wear, G/VG.	35.00
1937 February. Bug damage to about half of spine in a spotty pattern, front cover lite wear, G/VG.	35.00
1937 March. Page loose, browning, some flaking, FR.	15.00
1937 April. General wear, some staining to cover, G/VG.	35.00
1937 May. Small spine split, 1" tear, VG-.	45.00
1937 June. Aggressive tape to spine, moderate wear, creasing, G.	20.00
1937 July. Creasing to cover, edge wear, browning, G+.	30.00
1937 September. Damp stain to back cover, G.	30.00
1937 Dec 1937. First issue published under the editorship of John W. Campbell. Contains The *Galactic Patrol* part 4 by E. E. Smith. General Lite wear, VG+.	85.00
1937 December. Contains *The Galactic Patrol* part 4 by E. E. Smith. General wear, surface creasing, VG-.	65.00
1938 April. Moderate wear, creasing, G/VG.	30.00
1938 December. General lite wear chip off back cover, VG+.	45.00
1938 February. Mild damp stain, hole punch cover, VG.	35.00
1938 July. *Legion of Time* part 3 by Jack Williamson and The Dangerous Dimension 1st SF story by L. Ron Hubbard. General mild wear some surface creasing, VG.	125.00
1938 March. Mild damp stain, hole punch cover, VG.	35.00
1938 September. Contains *The Tramp* pt. 1 by L. Ron Hubbard. Creasing, mild damp staining, VG-.	75.00
1939 January. Contains *The Incorrigible* by L. Sprague de Camp, FN.	75.00
1939 January. Contains *The Incorrigible* by L. Sprague de Camp. General wear, chipping, dark paper, VG-	38.00
1939 January. Contains *The Incorrigible* by L. Sprague de Camp Moderate damp staining, wavy paper. G/VG.	30.00
1939 March. Moderate damp staining, wavy paper. G/VG.	30.00
1939 April. Contains *Cosmic Engineers* pt. 3 by Clifford Simak and *One Against The Legion* pt. 1 by Jack Williamson. Lite wear and handling, VG+	60.00
1939 May. General wear, small tape to foot of spine, VG.	45.00
1939 June. Contains *One Against the Legion* pt. 3 (end) by Jack Williamson and *Design for Life* by L. Sprague de Camp, and *Hermit Of Mars* by Clifford Simak. FN-.	75.00
1939 June. Hole punch cover, VG.	40.00
1939 Sept. Contains the first science fiction appearance in pulps of Theodore Sturgeon with the story, *Ether Breather*. Small paper perished from crown of spine, FN-.	125.00
1939 September. Contains *Ether Breather* by Theodore Sturgeon. Surface creasing, lite wear, VG.	75.00
1939 September. Contains *Ether Breather* by Theodore Sturgeon. General wear, some surface creasing. G/VG.	50.00
1939 October. Contains *Grey Lensman* by E. E. Smith. Classic cover. Mild wear, FN	125.00
1939 November. Contains *Grey Lensman* pt. 2 by E. E. Smith and *Misfit* by Robert Heinlein. General Lite wear and handling with minor loss of paper at foot and crown of spine, VG.	60.00

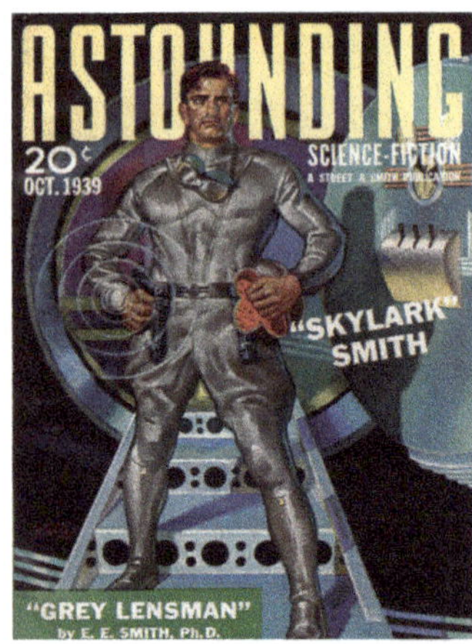

Astounding 1939 Oct

Astounding 1941 Sept

Astounding 1941 Dec

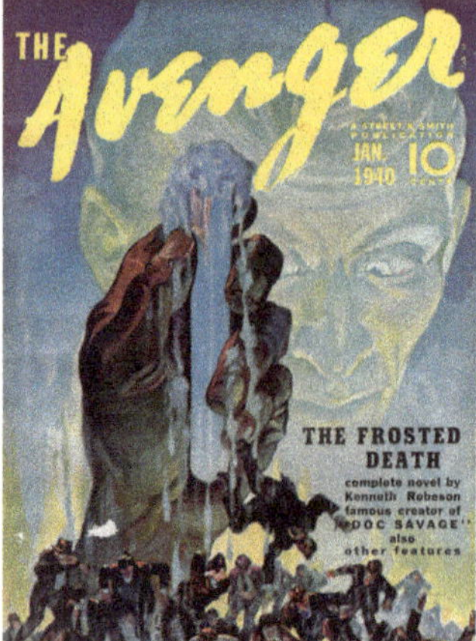

Avenger 1940 Jan

1940 January. Small chip off right edge, lite creasing, VG.	30.00
1940 February. Contains *The Professor Was A Thief* by L. Ron Hubbard, and *If This Goes On...* by Robert Heinlein. Lite wear, VG/FN.	85.00
1940 March. Contains the final part of *If This Goes On...* by Robert Heinlein. Mild damp staining, VG+.	60.00
1940 May. Contains *Final Blackout* pt. 2 by L. Ron Hubbard. Lite wear, surface creasing, VG+	75.00
1940 August. Contains *Vault Of The Beast* by A. E. Van Vogt. Some staining to logo, VG.	30.00
1940 Nov. Contains *Slan* pt. 3 by A. E. Van Vogt, and *One Was Stubborn* by L. Ron Hubbard writing as Rene La Fayette and *Sunspot Purge* by Clifford Simak. Lite wear, mild creasing, VG.	60.00
1940 Nov. Contains *One Was Stubborn* by L. Ron Hubbard, and *Slan* pt. 3 by A. E. Van Vogt. Lite surface creasing, VG/FN.	75.00
1940 December. Contains *Slan* pt. 4(end) by A. E. Van Vogt. Lite wear, small rub hole at top staple, VG.	60.00
1941 January. Moderate surface creasing to cover, dark tanning paper, G/VG.	35.00
1941 February. Contains *-And He Built A Crooked House* by Robert Heinlein and *Completely Automatic* by Theodore Sturgeon. General moderate wear, creasing, G/VG.	40.00
1941 April. Contains *The Mutineers* by L. Ron Hubbard writing as Kurt von Rachen. Hole in back cover, moderate creasing, G+.	35.00
1941 May. Contains *Universe* by Robert Heinlein. Lite wear and surface creasing, VG+.	50.00
1941 June. Contains *Artnan Process* by Theodore Sturgeon. Lite wear, mild creasing, VG+.	60.00
1941 June. Contains *Artnan Process* by Theodore Sturgeon. Moderate surface and readers creasing, G/VG.	35.00
1941 July Contains *Methuselah's Children* by Robert Heinlein, *The Probable Man* by Alfred Bester, *Spaceship in a Flask* by Clifford D. Simak and *The Seesaw* by A. E. Van Vogt. Lite wear, Creasing, VG+.	60.00
1941 July. Two sm binder holes at spine G/VG.	35.00
1941 August. Contains *Methuselah's Children* pt 2 by Robert Heinlein. Loss of paper at top right corner, half of pulp, FR.	10.00
1941 September. Contains *Nightfall* by Isaac Asimov. Two sm binder holes at spine, chipping to right edge, G/VG.	50.00
1941 October. Contains *Common Sense* by Robert Heinlein. Two sm binder holes at spine, G/VG.	35.00
1941 November. Contains *Second Stage* Lensmen by E. E. "Doc" Smith. Two sm binder holes, creasing G/VG.	30.00
1941 Dec. Contains *Second Stage Lensmen* pt. 1 by E. E. "Doc" Smith. General Lite wear, FN.	60.00
1941 Dec. Contains *Second Stage Lensmen* pt. 1 by E. E. "Doc" Smith. Two sm binder holes, G/VG.	35.00
Bedsheet size begins	
1942 January. Contains *The Invaders* by L. Ron Hubbard. Tos, aggressive chipping and paper perished from right edge, rough, FR.	15.00
1942 February. Glue repair near bottom of spine and onto fc, wear, G.	20.00
1942 March. General wear, creasing, G/VG.	35.00
1942 April. Contains *Strain* by L. Ron Hubbard. Two sm binder holes at spine, surface creasing, G/VG.	45.00
1942 May. Contains the first appearance of *Foundation* by Isaac Asimov. 1.5" repaired tear at crown of spine, general surface ceasing, G/VG.	150.00
1942 June. Contains *The Slaver* by L. Ron Hubbard. Moderate surface creasing, some chipping, G/VG.	45.00
1942 July. Flag cover. Contains *Space Can* by L. Ron Hubbard. Some surface creasing and mild chipping, VG.	60.00
1942 August. Contains *Waldo* by Robert A. Heinlein. Moderate creasing, 1" closed tear to right edge, G/VG.	45.00
1942 August. Contains *Waldo* by Robert A. Heinlein. Moderate creasing, 1" paper perished from spine, G+.	35.00
1942 September. Contains *Starvation* by Fredric Brown. Sm tp to spine, surface creasing, G/VG.	35.00
1942 September. Contains *Starvation* by Fredric Brown. Spine damage, 3" tape to cover, G.	20.00
1942 October. Contains *The Beast* by L. Ron Hubbard. Two sm binder holes at spine, G/VG.	45.00
1942 November. Two sm binder holes at spine, G/VG.	35.00
1942 December. Sm tear thru book at spine, general wear, G.	20.00
1943 January. Lite wear, sm rub hole at lower staple, VG.	40.00
1943 February. Tape to spine ends, aggressive chipping to right edge, G.	20.00
1943 March. Moderate creasing, chipping and some spine damage, G.	20.00
1943 April. Moderate creasing, chipping and sm tp to spine ends, G.	20.00
Bedsheet size ends	
1943 Aug. Contains *M 33 in Andromeda* by A. E. Van Vogt and The Mutant's Brother by Fritz Leiber jr. Lite wear and handling, some pages starting, VG-.	40.00

Avenger

1939 Nov (#3.) General Lite wear, damp stain to left edge, nice paper. VG.	100.00
1940 January. FN- with nice supple paper.	165.00
1940 February. Moderate surface creasing, 1" closed tear, VG-.	65.00
1940 March. Some cover creasing and interior tape with Lite tan supple paper. VG.	75.00

Avenger 1940 Apr

Avenger 1942 Jul

Big Book Detective 1945 Feb

Big Double Feature

1940 April. General wear and some surface creasing, VG.	80.00
1940 April. Hole punch cover, else near fine with nice supple paper.	75.00
1940 July. Classic torture cover. Store stamp, surface creasing, VG-	75.00
1940 November. Mild surface creasing, FN-.	125.00
1941 May. Mild wear and surface creasing, VG.	85.00
1941 July. Lite readers crease with tanning supple paper. VG+.	95.00
1941 November. General wear, some creasing and "5" marked to price. VG-.	55.00
1942 January. General wear, creasing with Lite tan supple paper. VG.	65.00
1942 January. General wear and surface creasing, VG-.	75.00
1942 March. General lite wear, small chip off top right corner of back cover, FN-	125.00
1942 July. Mild wear, small hope in spine, VG.	85.00
1942 July. General Lite wear and slight loss of paper to B. C. VG.	65.00
1942 September. 1" tear at lower spine, lower right corner off, VG-.	75.00

Baseball Stories

1947 Summer. General wear, creasing some small tears, VG-.	25.00

Battle Birds

1940 September. Contains *The High-Hat Squadron From Hell* by David Goodis. Small lower right corner tip off, lite wear, VG.	75.00
1942 August. Contains *Vickers Pay-Off* by David Goodis. Moderate wear, chipping, G/VG.	50.00
1943 March. Contains *Midnight Mission* by David Goodis. General wear, 1.5" stain at right edge, VG-.	35.00
1944 January. Contains *Wings Over Kiska* by David Goodis. General wear, VG	75.00
1944 March. Contains *Wings of the Free* by David Goodis. General wear, tos, some int tp, G/VG.	35.00

Battle Stories

1929 June. Mild wear and Lite creasing, VG/FN.	125.00
1930 June.. Back cover re-glued, general wear, VG+	75.00
1933 November. General wear, nice paper. VG+	60.00
1931 May. Lite wear and handling with nice paper. FN-.	95.00
1935 Jan. Toc missing.	15.00

Best Football Novels

1942 December. #1. Moderate wear, slight spine lean, some small tears, G/VG.	50.00

Best Western Magazine

1935 September, #1. Scarce. Red Circle (Marvel.) General lite wear and handling, FN.	60.00

Beyond Fantasy Fiction

1953 September. Contains *The King of the Elves* by Philip K. Dick. Moderate wear and cresting to cover, small piece off right edge, G/VG.	15.00

Big Book Detective

1944 December. Normal wear and some creasing, Canadian issue, VG.	25.00
1945 February. Poison cover. Max Brand story. Lite wear and .5" off bottom of spine, Can issue, VG/FN.	50.00

Big Chief Western

1940 October, #1. Mild chipping to extremities and mild interior flaking, stamped "serials division sample file, library of Congress" VG-.	150.00

Big Double Feature Magazine (Black Mask)

1939 one shot. Rare. Contains rebound (remaindered) copies of Black Mask and Ranch Romances. Lite wear and surface creasing with great spine, possible unread and exceptional condition for the thickness. A few flakes from top of book VG+.	750.00
Another copy. 1st ad pg and toc out, few small holes to cover.	250.00

Bill Barnes 1935 Jun

Black Book Detective 1939 Mar

Black Book Detective 1945 Win

Black Mask 1920 Apr

Big-Book Western Magazine

1949 January. General Lite wear, cream supple paper interior, VG.	20.00
1950 June. *The Devil Deals Bullets!* by Harry F. Olmsted. General wear, some tears, chipping to extremities.	15.00
1951 September. *Vengeance Bets a Blue Chip* by Robert Hogan. General Lite wear, VG+.	30.00
1952 May. *There's Hell over the Hump* by Roe Richmond. General Lite wear, some small tears and chipping.	15.00

Bill Barnes Air Adventurer

1934 February. #1. Metallic cover, moderate creasing, 2" spine split, G+.	250.00
1934 March. #2. Back cover almost detached, major chipping to front cover, 2" spine split, 3" paper perished from spine.	100.00
1934 November. General wear, some creasing and tears mainly at over hangs, G+.	65.00
1934 December. Bill Barnes Air Adventurer 1934 December. Small tp. to fc and int. tp., G/VG.	95.00
1934 December. Canadian Edition, Surface creasing, store stamp, VG.	65.00
1935 March. General wear, some staining to front cover, VG.	95.00
1935 April. Mild wear with some creasing and small tears to over hangs, VG.	95.00
1935 April. Canadian Edition, same cover as March issue. Moderate wear and creasing, store stamp VG-.	50.00
1935 June. Lite wear mainly at over hangs, FN-.	250.00
1935 June. Canadian edition same cover as May. Lite wear and surface Creasing, faint store stamp, VG/FN.	95.00
1935 July. Some chipping, small tears and creasing mainly at extremities, G/VG.	95.00
1935 August. Moderate interior tape , cover armature repair, G.	45.00
1935 September. Most of spine perished, FR/G.	35.00
1935 September. Canadian Edition. 4" tear, nbc, Aggressive chipping, FR	25.00

Black Book Detective

1938 July. Moderate wear, some chipping with tanning paper. G/VG.	60.00
1939 Mar. Bondage cover. Dealers label affixed to cover, general wear , surface creasing, VG.	75.00
1939 March. Bondage cover. General lite wear, some creasing, VG+.	85.00
1939 March. General wear, creasing, some chipping, back cover loose, VG-.	30.00
1941 March. General wear, Lite creasing and mild trim to right edge, VG.	50.00
1944 Fall. Lite wear, some creasing with mild trim to right edge, VG.	75.00
1945 Spring. General wear, mild trim to edge with light tan supple paper, VG.	75.00
1945 Summer. General wear, mild trim to edge, VG+.	75.00
1945 Winter. General wear, mild trim to edge, VG.	75.00
1946 Fall. Cool Black Bat cover art. Stamped "Checking Copy" Overall nice with mild trim, VG+.	50.00
1946 Winter. General Lite wear, mild trim, 1" paper perished from crown of spine, VG+.	60.00
1946 Winter. General Lite wear, mild trim, VG+.	50.00
1947 December. General wear, some tears & chipping, VG-.	45.00
1947 February. General wear, mild cover trim, Lite tan supple paper, VG-.	45.00
1948 April. General Lite wear, some surface creasing, VG+.	70.00
1948 November. 2" tear to cover, some creasing. VG-.	50.00
1948 September. General wear, moderate surface creasing with decent supple paper, VG-.	45.00
1949 March. 3" tear to cover, quarter size piece off, G.	25.00
1949 May. Large pieces off cover, front cover almost loose, G.	25.00
1950 Fall. Piece off, moderate trim, G+.	25.00
1951 Spring. Lite wear, creasing , VG+.	50.00

Black Mask (see also Big Double Feature Magazine)

1920 April, #1. First issue of the seminal detective noir pulp title. Some tape stains to cover edges, small paper perished from spine tips, excellent cream paper, shows well, VG+.	3,750.00
1938 May. Contains stories by Carroll John Daly, Frank Gruber, Donald Wandrei and others. Lite wear, 1" tear at lower left corner, some loss at over hangs, VG.	175.00
1939 April. Contains *Hide The Evidence* by Frederick C. Davis. 1" tear at spine, mild wear nice paper, FN-.	165.00
1947 September. General wear, surface creasing, readers crease, VG-.	50.00
1951 March. Black Mask 1951 March. Lite wear, surface creasing, nice paper, VG+.	50.00

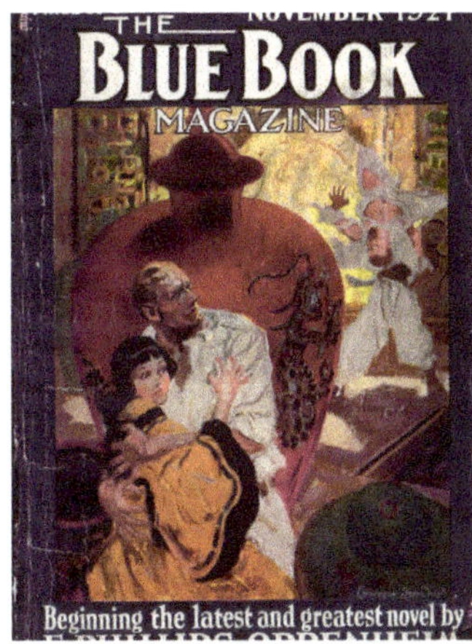

Blue Book 1921 Nov

Blue Book 1934 Jun

Blue Book 1936 Jan

Blue Book 1940 Aug

Blazing Western

1947 February, #1. Cover art by H. W. Scott. General mild wear, creasing, slight chipping to edge, VG+.   65.00

Blue Book Magazine

1921 November. Contains *The Great Prince Shan* pt. 1 by E. Phillip Oppenheim. General wear and creasing, mild flaking, VG-.   45.00

1928 August. Contains *The Hostile Island* by H. Bedford-Jones. General wear, creasing, VG-.   25.00

1932 April. Contains *The Cruise of the Sea Hawk* by H. Bedford-Jones. Some splitting at top of spine, VG.   25.00

1932 May. Front cover loose, G.   15.00

1934 April. Contains the last chapter of *After Worlds Collide* by Edwin Balmer and Philip Wylie. General wear, creasing, G+.   25.00

1934 June. General Lite wear and handling for fine condition with Lite tanning supple paper.   25.00

1935 November. Contains *Tarzan and the Immortal Men* pt. 2 by Edgar Rice Burroughs. General wear, slight wave to book, VG.   65.00

1935 November. *Tarzan and the Immortal Men* by Edgar Rice Burroughs. Readers crease, 2.5" tear, G/VG.   45.00

1936 January. Contains *Tarzan and the Immortal Men* pt. 4 by Edgar Rice Burroughs. Burn hole in cover and 1st few pages, VG-.   45.00

1936 January. *Tarzan and the Immortal Men* pt. 4 by Edgar Rice Burroughs. Lite wear, VG/FN.   75.00

1936 March. Contains *Tarzan and the Immortal Men* pt. 6 by Edgar Rice Burroughs. Lite wear, VG/FN.   75.00

1937 February. Contains *A Card From Mr. Lincoln* by H. Bedford-Jones. Topless female cover, unusual for this title. Lite wear, FN.   55.00

1938 March. General Lite wear and handling, VG+.   20.00

1938 April. Contains *Warriors in Exile* by H. Bedford-Jones. Lite wear, some creasing, VG/FN   35.00

1938 April. General Lite wear, markings to cover, G/VG.   20.00

1938 May. General wear, creases and markings, G+.   15.00

1938 June. General wear, creases and markings, G/VG.   20.00

1938 July. Lite wear, mild creasing, VG+.   25.00

1938 September. General Lite wear, mild creasing, VG+.   25.00

1939 February. Contains *The True Steel* by Max Brand. Tanning supple paper. FN-.   30.00

1939 April. Contains *Five Miles to Youth* by H. Bedford-Jones. Tanning supple paper, FN-.   30.00

1939 April. Contains *Five Miles to Youth* by H. Bedford-Jones. Lower right corner chipped away, VG-.   15.00

1939 May. Contains *The Wolf Woman* by H. Bedford-Jones. Lite wear, chip off right edge of cover, VG.   35.00

1939 May. Contains *Trumpets from Oblivion* by H. Bedford-Jones. FN.   25.00

1939 June. Contains *Man Bites Dog* by Ellery Queen. FN/VF.   85.00

1939 December. Contains *The Wings of Wrath* by H. Bedford-Jones and *The Trojan Horse* by Ellery Queen. Lite wear, very small piece off top right of back cover, VG+.   85.00

1940 August. Contains *Hell's Mouth* by H. Bedford-Jones. Lite wear, VG+.   25.00

1940 January. Contains *Three Black Sheep* by H. Bedford-Jones. General wear, chipping, creasing, VG.   15.00

1940 November. Contains *Two Swordsmen of Gascony* by H. Bedford-Jones. Lite wear, NF.   30.00

1940 October. Contains *First Woman* by H. Bedford-Jones. Lite wear, NF.   30.00

1940 September. Contains *The Bishop's Pawn* by H. Bedford-Jones. Lite wear, NF.   30.00

1941 February. Contains *A France Forever!* by H. Bedford-Jones. Lite wear, NF.   25.00

1941 September. Contains *He Who Turned Back* by H. Bedford-Jones. General wear, VG. Bedsheet size.   25.00

1941 October. Contains *Young Man With A Banjo* by H. Bedford-Jones and *The Plymouth Express* by Agatha Christie. Corner of cover cut off and cut into first page, VG-. Bedsheet size.   25.00

1941 November. Contains *Eight Are the Gates* by H. Bedford-Jones. Some splitting to top of spine, VG.   25.00

1941 December. Contains *A Son of Han* by H. Bedford-Jones and *The Italian Nobleman* by Agatha Christie. General wear , VG, Bedsheet size.   35.00

1942 July. Contains *The Man Responsible* by H. Bedford-Jones. General wear and handling and 1" paper perished from foot of spine, VG-. Bedsheet size.   25.00

1942 June. Contains *The King of Macassar Strait* by H. Bedford-Jones. General wear, VG. Bedsheet size.   25.00

1942 October. Contains *Fame and Honor...Gold and Pearls* by H. Bedford-Jones. General wear, 1" paper perished from foot of spine, VG-. Bedsheet size.   25.00

1943 June. Contains *So Gallantly Streaming* by H. Bedford-Jones. Lite wear, VG+. Bedsheet size.   25.00

1943 June. Contains *The Crescent* is For Hope by H. Bedford-Jones. Lite wear, VG. Bedsheet size.   25.00

1943 May. Contains *A Flag Bright with Stars* by H. Bedford-Jones. Lite wear, VG. Bedsheet size.   25.00

1944 December. Contains *The Gods Do Not Forget* by H. Bedford-Jones. Some splitting at crown and foot of spine, G/VG.   15.00

1946 August. *The Last Pharaoh* by H. Bedford-Jones. Some splitting at crown and foot of spine, VG-   20.00

1946 December. Contains *Assassination at Christmas* by H. Bedford-Jones. Lite wear, NF. Bedsheet size.   30.00

1946 July. Contains *Red Sky Over Thebes* by H. Bedford-Jones. Splitting at spine ends, VG-. Bedsheet size.   20.00

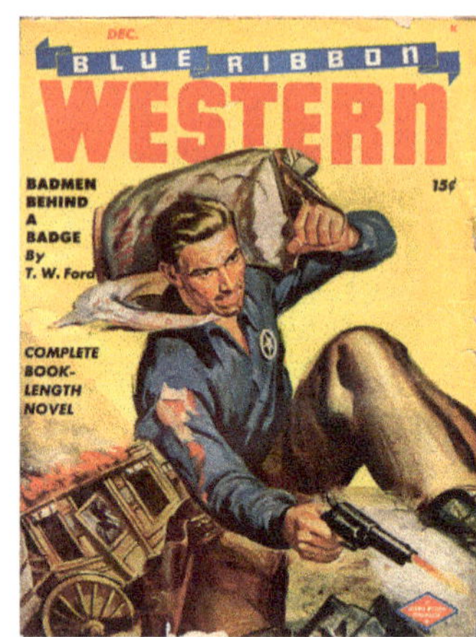

Blue Ribbon Western 1946 Dec

Bull's Eye Western 1935 Feb

Captain Future 1940 Win

Captain Future 1940 Sum

1948 January. Contains *The Thirsty Cup* by H. Bedford-Jones. Lite wear & creases to cover, VG+.	25.00
1948 February. Contains *The Pastel Production Line* by John D. MacDonald. Lite wear, VG/FN.	85.00
1949 December. Contains *Delilah and the Space-Rigger* by Robert Heinlein. Some wear & creasing, VG+.	75.00
1950 October. Contains *A Date At Shepheard's* by Sax Rohmer. Lite creasing, VG+.	45.00
1951 January. Contains *X. Y. Z. Calls* by Sax Rohmer. General wear, creasing , VG-.	45.00
1955 January. Contains *The Past Master* by Robert Bloch. NF.	85.00

Blue Ribbon Western

1941 October. Mild wear and handling, VG/FN.	30.00
1941 December. Mild edge wear, few very small holes at spine, VG/FN.	30.00
1943 February. Severe cover trim, G.	30.00
1944 February. 3" tear repaired with tape from reverse, chipping, G.	15.00
1944 October. General moderate wear, creasing, G/VG.	15.00
1945 February. Pieces missing from right edge of cover, G.	15.00
1945 April. Lite wear and creasing, VG+.	25.00
1945 October. General lite wear and mild surface creasing, VG+.	25.00
1945 October. General lite wear and chew mark to back cover, VG.	20.00
1946 February. 4" tear at spine, moderate chipping, G.	15.00
1946 April. Moderate wear, surface creasing, G/VG.	15.00
1946 June. Lite wear and handling, VG.	20.00
1946 August. Lite wear and handling, VG.	20.00
1946 December. General wear and some small chipping to edge, G/VG.	15.00
1947 May. Mild creasing, chew mark to top right corner, G/VG.	15.00
1947 July. Moderate wear, 5" split to back of spine, G+.	15.00
1947 September. Some edge wear and one chip off, VG.	25.00
1947 November. General wear, some damp staining to back portion of pulp, VG-.	25.00
1948 January. Lower right corner off, edge wear and chipping, G.	15.00
1948 October. General wear, some edge tears and creasing, G/VG.	15.00
1948 December. General lite wear, few sm tears to over hangs, VG+.	25.00
1949 February. Wraps starting to separate, G/VG.	15.00
1949 August. Contains *The Hounds of Hades* by James Blish. Some int. tape, chipping.	50.00
1949 October. General wear and handling, VG.	25.00
1949 December. General wear, surface creasing, VG.	25.00
1950 February. Some tears and chipping to right edge, some foxing at logo, G/VG.	15.00
1950 April/May. Moderate wear, damp staining, G.	12.00
1950 September. Mild chipping to right edge, NF.	25.00

Boy's Adventure

1936 September. #1. 2" spine split at foot, general wear, VG.	175.00

Buck Jones

1937 July. Very scarce. Piece off front cover, moderate wear and creasing. FR.	75.00

Bull's-Eye Western Stories

1935 February, #1. General wear, moderate creasing, G/VG.	100.00

Captain Future

1940 Winter, #1. Chip to top right corner, some loss at bottom of cover. Small writing in "F" of the logo.	300.00
1940 Summer #3. Rocket bondage cover. Mod wear and creasing. VG.	150.00
1941 Fall. 4" tear to cover, chipping, G+.	20.00
1942 Fall. Aggressive wear, chipping and tears, G.	15.00
1942 Winter. Some chipping, small tears to extremities, VG-.	50.00
1942 Winter. Some chipping, small tears to extremities, nice paper, VG.	60.00
1943 Summer. Lower right corner off and piece off back cover , G/VG.	45.00
1943 Winter. Tos, lower right corner off, G+.	20.00

Civil War 1940 Spr

Clues 1941 July

Comet 1940 Dec

Complete Detecctive Novel 1928

1944 Spring. Last issue. Contains *Nothing Sirius* by Fredric Brown. General lite wear, VG/FN.	95.00
1944 Spring. Last issue. Contains *Nothing Sirius* by Fredric Brown. General wear, creasing, few small tears at extremities, VG.	70.00

Captain Zero

1949 November. #1. Top left corner, moderate creasing, VG.	200.00

Champion Sports

1937 September. #4. Mild trim, FN-.	30.00

Civil War Stories

1940 Spring #1. 5" spine split, general wear, creasing, G/VG.	95.00

Clues Detective Stories

1939 November. Small hole at lower staple, FN-.	95.00
1939 December. Small hole at lower staple, FN-.	95.00
1940 April. Some paper perished from back cover, VG-.	60.00
1940 July. Some damp staining to cover, l.r. corner off, G/VG.	50.00
1941 July. Lite wear and some surface creasing, few small tears to right edge, VG+.	75.00
1941 September. Lite wear and some surface creasing, minor spine damage, VG+.	75.00
1942 May. Lite wear and some surface creasing, minor spine damage, VG+	75.00

Comet

1940 Dec, #1. Small puncture in cover, some grime to right edge, VG-.	75.00
1941 Jan, #2. Aggressive surface creasing, G+.	20.00

Complete Cowboy

1945 Spring. General Lite wear, mild damp staining, lite tanning supple paper interior.	20.00
1945 Winter. General Lite wear, some paper perished from spine, tanning supple paper interior.	20.00
1948 August. General wear, some creasing and tears, some tape to cover, tanning supple paper interior.	12.00
1949 February. General wear, some creasing and tears, tanning supple paper interior.	12.00

Complete Detective

1938 November. General wear, center crease, very nice paper, VG.	200.00

Complete Detective Novel

1928 Sept, #3. *The Star Of death* by R. T. M. Scott. ½" off foot of spine, general wear, mild creasing, VG.	150.00
1928 Sept, #3. *The Star Of death* by R. T. M. General wear, some chipping to edge, G/VG.	75.00
1929 January. Front cover detached, moderate creasing to cover at logo, G.	25.00
1932 July. Craig Kennedy in *Murder under the Southern Cross*. General wear, creasing, chipping , bc loose , G/VG.	45.00
1934 July. Lite wear and handling, mild trim, VG.	55.00

Complete Northwest.

1939 July. RCMP Cover. Tape to repaired tear on fc, spine split, G.	30.00

Complete Northwest Novel Magazine.

1935 September, #1. RCMP cover. Lite wear and mild chipping, VG/FN.	250.00
1936 October. RCMP Cover. Chipping at top edge, some creasing, VG-.	75.00
1937 November. RCMP Cover. Back cover loose, damp staining, G+.	40.00

Complete Novel

1925 August, #4. General wear, Lite tan supple paper, excess glue to inside fc, about an 1"onto 1st page, G/VG.	75.00
1926 October #18. Three Bad Men adapted photoplay. General wear, some creasing, VG-.	150.00
1927 June. Boxing cover. Knock-Out Reilly. General wear, creasing, G/VG.	100.00

| Cowboy Stories 1925 May | Crack Detective 1947 Jan | Crime Busters 1938 Oct | Cupid's Capers 1934 Jun |

Complete Stories
1936 September. Great cover of a blonde defending herself with a knife by R. G. Harris. Some chipping &
     small tears to extremities, top right corner off back cover, 1.5" spine split, VG-.   60.00
1937 Sept/Oct. Last issue, skull cover, moderate surface creasing, VG-.   95.00

Confession Novel of the Month
1940 May, #1. Swastika Bride cover. Moderate surface creasing, VG-.   95.00

Cosmos Science Fiction
1953 September, #1.Cover by Alex Schomburg. Includes *The Troublemakers* by Poul Anderson,
    The Great C by Philip K. Dick; *The Curse* by Arthur C. Clarke. General wear, some creasing, VG.   20.00
1953 September, #1. Cover by Alex Schomburg. Includes *The Troublemakers* by Poul Anderson;
    The Great C by Philip K. Dick; *The Curse* by Arthur C. Clarke, FN+.   35.00
1953 Nov, #2. Contains *The Gentleman Is an Epwa* by Carl Jacobi, *Shape Up* by Jack Vance,
    With Intent to Kill by John Jakes, *Outside in the Sand* by Evan Hunter (Ed McBain) VF.   30.00

Courtroom Stories
April 1932. Considered "very rare." This Harold Hersey pulp is rarely encountered in any
    condition let alone in high grade as this issue is. Last issue of the short run. Very minor wear mainly
    to extremities with 1/2" perished from foot of spine and nice supple paper. FN-.   1,250.00

Cowboy Romances
1937 August, #1. Wrap coming loose, ½" tear to spine, VG.   100.00

Cowboy Stories
1925 May. A very rare one shot. General Lite wear and mild surface wear to spine. A solid hefty book with
    perhaps just a few know copies VG+.   995.00

Crack Detective (And Mystery)
1944 May. Some int. tp, chipping, VG-.   45.00
1944 July. General wear, piece off lower right corner, VG.   40.00
1945 November. General wear, creasing, edge wear, slight spine cock, VG-.   40.00
1947 January. Classic magician cover. General wear, some small tears. VG-   50.00
1947 June. General wear, browning, G/VG. Nice spider cover.   45.00
1947 October. General wear, chip off right edge of front cover, VG-.   30.00
1948 February. Skeleton cover. 1.5" tear thru book at spine. G   25.00
1948 November. John D. MacDonald. Some cresting and chipping to cover, VG-.   40.00
1949 March. Bondage bathtub cover. General wear, chipping to extremities, supple paper. VG   75.00
1956 December. Restart issue. General wear, readers crease at spine. VG.   40.00
1956 Dec. Surface creasing, some chipping, lr corner off, G/VG.   25.00
1957 July. General wear, chip off near top right corner, G/VG.   45.00

Crack Shot Western
1941 September. Some minor creasing and trim to right edge, VG+.   50.00
1941 September. 2" tear at foot of spine, general wear, G/VG.   35.00
1941 October. Gene Autry cover. Long chip off top right corner and small chip and tear at bottom, G/VG.   40.00

Crime Busters
1938 December. Norgil the Magician by Walter Gibson (Maxwell Grant.) 1" piece of spine loose and laid in, VG.   125.00
1938 October. Gadget Man by Lester Dent. General wear, some creasing, VG+.   175.00

Cupid's Capers
1934 June. Probably the 7th of possibly 8 issues, though more may exist. A very difficult title to put together a run of. All issues seem
    to be very scarce to rare. Stamped sample copy to top right corner and closed spine split above top staple, Shows extremely
    well with great vibrant colors to cover. Appears fine or better but because of the split we will call it VG+.   1,500.00

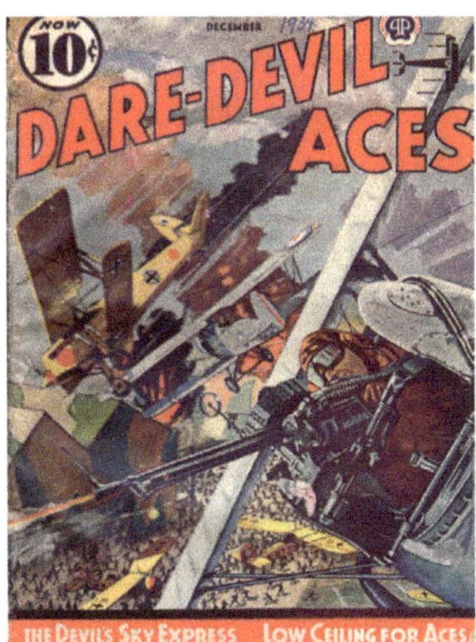
Dare-Devil Aces 1939 Dec

Dare-Devil Aces 1940 Aug

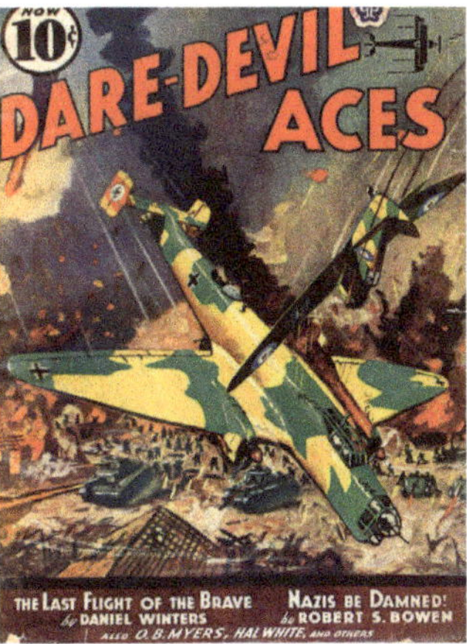
Dare-Devil Aces 1940 Oct

Dare-Devil Aces 1941 Nov

Dare-Devil Aces

1933 July. Some interior tape, VG.	75.00
1936 March. NF.	60.00
1936 April. FN.	70.00
1936 April. Mild spine lean, lite wear, VG/FN.	60.00
1936 May. Surface creasing, VG.	50.00
1936 June. 4" spine split, moderate chipping, G.	20.00
1936 August. Lite foxing to cover, VG/FN.	60.00
1936 December. Moderate creasing to cover, VG.	50.00
1937 May. Back cover almost loose, G.	20.00
1937 September. Moderate creasing to cover, G/VG.	30.00
1937 September. Mild surface creasing, some chipping to over hangs, VG.	40.00
1937 October. Some interior tape, VG.	40.00
1937 Nov. Few sm tears above logo at edge, VG/FN.	60.00
1937 Dec. Moderate creasing, VG.	40.00
1939 Jan. SM lower left corner off, mild damp staining at logo not too noticeable from outside, VG.	40.00
1938 February. Some loss at over hangs, VG+.	50.00
1938 March. Lite surface creasing, 1" split to foot of spine, VG.	40.00
1938 April. 1" x 3" piece off bc, G/VG.	30.00
1938 December. Lite wear, some mild staining to spine, VG/FN.	60.00
1939 February. Surface and readers creases, VG-.	35.00
1939 April. "1939" written in ink above logo, mild wear, VG.	40.00
1939 April. Spine lean, creasing, chipping to top edge, G/VG.	30.00
1939 May. Chipping and loss of paper to over hangs, few small tears, G/VG.	30.00
1939 June. Chipping and loss of paper to over hangs, few small tears, G/VG.	30.00
1939 July. Interior tape, G/VG.	30.00
1939 August. Moderate chipping to both covers and 1" x 2" piece off bc, G+.	20.00
1939 September. Moderate chipping to extremities, G/VG.	30.00
1939 October. Large corner off bc, 2 1" tears to fc, chipping, G/VG.	30.00
1939 October. General wear and creasing, VG.	40.00
1939 December. Moderate damp staining, chipping, G+.	20.00
1940 January. Large ship off right edge, VG.	30.00
1940 February. Damp staining to fc, 1" x 2" piece off bc & 2" tear , G+.	20.00
1940 March. Mild spine lean, some damp staining, VG-.	25.00
1940 May. Mild loss at over hangs, VG.	30.00
1940 June. Moderate chipping to extremities, some damp staining, G/VG.	25.00
1940 July. Lite wear, 2" tear to right edge, G/VG.	25.00
1940 August. Mild wear, small piece off lower left corner, VG.	30.00
1940 September. 2.5" spine split, 3" jagged tear to right edge, some damp staining, G+.	15.00
1940 October. Small chipping and few small tears to extremities, sm piece off near top right corner, G/VG.	25.00
1940 November. Mild chipping to bottom edge, VG/FN.	45.00
1941 January. Pencil writing to bc, lite surface creasing, VG.	30.00
1941 February. Moderate surface creasing, VG-.	25.00
1941 March. Crease to back cover, NF.	55.00
1941 April. FN.	60.00
1941 May. Moderate surface creasing, VG.	30.00
1941 July. Contains *Bombs Over Burma* by David Goodis writing as David Crewe. 1.5" tear at bottom of cover, moderate surface creasing, few tears to cover, G+.	30.00
1941 Nov. Very small lower left corner tip off, VG+.	40.00
1942 January. Moderate chipping, lower right corner off, G+.	20.00
1942 March. Moderate chipping, lower right corner off, G+.	20.00
1942 May. Contains *Fly It, Sailor!* by David Goodis writing as David Crewe. 5" tear at logo, browning flaking paper, G.	25.00
1942 July. Small tp to cover, VG+.	35.00
1942 September. General lite wear, mild creasing mainly to over hangs, 2 1" spine splits, VG-.	25.00

Dare-Devil Aces 1946 Nov

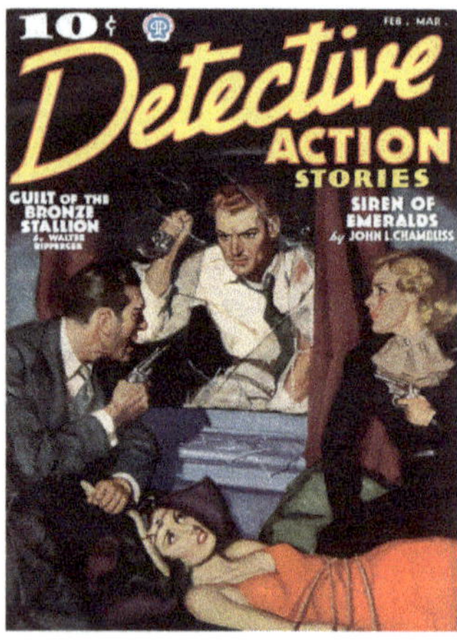

Detective Action 1937 Feb

Detective Book 1930 Aug

Detective Book 1953 Win

1942 November. Moderate creasing, tears, G+.	20.00
1943 January. FN.	60.00
1943 May. Moderate surface creasing, some damp staining, G/VG.	25.00
1943 August. Aggressive wear, FR/G.	10.00
1943 Oct. 1" tear thru book at spine, FR/G.	10.00
1943 December. Contains *Grandstand Ace* by David Goodis. Moderate surface creasing, 1" x 1" corner off bc, G.	30.00
1944 February. Moderate surface creasing, 2" x 2" corner off bc, G+.	20.00
1944 April. Lite creasing and wear, VG+.	35.00
1944 June. Lite creasing and wear, VG+.	35.00
1946 January. Half of last page perished, FR.	10.00
1946 February. Contains *The Last Dogfight* by David Goodis. Lite wear and handling, VG/FN.	75.00
1946 March. Contains *Marauders Never Retreat* by David Goodis. Aggressive wear, FR.	15.00
1946 July. Contains *Boches For Breakfast* by David Goodis. General wear and surface creasing, VG.	60.00
1946 September. Diagonal crease to cover,1" tear, few sm chips, G/VG.	25.00
1946 Nov. Final issue. Contains *Raiders Fight Alone!* By David Goodis. Lite wear and creasing, VG/FN.	95.00

Detective Action

1936 October. General mild wear and handling, small split at foot of spine with nice supple paper. VG/FN.	225.00
1937 January. Moderate wear & surface creasing, 1" tear at right edge, G/VG.	85.00
1937 Feb/Mar. Bondage torture cover, VF.	300.00

Detective and Murder Mystery

1941 February. Lite wear and handling, VG/FN.	125.00

Detective Book

1930 August, #5. Partial spine, moderate flaking to paper, some chipping, FR/G.	40.00
1930 October. Damp staining to cover and interior, rusty staples, 2" tear at foot of spine, FR.	25.00
1931 April. Covers loose, some loss of paper at extremities, FR.	25.00
1931 August. Some spine damage, small tears and chipping to extremities, G/VG.	85.00
1940-1941 Winter. Some paper perished from spine, splits at ends, interior brown tape to edges, G.	25.00
1942 Summer. Moderate surface creasing, VG-.	30.00
1945 Winter. 2" ss, some surface creasing and creasing to right edge, VG-.	35.00
1945 Winter. Damp stain, rusty staple, G/VG.	25.00
1945 Spring. Small piece off spine, general wear, creasing, some chipping, G+.	25.00
1946/47 Spring. Moderate wear and creasing, G/VG.	30.00
1949 Fall. Excess glue to inside fc, general wear, large grease pencil , G/VG.	35.00
1949 Fall. Some damp staining to cover with surface abrasion to lower cover, G+.	25.00
1951/52 Winter. Contains *The House that Stood Still* by A.E. Van Vogt. Moderate wear and creasing, G/VG.	30.00
1952/53 Winter, final issue. Trim to bottom edge & some loose of paper at top of pulp, G+.	30.00

Detective Dime Novels

1940 April, #1. Shadow above logo and lower ½" as if something was laying on top of the pulp for years. Else lite wear, VG+.	75.00

Detective Fiction Weekly

1929 May 18. Moderate wear, ½" tips off spine ends, G+.	25.00
1930 March 15. General lite wear, VG+.	40.00
1930 September 20. Moderate chipping, fc, loose, G.	15.00
1930 November 22. Moderate wear, creasing, some chips to extremities, G/VG.	25.00
1931 October 10. Death skeleton cover, 4" tear to cover, few tears, G/VG.	25.00
1932 February 6. Contains *It Takes a Crook* by Erle Stanley Gardner. Bc loose, paper flaking, lr corner off, G+.	25.00
1932 April 23. Lite wear, mild chipping to extremities, VG+.	40.00
1932 April 23. General wear & creasing, dingy cover, VG-.	25.00
1932 May 21. Lite wear, mild chipping to extremities, VG+.	40.00
1932 June 11. Lite wear, mild chipping to extremities, VG+.	40.00

Detective Dime Novels 1940 Apr

DFW 1931 Oct 10

DFW 1937 Oct 2

DFW 1938 Sept 17

1933 May 27. General wear, mild flaking some spine damage, VG.	35.00
1933 June 17. Moderate wear, creasing and sm tears to cover, G+.	15.00
1934 April 14. Excess glue to first page, some paper perished at spine, G/VG.	25.00
1934 July 21. General wear, sm paper off tips of spine, mild flaking, G/VG.	25.00
1934 December 29. General wear, splits to back cover, mild flaking, VG-.	30.00
1935 April 13. Contains *Spy!* By Max Brand. General wear, quarter size pobc, some staining, VG-.	30.00
1935 April 27. Electric chair cover. General lite wear, 1" tear, some chipping, VG.	50.00
1935 May 11. Contains *Spy!* By Max Brand. General wear, 1" chip off right edge, couple ½" tears, VG-.	30.00
1935 June 29. General lite wear, mild creasing, VG/FN.	45.00
1935 August 31. 1.5" tear, some chipping to extremities, VG.	35.00
1936 January 25. Cornell Woolrich, large tear to cover, wear, chipping. G/VG.	40.00
1936 November 21. Contains the conclusion of Seven Faces by Max Brand. General wear, creasing, sm tears, G/VG.	25.00
1936 February 1. General lite wear, nice paper, VG/FN.	45.00
1936 August 29. Interior tape, chip of lower left corner, G/VG.	25.00
1936 August 29. Max Brand, Paul Ernst. Moderate wear, chipping, flaking, G/VG.	25.00
1936 November 7. Max Brand. Top left corner off back cover, nice paper, VG-.	35.00
1936 December 12. Table of contents page loose, dark flaking paper. G+.	20.00
1937 January 9. Candid Jones. General wear, mild trim, mild flaking to paper. G/VG.	40.00
1937 February 20. Tos , 2" spine split, mild flaking. G+.	15.00
1937 March 13. Bulldog Drummond cover. Front cover half off. Spine split, moderate wear, G+	30.00
1937 March 20. Sm corner off bc, general wear, VG-.	25.00
1937 August 21. Hooded skeleton cover. General lite wear, some creasing, VG/FN.	75.00
1937 August 28. Nice lite handling, lite tan supple paper. FN-.	45.00
1937 September 4. Bulldog Drummond. 1" spine split, mild wear & surface creasing, nice paper.	30.00
1937 October 2. Some damp staining to cover, couple of small holes, general wear, G/VG.	20.00
1937 October 23. General wear, few small tears, G/VG.	20.00
1937 November 6. Mild wear, some flaking, VG.	25.00
1937 December 18. Readers and surface creasing, VG.	25.00
1937 December 25. Small chip off right edge, small tears to over hangs, VG.	25.00
1938 January 22. Moderate wear, pencil marks to logo, G/VG.	20.00
1938 March 19. Tos, int. tp., repaired tear, writing to logo, G.	15.00
1938 April 9. Contains *Match Ya for It* by Hugh B. Cave. Some chipping to over hangs, else very nice looking pulp, VG.	35.00
1938 August 27. Contains *Make Way For a Dagger* a Candid Jones story By Richard Sale. ½" X 3"off tr corner, G/VG.	30.00
1938 March 26. Contains *Coffins For Three* conclusion by Frederic C. Davis. General wear, creasing, VG.	30.00
1938 May 7. Mild wear, small tears, FN-.	40.00
1938 May 7. Moderate wear and creasing, G/VG.	20.00
1938 May 28. General lite wear and surface creasing, VG+.	30.00
1938 July 9. General wear and surface creasing, VG.	40.00
1938 July 16. General wear, creasing, mild chipping, VG.	25.00
1938 July 30. Moderate creasing, mild trim, VG.	25.00
1938 August 6. Contains *The Saint at Bay* by Leslie Charteris. Small lower right corner off, VG.	60.00
1938 September 17. 1st Dr. Skull. Store stamps to cover, lower corners off, 3" tear, G/VG.	50.00
1938 October 29. Moderate wear and chipping, G+.	18.00
1938 December 3. General wear, 1" tear to bc, VG.	30.00
1938 December 31. Moderate wear, some loss to over hangs, G/VG.	20.00
1939 February 25. Damp staining, rusty staples, G+.	15.00
1939 April 15. Contains *Death Comes For a Diva* by Hugh B. Cave. Moderate pieces missing from cover, G+.	20.00
1939 April 22. Contains *The Mystery of the Maudlin Mermaid* by Hugh B. Cave. L.l. Corner off, some chipping, VG.	25.00
1939 May 6. Nbc, G.	15.00
1939 May 20. General wear, moderate chips off bc, VG-.	25.00
1939 June 3. Surface creasing, chipping to extremities, VG-.	25.00
1939 August 5. Mild wear, VG/FN.	45.00
1939 August 19. Mild wear, VG/FN.	45.00
1939 August 26. General wear, some damp staining, scuff marks to logo, VG.	30.00
1939 September 30. General lite wear and handling, top left corner off bc, VG-.	25.00

Detective Novel 1938 Jan

Detective Novel 1944 Apr

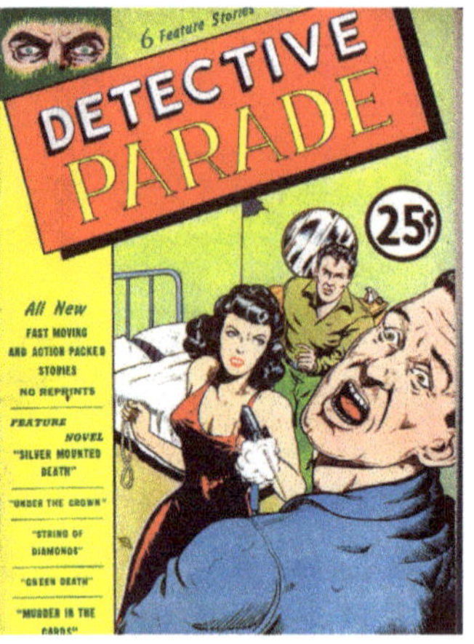

Detective Parade 1945

Detective Story 1929 Dec

1939 October 7. Moderate wear and creasing, tears to over hangs, VG-.	20.00
1939 October 21. Lite wear, VG/FN.	45.00
1939 November 25. Hugh B. Cave. Lite wear, FN.	60.00
1939 December 23. Hugh B. Cave. Lite wear with mild chipping, VG+.	40.00
1940 May 25. Contains *The Bloody Isle* pt. 1 by T. T. Flynn. ½" off foot of spine, Lite wear, VG.	30.00
1940 October 19. Contains *Herbie Rides His Hunch* by Fredric Brown. 2 chips off edge, VG.	40.00

Detective Mystery Novel.

1948 Spring. Stories by Leslie Charteris and Robert Leslie Bellem. Some chipping, mild creasing, VG.	25.00
Winter 1949. 1" tear at bottom edge, Lite wear, VG+.	35.00

Detective Novel

1938 January-February, #1. Lite wear, mild creasing, small tears, 1.5" tear at top of spine, VG.	150.00
1940 August. 1st appearance of the Crimson Mask. General wear and some creasing to cover, VG.	175.00
1943 September. Candid camera kid story by John L. Benton. Mild wear, nice paper, Printed in Canada. VG+	50.00
1944 March. Candid camera Kid story by John L. Benton. Mild wear, small tp to crown of spine, printed in Canada, VG.	40.00
1944 April. Last Crimson Mask. Few pages loose and interior tears, general moderate wear, G+.	60.00
1944 June. Nazi cover. Candid Camera Kid story. General wear and creasing, VG-.	75.00
1946 February. Cobra cover, Old tape to spine, back cover almost loose, G/VG.	40.00
1946 August. Great Skull cover by Belarski. Lite wear, small tears, creases, VG.	40.00
1946 August. Moderate damp staining, wear. G/VG	30.00
1947 January. Lite wear, FN-.	55.00
1947 January. General wear, tanning supple paper. Mild chipping to edges. VG-	40.00
1947 March. Moderate wear, chipping and creasing, tanning supple paper. G/VG.	30.00
1947 March. 2" tear at top left corner, creasing, G/VG.	25.00
1947 November. General mild wear, some chipping. VG	40.00
1947 November. General wear, small paper perished from foot of spine, 1" tear to right edge, G/VG.	20.00
1948-Fall. General lite wear, small tear at foot of spine, VG+.	40.00
1948 Fall. Small corner off, lower left, mild chipping and mild flaking to paper. VG-	35.00
1949 February. Split, quarter size piece off lower left corner, G/VG.	25.00
1949 Spring. General wear, some chipping, VG.	35.00
1949 Winter. Bondage cover. Piece off at lower left corner, chipping, G/VG.	30.00

Detective Parade

1945, #1. Rare one shot from Frank Comunale Publishing Co. Lite wear with great off white paper, FN/VF.	1,500.00

Detective Reporter

1937 September. Damp staining to covers, 2" spine split, mild trim to covers G/VG. Scarce to very scarce.	150.00

Detective Short Stories

1939 March. Center crease, edge chipping, VG-.	80.00

Detective Story Magazine

1921 March 26. Few tears at extremities, some creasing and stain to back cover, VG-.	40.00
1921 Oct 1. Contains *The Man in Purple* by Johnston McCulley. General wear, some chipping, VG-.	150.00
1922 Sept 2. Moderate wear and creasing, G/VG.	45.00
1922 November 11. Large tear, interior tape, aggressive wear, G+.	20.00
1929 February 2. ½" off crown of spine, few small tears, VG-.	45.00
1929 December 7. 1" tear at logo, lite wear, mild loss of paper to over-hangs, VG.	50.00
1935 December. Coughlin cover, multiple vertical creasing, nice paper, VG.	75.00
1936 April. Lovell cover, lite wear, lite trim, nice paper, VG+.	95.00
1941 April. Contains *Death On Post* #7 pt. 1 by Frank Gruber. Spine damage, creasing, bc loose, G/VG.	10.00
1941 May. L.l. corner off, chip off top edge, VG-.	25.00
1941 Oct. Surface creasing, lite readers crease, VG-.	25.00
1949 Spring. Second to last issue, scarce. Small tears mainly to over hangs, VG.	150.00

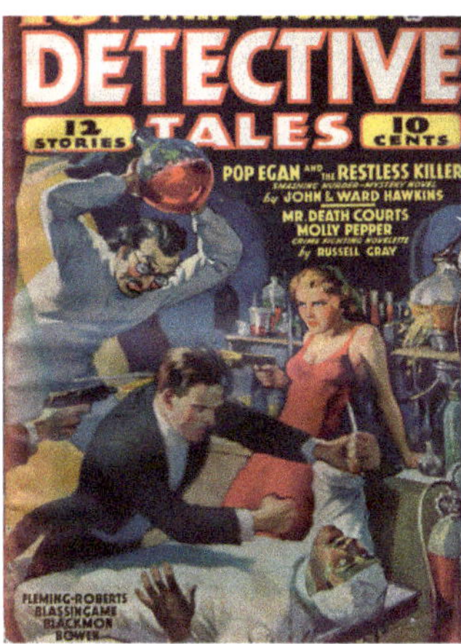

Detective Tales 1939 Feb

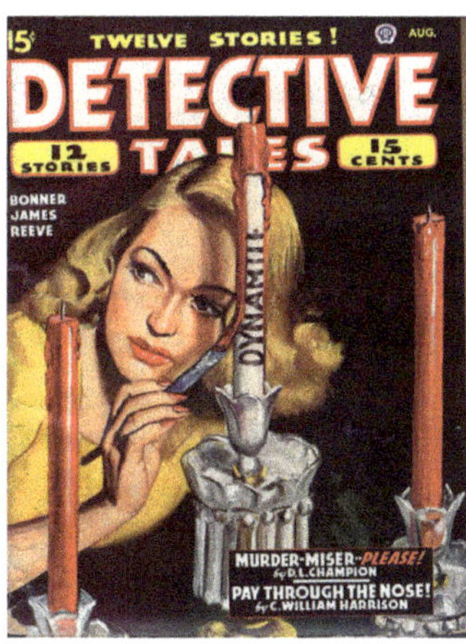

Detective Tales 1944 Aug

Detective Tales 1948 Oct

Dime Adventure 1935 June

Detective Tales

1935 December. Coughlin cover, multiple vertical creasing, nice paper, VG.	85.00
1936 March. Oriental menace cover. General wear, some creasing, sm tears to extremities, G/VG.	60.00
1936 April. Lovell cover, lite wear, lite trim, nice paper, VG+.	95.00
1937 June. Branding Cover. Branding cover. Moderate creasing, small tears to extremities, G/VG.	60.00
1938 May. Period based oriental menace cover. Surface creasing, nice paper VG+.	80.00
1939 February. Some damp staining, mainly to lower cover and some pages, G/VG.	60.00
1939 August. Nude cover. Piece off lr edge, general creasing, few small tears, VG-.	100.00
1941 June. Moderate wear, chipping G/VG.	25.00
1941 January. Damp staining to pulp, G+.	25.00
1942 September. Tear to lower corner, small interior tape, VG.	50.00
1943 September. Aggressive wear, covers almost loose, G+.	15.00
1943 September. Readers crease, surface creasing, VG.	50.00
1944 August. Dynamite candle cover. Front cover cut a bit off center, chipping to back cover, VG.	95.00
1944 January. Staining to logo, aggressive interior tape, G+.	25.00
1944 June. General wear, readers crease, G/VG.	35.00
1946 July. VG+ with decent cream supple pages.	45.00
1946 May. John D. MacDonald 1st pulp appearance. Moderate creasing and readers crease, G/VG.	250.00
1946 Oct. 1.5" spine split to back cover, few small tears and creasing, VG+.	50.00
1947 May Contains the first appearance of *Giant Killer* by D. L. Champion, VG+.	55.00
1947 May. General lite wear, mild trim, VG+.	45.00
1947 December. Moderate creasing, medium chip off top left corner, G+.	25.00
1948 January. Lite wear, some creasing, VG+.	35.00
1948 October. Contains *If Looks Could Kill!* By Fredric Brown. General lite wear, mild trim, VG.	65.00
1948 October. Contains *If Looks Could Kill!* By Fredric Brown. L.r. corner off, moderate creasing, G.	25.00
1949 February. Contains *Killers' Nest* by John D. MacDonald. Moderate surface creasing, VG.	50.00
1949 October. *Blue Stars for a Dead Lady* By John D. MacDonald. Trim to right edge, else VG+.	50.00
1950 June. Contains *Blind Lead* by Fredric Brown. Some chipping, ½" loss at foot of spine, VG-.	45.00
1950 Oct. Slight spine lean, readers crease, 1" tear to right edge, VG-.	35.00
1951 February. John D. MacDonald, Hugh B. Cave. FN.	60.00
1951 April. Contains *The Deadliest Game* by John D. MacDonald, *Seven Dirty Dollars* by Hugh B. Cave, and *If I Should Die Before I Wake* by Cornell Woolrich. Lite wear, FN.	125.00
1951 Dec. Some surface creasing, mild readers crease, VG.	35.00
1952 February. Moderate surface creasing, few small tears, G/VG.	25.00
1952 June. Good condition with nice cream supple pages.	35.00

Detective Yarns.

1939 April. Small burn mark to cover with nice paper. G/VG. Scarce.	125.00

Dime Adventure

1935 June, #1. Mild center crease, slight spine lean, VG+.	150.00

Dime Detective

1933 February 15. Browning paper, flaking, nice looking cover, G+.	95.00
1933 Dec 15. Book trimmed, G.	75.00
1934 May 15th. Some chipping, interior tape. G+.	75.00
1934 August 15. Howitt cover. Aggressive creasing, VG-.	110.00
1934 October 15. Howitt cover. Slight spine lean, readers crease, mild wear, VG-.	125.00
1934 December 15. Baumhoffer cover. Readers crease, slight spine lean, store stamp to logo VG-.	150.00
1935 January 1. Tattoo cover, readers crease, lite wear, mild trim, VG+.	275.00
1935 January 15. Lite pencil writing, lite diagonal crease to lr corner, shows well, VG.	200.00
1935 February 1. Baumhoffer bondage & ghost cover. Lite wear, readers crease, VG+.	275.00
1935 April 15. Baumhoffer bondage cover. Couple of vertical creases, general wear, VG.	250.00
1936 March. Book trimmed, G.	55.00

Dime Detective 1935 Jan 15

Dime Detective 1939 Oct

Dime Detective 1943 Jul

Dime Mystery 1934 Nov

1936 April. Contains the Race Williams story *Just Another Stiff* by Carroll John Daly, a Cardigan story *Lead Poison* by Frederick Nebel the *The Living Lie Down With the Dead* by Cornell Woolrich. Readers crease, some creasing to lr corner, VG-.	175.00
1937 March. Contains a Cardigan story by Frederick Nebel. Loss of paper to right edge, G/VG.	75.00
1938 February. Baumhoffer. Lite wear to extremities, readers crease, some damp staining, G/VG.	75.00
1939 February. Bondage cover. Moderate damp staining, mild flaking & wear G/VG.	85.00
1939 October. Bondage cover. Lite wear mainly to extremities, some loss to over hangs, mild flaking, VG+.	295.00
1942 October. Int. tp starting to bleed thru, 3" spine split, shows well, G/VG.	40.00
1943 July. Lite wear mild trim FN-.	95.00
1944 Jan. Moderate creasing, some chipping, G/VG.	40.00
1945 February. Nice séance cover image. Lite wear, VG+ Printed in Canada.	65.00
1945 June. General wear and some creasing with lite tan supple paper. Printed in Canada, VG+.	40.00
1945 October. General wear, some creasing, few small tears. Printed in Canada, VG.	55.00
1946 March. Contains *Some Like 'Em Dead* by Frederick C. Davis. Lite wear, VG+.	75.00
1947 Jan. Mild surface creasing, slight spine lean, VG.	60.00
1947 March. Readers creases, some chipping, VG-.	55.00
1947 June. Lite creasing , mild trim, VG.	45.00
1948 March. Contains *With Soul So Dead* by John D. MacDonald, Nine Toes Up! by Frederick C. Davis. Lite wear & creasing, VG.	65.00
1948 April. Evil clown cover by Normal Saunders. General wear, VG.	60.00
1948 June. Readers crease & general wear, surface creasing, paper pull to back cover, VG-.	45.00
1949 January. Contains Kill-And-Run Blond by Frederick C. Davis. Moderate wear and creasing, G/VG.	40.00
1949 October. Contains *Race Williams Cooks A Goose* and *Target For Tonight* by John D. MacDonald. Lite wear and handling, VG+.	125.00
1949 Dec. Contains *Take a Powder, Galahad!* By John D. MacDonald. Sm l.l. corner off, VG.	45.00
1950 February. Contains *Blind Witness* by Frederick C. Davis. Lite wear and surface creasing, VG/FN.	60.00
1950 June. Contains *College-Cut Kill* by John D. MacDonald. Rub mark to lower staple, FN-.	60.00
1951 April. Sm chip to lower edge, FN-.	50.00
1951 June. Contains *Guns Across the Table* by Frederick C. Davis. FN/VF.	95.00
1951 April. Lite readers crease and mild wear, VG/FN.	50.00
1951 Oct. Contains *Death, My Darling Daughter* by Frederick C. Davis. Mild wear, FN.	65.00

Dime Mystery

1933 April. Mild wear & some creasing, shows well, VG+.	200.00
1934 January. Mild damp staining, lite wear, VG.	140.00
1934 May. Chip off back edge, small corner off, G/VG.	110.00
1934 June. Bondage cover. Moderate wear, creasing, sm tears to edge, 1.5" tear at logo, internal tape, G/VG.	100.00
1934 July. Cover a bit dingy, some creasing to extremities, VG-.	125.00
1934 October. Bondage, hooded Menace Cover. Sm lower left corner off, moderate surface creasing, 1" off foot of spine, VG-.	150.00
1934 November. Hooded menace cover, mild flaking, great cover, VG+.	150.00
1934 Dec. Sea creature menacing girl. Diem size chip at logo, Canadian printing, VG-.	75.00
1935 April. Hooded menace cover, mild flaking, great cover, some paper perished from overhangs, VG.	150.00
1935 April. Hooded menace cover. Trim to right edge, lite surface creasing, VG-.	120.00
1935 September. Readers crease at spine, mild wear, shows very well, VG/FN.	200.00
1935 October. Fireplace and devil cover. Contains *Mistress of the Dead* by Hugh B. Cave. Moderate creasing, G/VG.	125.00
1935 November. Hypo cover. Moderate chipping, some creasing, VG-.	175.00
1935 Oct. Bondage cover. Moderate creasing, name in ink, G/VG.	95.00
1936 November 1936 November. Classic rat cage cover. Moderate wear and creasing, G/VG.	175.00
1937 January. Bondage cover. Moderate wear and creasing, VG-.	145.00
1937 February. Small tear to right edge and 2" crease, VG+.	125.00
1937 February. Moderate readers creasing, creasing, tear to right edge, G/VG.	125.00
1937 March. Bondage, nude statue cover. Contains *When The Bat Man Thirsts* by Frederick C Davis. Surface creasing, sm tears to extremities, VG-.	175.00
1937 October. Moderate creasing, lr, corner off, G/VG.	75.00
1937 Nov. Bondage torture cover. Spine lean, creasing and sm tears to extremities, G/VG.	125.00
1937 December. Torture cover. Large piece off right edge, G+.	60.00
1938 September. Classic bondage torture skeleton cover. Small lower left corner off, mild wear, VG.	300.00

Dime Mystery 1935 Apr

Dime Mystery 1938 Sep

Doc Savage 1936 Apr

Doc Savage 1936 Jun

1939 March. Bondage cover, some loss of paper to back cover, general wear, VG.	195.00
1939 May. Classic X-Ray cover. Mild wear, FN.	350.00
1939 Oct. Moderate chipping and two corners off, G+.	45.00
1940 July. Midget attack cover. Some interior tape, 2 small holes in cover and 1st few pages, VG-.	100.00
1940 July. Store stamp, small tape to spine, Lower left corner off of back cover, G/VG.	75.00
1940 December. Mild wear and handling for Fine condition.	150.00
1941 March. Mummy Amputee Cover. General wear, some chipping, VG.	150.00
1941 May. Oriental menace cover. Two hole punches, moderate chipping, G+.	50.00
1941 July. Stain to cover, wraps coming loose from book block, G/VG.	75.00
1942 January. Bondage cover. Small tape at crown of spine, some creasing lite tan supple paper. VG.	125.00
1942 May. Few sm tears at edge, lite wear, VG/FN.	75.00
1944 July. Mild wear, NF.	75.00
1946 Jan. Skull cover. FN.	85.00
1946 Feb. Contains *The Noose Hangs High* by Robert Bloch. NF.	85.00
1946 May. Slight browning to edges, VG+.	60.00
1947 March. Miniature couple with giant hand. Mild wear, NF.	125.00
1947 January. Mummy cover. Mild wear and creasing, VG.	75.00
1947 Sept. Moderate surface creasing and readers crease, G/VG.	35.00
1947 Dec. Girl trapped in spider web. Lite wear, slight spine lean, FN-.	85.00
1948 February. General wear, mild chipping, VG.	60.00
1949 June. Flaking paper, chipping, G/VG.	30.00
1949 Oct. Mummification cover, FN.	85.00

Dime Sports

1937 March. Dime Sports 1937 March. 3" tear to cover, G/VG.	15.00
1937 May. 1" tear to back cover, otherwise, FN.	30.00
1937 October. Some creasing and small tears to extremities, VG.	20.00
1938/39 December/January. Some damp staining to lower left of cover, G/VG.	15.00
1939 November. Some chipping and small tears to over hangs, G/VG.	15.00
1940 March. 1" tear at spine, some creasing, VG+.	22.00
1943 October. Moderate surface creasing, VG.	20.00
1944 February. Lite wear, FN.	30.00

Doc Savage

1934 November. Light wear, over-hangs a bit tender, one missing, decent paper. VG/FN.	200.00
1935 September. *The Mystery of the Majii.* Some chipping, creasing and small tears to over hangs, G/VG.	85.00
1936 April. Trim, 1 non-Doc story page out. G.	40.00
1936 June. Slight loss at lower left corner, very mild loss to over hangs, shows well, VG/FN.	185.00
1938 June. *The Submarine Mystery.* Sm tp to spine ends, surface creasing, G/VG.	50.00
1938 Dec. *The Devil Genghis.* Moderate surface creasing, few tears to right edge, VG-.	65.00
1939 July. *Merchants of Disaster.* Lite wear, very mild trim, nice looking. VG/FN.	75.00
1939 May. *The Gold Ogre* 1" tear at bottom edge, shows well. VG/FN.	95.00
1940 August. *Tunnel Terror.* Ham cover. General Lite wear. FN-.	95.00
1940 December. *The Men Vanished.* Small tape on spine, mild interior tape, Lite wear, VG.	50.00
1940 February. *The Angry Ghost.* Minor paper perished from spine, 1" spine split. VG+.	55.00
1940 May. *The Boss of Terror.* Lite wear, few small closed tears, VG+.	55.00
1940 June. *The Awful Egg.* Monk cover. General Lite wear. FN-.	95.00
1941 April. *The Golden Man.* Minor spine damage, Lite wear. VG+.	50.00
1941 July. Doc Savage 1941 July. Moderate wear, creasing some chips off, G/VG.	40.00
1941 June. *The Headless Men.* General wear and creasing, VG.	45.00
1941 August. General wear, some creasing, 1.5 " spine split, Lite tan supple paper, VG.	60.00
1941 September. *The Mindless Monsters.* Lite wear, minor staple wear, VG/FN.	70.00
1942 January. General Lite wear, some creasing, VG/FN.	70.00
1942 August. *The Three Wild Men.* General Lite wear, name stamp to cover and some pages, VG/FN.	70.00
1942 October. The Laugh of Death. Lite wear, FN.	95.00

Doc Savage 1949 Sum

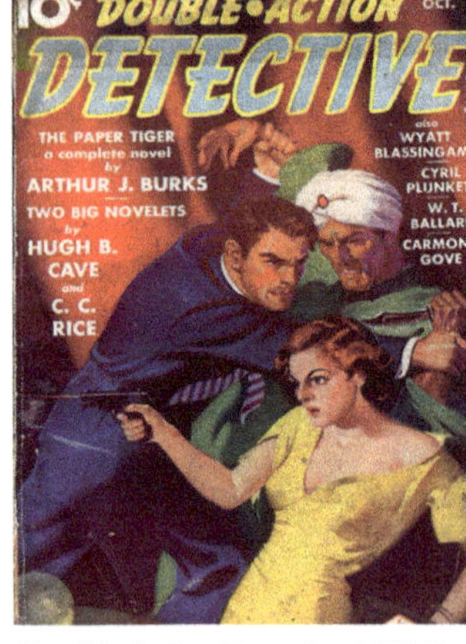

Double Action Detective 1938 Oct

Double Action Gang 1936 May

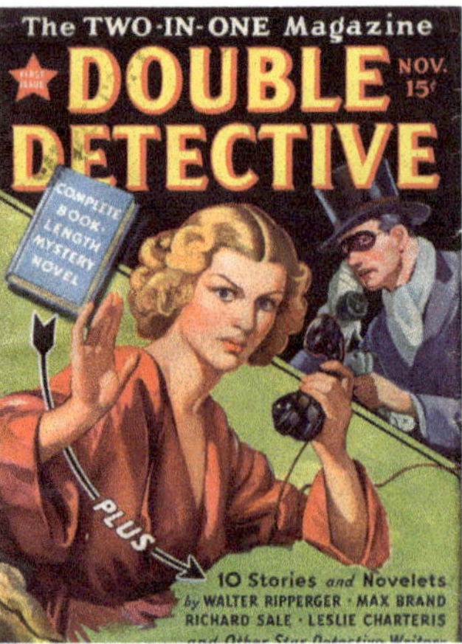

Double Detective 1937 Nov

1943 January. *The Time Terror.* Lite wear dinosaur cover, FN-	125.00
1943 July. *Mystery on Happy Bones.* Small tape on spine, Lite tan supple paper. VG/FN.	80.00
1943 May. *The Talking Devil.* Lite wear, mild creasing, VG/FN.	85.00
1943 September. *Hell Below.* General Lite wear, minor damage to spine, G/VG.	45.00
1944 June. *The Pharoah's Ghost.* Lite wear, very nice paper, FN.	60.00
1944 October. *Jui San* Lite crease at center of cover, mild surface creasing, nice paper, VG/FN.	70.00
1944 October. *Jui San.* Piece off back cover, VG.	40.00
1945 April. *Cargo Unknown.* Top right corner off, VG.	50.00
1945 December. *The Screaming Man.* Very Lite wear, FN/VF.	80.00
1945 May. *Rock Sinister.* Lite wear, nice paper, FN.	60.00
1946 March. *Terror and the Lonely Widow.* FN/VF.	80.00
1946 April. *Five Fathoms Dead.* Also contains the Frank Herbert short story *Jonah and the Jap* his first pulp appearance. Mild center crease. FN-.	150.00
1946 July. *Fire and Ice.* Mild wear, nice, FN.	60.00
1947 Nov/Dec. *Once Over Litely.* Also *Or The World Will Die* by John D. MacDonald. Lite wear, sm paper off top of spine. FN-	100.00
1947 Sept/Oct. *Let's Kill Ames.* Also *The Chinese Pit* by John D. MacDonald. Lite wear. FN-	100.00
1948 Mar/Apr. Moderate wear, some chipping to spine, G.	25.00
1948 March/Apr. Only Cartier Doc Savage cover. The Pure Evil. Lite wear, mild readers crease, VG/FN.	125.00
1948 March/Apr. Scarce. Mild readers crease, lite wear, VG+.	115.00
1948 July/August. Scarce. Mild damage to spine, mild vertical crease to center of cover, VG.	120.00
1949 Winter. *The Green Master.* Some loss at bottom extremities of cover and some pages, chipping to right edge and some damp staining most evident to back cover, G/VG.	150.00
1949 Spring. *Return from Cormoral.* 2" paper off spine, extra staples, general wear. G/VG.	200.00
1949 Spring. *Return from Cormoral.* Lite wear and handling, some chipping to bottom edge of cover, few small tears to over hangs, VG.	225.00
1949 Spring. *Return from Cormoral.* Top corners off cover, scarce, VG-.	200.00
1949 Summer. *Up from Earths Center.* Last scarce issue. Moderate loss of paper to bottom edge of cover and several pages, nice paper, G/VG.	250.00

Double Action Detective

1938 October, #1. Hugh B. Cave. General wear and handling, creasing, G/VG.	150.00

Double Action Gang

1936 May, #1. Double Action Gang 1936 May, #1. lite wear, VG+.	250.00
1937 December. #1. Contains *White Way To Hell* by E. Hoffmann Price. Diagonal crease, mild wear, mild trim, VG-.	60.00

Double Action Western

1934 September, #1. Mild flaking to dark paper, VG-.	200.00
1939 November. General wear, some creasing and tears, tape to cover, G.	10.00
1942 January. some creasing and tears, pencil marks to cover, VG.	15.00
1944 January. General wear, some creasing and tears, tanning supple paper interior, VG.	15.00
1944 March. General wear, some creasing and tears, lower left corner off, tanning supple paper interior., VG-.	12.00
1945 March. General wear, some creasing and tears, tanning supple paper interior, VG.	12.00
1946 January. General wear, some creasing and tears, quarter size piece off above logo, G/VG.	10.00
1951 January. General wear, some creasing and tears, some paper perish from spine, VG-.	10.00
1953 May. General wear, some creasing and tears, some paper perish from spine, VG.	15.00
1954 March. General wear, some creasing and tears, some paper perish from spine, tape on spine, G/VG.	10.00
1954 May. General wear, some creasing and tears, one fifth cover missing from bottom, g.	5.00
1957 April. General wear, some creasing, mild damp stain, G/VG.	10.00
1957 February. General wear, some creasing and tears, slight loss of paper at bottom left corner, VG+.	15.00
1957 February. Some creasing and tears, spine split half way up plus two inch tear into cover, G/VG.	10.00

Double Detective

1937 November. #1. Stamped "Sample Copy" to bc, lite dealers stamp to logo Shows very well with great colors, VG/FN.	200.00

Dusty Ayres 1934 Nov

Dynamic Adventures 1935 Oct

Exciting Mysteries 1942 Oct

Exciting Mystery 1943 Win

Dusty Ayres and His Battle Birds
1934 July. 1st issue. Moderate creasing, some int tp., G/VG.	225.00
1934 August. Science Fiction cover. Moderate wear and creasing, top left and lower right corners off, G.	50.00
1934 August. Science Fiction cover. Large tear in cover mended with tp on verso. FR/G.	30.00
1934 November. Science Fiction Cover. General wear, readers crease and some surface creasing, VG-.	150.00
1935 January. Science Fiction Cover. Aggressive wear, and creasing, tape to spine, G.	65.00

       Also see sets and runs section.

Dynamic Adventures
1935 October. #1. Scarce. Saunders Mountie cover. Edge wear, hole in back cover penetrates a few pages, G/VG.	200.00

Dynamic Science Stories
1939 February, #1. Contains *Mutineers Of Space* by Lloyd Eshback. Lite wear, mild trim, FN-.	75.00
1939 April/May, #2. Contains *Prison Of Time* by Eando Binder. Lite wear, mild trim, VG/FN.	100.00
1939 April/May, #2. Moderate surface creasing, some tos, G/VG.	40.00

Exciting Baseball
1951 #4. Moderate wear, 1.5" tear to right edge, some creasing, VG-.	25.00

Exciting Detective
1942 March. The Purple Scar story. Damp staining mainly to bc and last few pages, chipping, G/VG.	60.00

Exciting Football
1948 Winter. Lite wear, creasing, VG+.	25.00
1951 Fall. Moderate wear, creasing to cover. G/VG.	20.00

Exciting Love
1941 Winter, #1. Mild chipping to overhangs. VG+.	75.00
1941 Winter, #1. Moderate creasing, 1" tear to right edge, G/VG.	45.00

Exciting Mystery
1942 October, #1. Moderate wear, surface creasing, 1.5" tear to bottom left corner, some chipping, G/VG.	75.00
1943 Spring. Nazi Cover. Hole in back cover, few small tears to extremities, VG+.	125.00
1943 Winter. Nazi Cover. Nazi cover. Some chipping to extremities, 1. 5" tear to back cover, VG+.	125.00

Exciting Navy Stories
1942 April, #1. Lite wear and chipping to extremities, VG/FN.	95.00
1942 April, #1. Bc loose and in tow pieces with some loss, FR.	25.00
1942 Winter, #2. Moderate surface creasing, some chipping, G/VG.	40.00
1942 Winter, #2. Moderate wear and chipping, 3" spine split, G+.	25.00
1943 Spring, #3 (final.) Scarcest of the three issues? Piece off fc, general wear, VG-.	100.00

Exciting Sports
1941 Winter, #1. Date written on cover, else very nice FN.	100.00
1941 Winter, #1. Dust shadows to extremities, mild flaking, VG.	85.00
1941 Winter, #1. General wear, chipping, very small tape to foot of spine, VG-.	75.00
1941 Fall , #4. Some surface cresing, 1" tear to right edge, VG-.	25.00
1943 Summer. Moderate wear, lr corner off, G/VG.	20.00
1943 Fall. Lite wear and surface creasing, VG/FN.	40.00
1944 Fall. General wear, some creasing to cover, VG.	25.00
1946 Summer. 2" tear to right edge, creasing, G/VG.	20.00
1947 December. General wear, some creasing to cover, VG	25.00
1949 Fall. One inch tear to right edge, some surface creasing with Lite tan supple paper, VG+.	30.00
1950 Spring. Slight spine lean, Lite wear, tanning supple paper, VG.	25.00
1950 Summer. General wear, some creasing to cover, VG.	25.00

Exciting Western 1940 Fall

Famous Detective 1949 Nov

FFM 1942 Feb

FFM 1942 Sep

Exciting Western
1940 Fall #1. Robert Leslie Bellem. Tanning, mild staining to extremities, VG+.   150.00

Fact Detective
1939 March, #1. Photo cover. 2" tear to b.c., wear marks to front, VG-.   85.00
1939 March, #1. Photo cover. FN.   125.00

F. B. I. Detective
1950 December. Readers crease, overall very nice issue, VG/FN.   75.00
1950 June. General wear, creasing, small chip off edge, nice paper, VG.   75.00

Famous Detective
1949 Nov. #1. Skeleton cover. 4" tear to bc, shows well, VG.   100.00
1949 Nov. #1. Skeleton cover. General lite wear with small tears to over-hangs, VG.   55.00
1949 Nov. #1. Skeleton cover. Water damage to pulp, staining, rusty staples, G+.   35.00
1950 January. General wear and creasing, some chipping to extremities. VG-.   35.00
1950 June. General wear and surface creasing, some chipping to extremities. VG-.   35.00
1950 November. Aggressive creasing, sm tape to edge, G+.   20.00
1952 Feb. Lite wear, few small tears, creases mainly to extremities, VG+.   75.00
1954 Dec. Contains *Murder Yet To Come* by Carroll John Daly. Lite wear and blemish/rubbed area to tr corner, VG+.   45.00
1955 April. Showgirl cover. Lite wear and mild surface creasing, VG.   40.00
1956 April. Showgirl cover. FN.   60.00

Famous Fantastic Mysteries
1939 September, #1. See Yakima section.
1939 November, #2. Top corners off, sm tos, ½" paper perished to spine, G.   15.00
1939 December, #3. FN.   75.00
1940 January, #4. FN.   60.00
1940 February. FN.   50.00
1940 March. 1.5" closed tear at spine, VG+.   35.00
1940 April. Frank R. Paul cover art. FN.   75.00
1940 May-June. Mild wear and few sm tears to over hangs, VG+.   40.00
1940 August. Finlay cover art. Mild wear, surface creasing, VG.   45.00
1940 October. Classic Finlay cover. Tape to right edge, lower right corner off, G+.   20.00
1940 December. Frank R. Paul cover art. Mild chipping to extremities, VG+.   40.00
1941 February. Finlay cover art. Surface creasing, mild damp staining at logo, VG-.   30.00
1941 April. Finlay cover art. Lite wear to extremities, VG/FN.   45.00
1941 June. Finlay cover art. Some chipping to extremities, mild creasing, VG+.   40.00
1941 June. Finlay cover art. Moderate trim to pulp, G.   10.00
1941 August. Finlay skeleton cover. Mild cover trim and some chipping, VG.   45.00
1941 August. Finlay skeleton cover. Moderate wear, 2" split at top rear of spine, G+.   15.00
1941 Oct. Finlay nude cover. Reprints *The Colour Out of Space* by H. P. Lovecraft. Some wear, chipping to edges, VG.   85.00
1941 December. Finlay cover art. Mild trim to cover, some paper perished from spine, VG-.   35.00
1942 February. Finlay cover art. Lite wear and surface creasing, VG+.   45.00
1942 April. Finlay cover art. Sm tp to crown of spine, lite wear, VG.   40.00
1942 June. Finlay cover art. FN.   60.00
1942 July. Finlay cover art. Lite wear, store stamp to back cover, FN-.   50.00
1942 August. Finlay cover art. NF.   50.00
1942 September. Finlay cover art. Lite wear, NF.   50.00
1942 December. Finlay cover art. Some tp to spine ends, mild creasing, G/VG.   25.00
1943 March. Finlay cover art. Readers crease, some edge wear, VG.   40.00
1943 September. Finlay cover art. Some readers creasing, mild edge wear, VG-.   35.00
1943 December. Ray Bradbury. Moderate surface creasing, store stamps, general wear, G/VG.   35.00
1944 June. Dinosaur cover. Lite surface creasing, mild wear to extremities, VG+.   25.00
1944 September. Slight spine lean, readers crease, VG.   20.00

FFM 1946 Dec

FFM 1949 Feb

FFM 1950 Jun

FFM 1952 Dec

1944 December. Readers and surface creasing, 1" tear at top left corner, G/VG.	15.00
1945 March. Mild surface creasing and wear to extremities, VG.	20.00
1945 September. Slight spine lean, mild surface creasing, VG.	20.00
1945 December. Lite wear and surface creasing, VG+,	25.00
1946 February. Slight spine lean, mild wear to extremities, VG+.	25.00
1946 April. Slight spine lean, some creasing to extremities, VG.	20.00
1946 June. Moderate creasing, G/VG.	15.00
1946 October. Readers crease, lite wear, VG+.	25.00
1946 December. Classic Finlay hooded skull skeleton cover. 3" back spine split, some edge wear, G/VG.	30.00
1947 February. Finlay cover art. Moderate creasing and edge wear, G/VG.	20.00
1947 April. Spine lean, surface creasing, edge wear, G+	15.00
1947 June. Finlay cover art. Readers and surface creasing, G/VG.	20.00
1947 August. Finlay cover art. Lower right corner off, moderate creasing, G+	15.00
1947 October. NF.	40.00
1947 December. Surface creasing, some wear to right edge, few small tears, VG.	20.00
1948 February. Spine slant, surface creasing, 1.5" split to lower rear spine, G/VG.	15.00
1948 April. General wear, creasing, G/VG.	15.00
1948 June. Classic Finlay devil cover. Readers and surface creases, sm tears to edge, G/VG.	30.00
1948 August. NF.	40.00
1948 August. Moderate creasing, wear, G/VG.	15.00
1948 October. Mild surface creasing, sm tip off lower right corner, VG.	20.00
1948 December. Mild creasing, mainly to extremities, VG.	20.00
1949 February. Girl laying on bloody earth cover. Sm tp to spine ends, some chipping, G/VG.	30.00
1949 April. Sm wear hole near spine, VG/FN.	25.00
1949 June. SM tp to top of spine, mild chipping to extremities, VG-.	15.00
1949 August. FN.	40.00
1949 October. Lite vertical crease, some creasing to lower right corner, VG-.	15.00
1949 December. Lite wear, few small tears to extremities, VG.	20.00
1950 February. Lite wear and mild surface creasing, VG.	20.00
1950 April. FN.	40.00
1950 June. Robot cover. Mild readers and surface creasing, VG/FN.	50.00
1950 August. Slight spine lean, mild wear, VG.	20.00
1950 October. Readers and surface creasing, VG.	20.00
1951 January. FN.	40.00
1951 March. Lite wear and handling, VG/FN.	30.00
1951 May. Mild handling, FN.	40.00
1951 July. *War of the Worlds* cover. Mild surface creasing and handling, VG/FN.	40.00
1951 July. *War of the Worlds* cover. Some chipping to right edge, VG.	30.00
1951 October. Aggressive wear and creasing, G.	10.00
1951 Dec. Contains *Pickman's Model* by H. P. Lovecraft. Center crease, general wear, G/VG.	25.00
1952 February. Back cover almost loose, some chipping also to back cover, G.	10.00
1952 April. Small wear hole at bottom staple, NF.	35.00
1952 August. Moderate surface creasing, G/VG.	15.00
1952 October. NF.	35.00
1952 December. Contains Skull-Face by Robert E. Howard. Mild vertical crease, creasing to lower right corner, VG.	45.00
1953 April. Lite wear, VG/FN.	30.00
1953 June. Contains *Anthem* by Ayn Rand. Lite wear & creasing, small chip off right edge near lower corner, VG.	100.00

Famous Spy Stories

1940 January, #1. Aggressive tp to right edge, sm piece off top left corner, G+.	40.00

Famous Western

1947 September. Contains *Vengeance Bound General* wear, some small tears.	20.00
1956 December. Contains *Lonely Guns General* wear, some small tears, creasing.	20.00

Fantastic Adventures 1940 Jan

Fantastic Adventures 1940 Apr

Fantastic Adventures 1941 Nov

Fantastic Adventures 1942 Mar

Fantastic Adventures

1939 May, #1. Slight spine lean, small tear at spine, VG-.	125.00
1939 July, #2. Contains *The Scientists Revolt* by Edgar Rice Burroughs. Moderate creasing to over, VG.	150.00
1940 January, #5. Robot Cover. Lite wear and surface creasing, VG/FN.	95.00
1940 April, #8. Dinosaur Cover. Dinosaur cover. General lite wear, VG/FN.	100.00
1940 May, #9. Gorilla Cover. Moderate surface creasing, VG.	80.00
1940 June. (1st regular size issue) Moderate cover creasing, VG.	45.00
1940 Aug. Mild damp staining, creasing, VG.	35.00
1940 Oct. J. Allen St. John dinosaur cover. Sm tos at foot, VG.	50.00
1941 Jan. Mild trim, VG+.	40.00
1941 Mar. Contains *Slaves of the Fish Men* by Edgar Rice Burroughs. J Allen St. John cover. Moderate Cover creasing, small int. tp which has bleed thru, G/VG.	50.00
1941 July. Contains *Goddess of Fire* by Edgar Rice Burroughs. Mild wear and handling, FN-.	75.00
1941 November. Contains *The Living Dead* by Edgar Rice Burroughs. Mild trim, lite wear, VG.	95.00
1941 Aug. Moderate creasing, few closed tears to extremities, G/VG.	25.00
1941 Sept. Top right corner off, some chipping, G/VG.	25.00
1941 Dec. Lite wear and creasing, VG+.	40.00
1942 March. Contains *War on Venus* by Edgar Rice Burroughs. Mild trim, lite surface Creasing, VG-.	80.00
1942 June. 244 pages. Stories by Robert Bloch and Edmond Hamilton. 2.5" tear to lower left corner, VG.	40.00
1942 July. 244 pages, dragon cover by J. Allen St. John, VG+.	60.00
1942 Sept. 244 pages. *Son of a Witch* by Robert Bloch. Lite wear and slight loss at spine ends, VG+.	60.00
1942 Oct. Tos, moderate creasing, G+.	20.00
1942 Nov. *The Golden Opportunity of Lefty Feep* by Robert Bloch. Lite creasing mainly to lower right corner, VG+.	60.00
1942 Dec. Slight spine lean and readers crease, creasing to bc, VG-.	25.00
1943 March. Lite wear, some fading to spine, VG+.	40.00
1943 May. Readers crease, mild fading to spine, VG+.	40.00
1943 July. Moderate wear, 1" closed tear at top right corner, VG.	30.00
1943 August. Flag cover. 1" closed tear at top edge, lite creasing, VG.	40.00
1943 October. Lite wear, some scratches to cover, VG.	30.00
1944 October. Skull cover, NF.	70.00
1945 July. NF.	60.00
1946 May. Very mild center crease, VG/FN.	50.00
1946 July. Contains *Tree's A Crowd* by Robert Bloch. Sm tp at spine ends, VG-.	35.00
1947 January. Moderate readers creasing to cover, VG-.	30.00
1947 March. Creasing to lower area of cover, VG-.	30.00
1947 July. Dragon cover. Contains *Largo* by Theodore Sturgeon. Moderate creasing to cover, G/VG.	35.00
1947 Nov. Crease to bottom right corner, small tears to overhangs, 1" closed tear to bottom edge, VG-.	25.00
1947 Dec. Damp staining to covers, 4" tear to bc, G+.	15.00
1948 January. Nude and snake cover. Readers crease, mild spine lean, VG.	40.00
1948 February. Mild surface creasing, VG.	30.00
1948 March. Sm tips off corners, 3" spine split, some paper perished from bc, G/VG.	25.00
1948 April. Wear hole at bottom staple, wrap around starting to loosen, VG.	30.00
1948 September. Mild wave to pulp, bc a bit dingy, and 5" crease. VG-.	25.00
1948 October. General lite wear, ½" closed tear at spine near logo, VG.	30.00
1949 January. Moderate creasing to cover, VG-.	25.00
1949 February. 2" spine split, lite wear to extremes, VG.	30.00
1949 March. Topless mermaid cover. Moderate creasing, VG-.	30.00
1949 April. Gorilla cover. Mild creasing, ¼" paper perished from crown of spine, VG.	35.00
1949 May. Few tears to right edge, sm tip off l.r. corner, G/VG.	25.00
1949 June. 1" closed tear near lower left corner, shows well, FN-.	55.00
1949 July. Some bug damage to bottom edge of front cover, G/VG.	25.00
1949 October. NF.	50.00
1949 December. Moderate wear, 1" tear at bottom of cover, G+.	20.00
1950 January. Rubber stamp to cover, mild trim, VG-.	25.00
1950 February. Contains *The Dreaming Jewels* by Theodore Sturgeon. Moderate surface creasing, G/VG.	30.00

Fantastic Adventure 1951 Jul

Fantastic Novels 1941 Apr

Fantastic Novels 1949 Mar

Fantastic Novels 1949 Nov

1950 March. Lite wear, few sm tears to over hangs, VG+.	40.00
1950 April. Mild surface creasing and edge wear, VG-.	25.00
1950 May. Contains *Vanguard Of the Lost* by John D. MacDonald. Pencil markings to toc, lite surface creasing, VG.	30.00
1950 June. Toffee cover and story. ½" off crown of spine, lite creasing, VG-.	25.00
1950 July. Contains *End Of Your Rope* by Robert Bloch. 1" splits at spine ends, lite wear, VG-.	25.00
1950 Oct. Contains *The Masters of Sleep* by L. Ron Hubbard. Lite wear, some chipping to extremities, VG-.	75.00
1950 September. Moderate creasing, VG-.	25.00
1951 February. Egyptian mummy cover, NF.	55.00
1951 April. Some edge chipping, small tears, VG-.	25.00
1951 May. Contains *Make Room For Me!* By Theodore Sturgeon. General handling, some chipping, VG-.	30.00
1951 July. Skeleton cover. Contains *The Dead Don't Die!* By Robert Bloch. Some creasing, small chip at l.l., VG-.	50.00

Fantastic Novels

1940 July, #1. Finlay cover art. Lite wear and creasing, VG+	75.00
1940 September, #2. Sm paper pull at spine, general lite wear, ½" tear at right edge, VG-.	25.00
1941 January, #4. Finlay cover art. 2" sealed tear at middle of spine, VG.	30.00
1941 April. Finlay topless fire hair girl. Mild chipping, NF.	95.00
1948 March. Mild wear and chipping, VG-.	18.00
1948 May. Mild wear, writing to top of 1st page, VG/FN.	30.00
1948 July. Moderate surface creasing, VG.	20.00
1948 September. Stevens cover of woman and frog men army. Lite wear, sm tears to over hangs, VG.	30.00
1948 September. Stevens cover of woman and frog men army. Sm tape to spine ends, readers crease, G/VG.	20.00
1948 November. Finlay spider cover. Lite creasing, VG+.	60.00
1949 January. Stevens cover. Sm dust shadow, lite wear, VG.	25.00
1949 March. Finlay skeleton cover. Mild chipping creasing to extremities, VG-.	50.00
1949 May. Stevens Pterodactyl cover. 1.5" tear mended on verso with tp, , shows well, VG.	30.00
1949 July. Stevens cover. Readers crease, slight spine lean, general wear, G/VG.	20.00
1949 September. Dust shadow to top of cover, some loss to over hangs, VG.	20.00
1949 November. Finlay nude cover. NF.	95.00
1950 January. Lite wear, NF.	40.00
1950 March. 3" tear at lower left corner, few sm tears at extremities, G/VG.	15.00
1950 May. Mild diagonal crease, mild wear, VG-.	20.00
1950 July. Lite wear, few sm tears at over hangs, VG+.	25.00
1950 September. NF.	40.00
1950 November. Loss at lower right corner, 2" tear to bc, G/VG.	15.00
1951 January. Lite wear, mild creasing, VG.	20.00
1951 April. Lite wear, few sm tears at over hangs, VG/FN.	30.00
1951 June. Last issue, General wear, readers crease, 1" tear at right edge and few sm ones. G/VG.	15.00

Fantastic Story Magazine

1953 July. Contains The Indefatigable Frog by Philip K. Dick. Lite wear, VG/FN.	40.00

Fantastic Universe

1954 January, #4. Contains *Beyond the Door* by Philip K Dick. Price label taped to cover by logo, G/VG.	15.00
1954 May. Contains *Survey Team* by Philip K. Dick. Moderate surface creasing, readers crease, G.	10.00
1954 May. Contains *Survey Team* By Philip K Dick. General wear and creasing, VG-.	20.00
1954 October. Contains *Souvenir* By Philip K Dick. General wear and creasing, G/VG.	15.00

Fantasy & Science Fiction

1952 Nov. Contains *The Little Movement* by Philip K. Dick. Couple small paper pulls to bc, lite wear, FN.	20.00
1953 February. Contains *Roog* by Philip K. Dick. Lite wear, medium crease to lower right corner area, VG.	15.00
1953 February. Contains *Roog* by Philip K. Dick. Very lite wear, appears unread, VF.	30.00
1953 June. Contains *The Cookie Lady*. By Philip K Dick. Two small pieces of tape at spine ends, VG.	28.00
1953 July. Contains *Expendable* by Philip K. Dick. Lite wear, minor surface creasing, VG+.	20.00
1953 July. Contains *Expendable* by Philip K. Dick. Lite wear, grease pencil, slight lean to spine, VG.	20.00

Federal Agent 1936 Aug

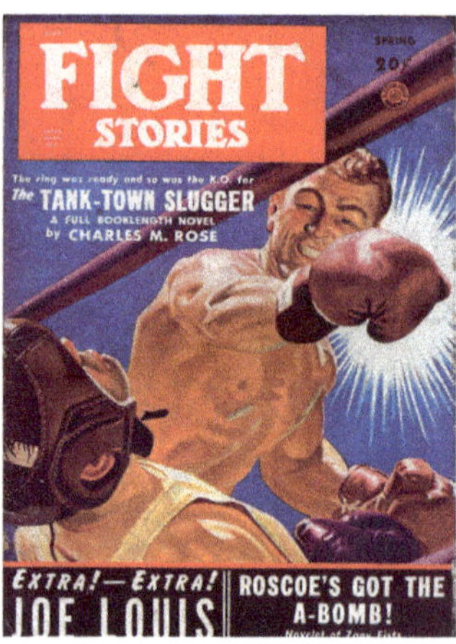

Fight 1950 Spr

Fighting Western 1945 Feb

Fighting Western 1950 Sep

1953 August. Contains *Out in the Garden* by Philip K Dick. Also the Conan story
    The Frost Giants Daughter by Robert E. Howard. Lite wear and mild surface creasing, VG/FN.   45.00
1954 December. Contains *The Father-Thing* by Philip K. Dick. Very lite wear, FN/VF.   25.00
1954 January. Contains *The Short Happy Life of the Brown Oxford* by Philip K. Dick. Lite wear, FN-.   20.00
1959 January. Contains *Explorers We* by Philip K. Dick. Mild bend to magazine, VG+.   18.00
1959 January. Contains *Explorers We* by Philip K. Dick. General lite wear, lean to spine, spot to cover, VG-.   10.00
1964 July. Contains *Cantata 140* by Philip K Dick. Lite wear and wave to magazine, VG.   16.00
1968 August. Fantasy & Science Fiction 1968 August. Philip K Dick letter published. FN.   12.00
1969 October. Contains *The Electric Ant* by Philip K Dick. FN-.   24.00
1981 October. Contains *The Alien Mind* By Philip K Dick. Also *The Needle Man* by George R. R. Martin. VG.   20.00

Fast Action Detective & Mystery
1957 January. General wear, moderate creasing, G/VG.   40.00

FBI Detective Stories
1950 June. Some chipping, VG/FN.   40.00

Federal Agent
1936 August. #1. Scarce. Some damp stain and few chips, VG.   300.00

Fight Stories
1941 Summer. Sm paper perished from crown of spine, general lite wear, VG.   45.00
1942 Fall. Lite creasing, off white paper, VG+.   50.00
1942 Fall. Lite wear. With certificate from the Glenn Lord collection, VG.   45.00
1943 Fall. 3.5" spine split, some chipping to over hangs, G/VG.   35.00
1945 Winter. Damp staining to bc, and corner of fc, G/VG.   35.00
1949 Fall. 4" tear to spine and lower cover. G.   25.00
1950 Spring. Sm paper perished from spine tips, general lite wear, VG.   40.00

Fifteen Sports Stories.
1948 August. Boxing Cover. Appears to be in unread file copy type condition, FN/VF.   40.00
1949 March. Basketball Cover. Appears to be in unread file copy type condition, FN/VF.   40.00
1951 April. Contains *Salute to Courage* by John D. MacDonald. Unread file copy type condition, FN/VF.   60.00
1951 December. Boxing Cover. Appears to be in unread file copy type condition, FN/VF.   50.00
1951 January. Football Cover. Appears to be in unread file copy type condition FN/VF.   40.00
1948 August. General wear, 1.5" tear at lower left corner, tanning Supple paper. VG.   25.00
1948 July. General wear moderate pencil marks to cover, tanning supple paper. G/VG.   15.00
1949 May. General Lite wear, moderate tanning with mild flaking to extremities. VG-.   25.00

Fighting Western
1945 February #1. Mild trim slight damps stain, VG+.   125.00
1945 August #3. General lite wear and handling, VG.   100.00
1946 August. Some loss at right edge and spine ends, G/VG.   25.00
1946 June. Moderate creasing, G/VG.   25.00
1946 March. Moderate wear and creasing, VG-.   30.00
1946 May. Lite wear and handling with lite tan supple paper. VG+   25.00
1948 July Szokoli bondage cover. General wear, very nice paper, VG+.   85.00
1950 March. Moderate creasing to cover, VG-.   40.00
1950 September. Last issue. Mild trim and creasing, VG.   95.00

Five-Novels
1934 July. Canadian printing, G/VG.   25.00
1942 March. Lite wear, FN+.   50.00
1947 March. Five-Novels Monthly 1947 March. Mild cover creasing, small tip off l.l of bc, VG/FN.   30.00

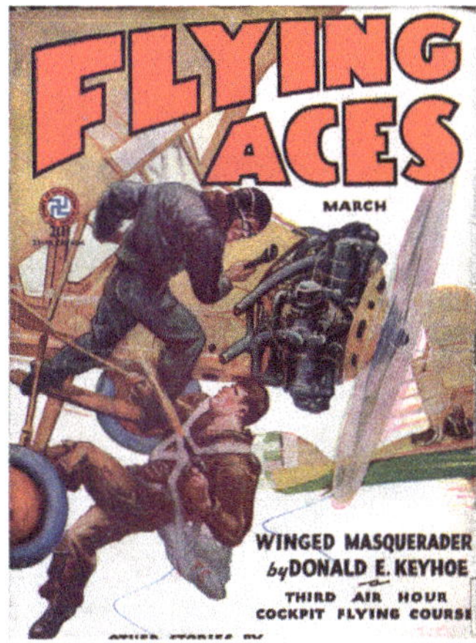

Flying Aces 1930 Mar

Flynn's 1924 Sep

G-8 1934 Nov

G-8 1944 Jun

Flying Aces
1930 March Scarce. 1" closed tear to right edge, couple pen marks to fc, minor paper perish from spine, VG+. 295.00
1932 August. Some creasing to cover, very nice paper, Canadian edition, VG+. 85.00
1932 December. Some creasing, 2.5" tear to cover at logo, Canadian edition, VG-. 65.00

Flynn's (Weekly)
1924 September, #1. Very scarce. Mild wear and small tears at extremities, Great condition for its age, FN-. 750.00

Foreign Legion
1940 August, #1. Some chipping to extremities, lite wear, VG. 150.00
1940 Oct, #2. Diagonal crease to top right corner, general wear, VG-. 85.00

Fortune Story Magazine
1929 September. Beautiful looking pulp, mild trim to cover, FN-. Rare. 495.00

Frontier (Frontier Stories)
1924 October. #1. First issue of what would end up being about a 160 issue run published by Doubleday, Page & Co, and later also Fiction House. Lite wear above average condition for the age. VG/FN. 450.00
1941 Spring. Covers separated in two pieces with spine damage, FR. 10.00
1942 Spring Mild damp stain, general wear, VG-. 20.00
1945 Spring. Front cover detached, interior tape, FR. 10.00
1949 Spring. Moderate wear, some tears and chipping, G/VG Canadian. 15.00

Future (Fiction)
1940 March, #2. Mild wear and few sm tears to over hangs, FN-. 95.00
1940 March, #2. Diagonal crease to cover, slight spine lean, lite wear, VG. 40.00
1940 July, #3. Bondage cover. 2.5" split at bottom of spine, mild creasing, VG. 50.00
1940 Nov. Frank R. Paul cover. Edge wear, few small tears, VG. 50.00
1954 October. Contains Meddler by Philip K Dick. Lite wear and mild surface creasing, VG/FN. 35.00
1956 #29. Contains Vulcan's Hammer by Philip K Dick. Lite wear FN-. 45.00

G-8 and His Battle Aces
1934 November. 1934 November. Damp staining to front and back cover and some interior pages. G/VG. 75.00
1935 October. General wear and creasing, interior tape with nice supple paper, G/VG. 145.00
1937 March. Leopard cover. Trim to book, nice paper. VG-. 60.00
1937 August. Damp staining to front and back cover and some interior pages, G+. 50.00
1937 October. General wear and some creasing with nice supple paper, VG. 95.00
1938 July. Label affixed to top right corner and masking tape to interior front cover edge, G+. 60.00
1939 April. Damp staining to cover, general wear, G+. 50.00
1940 July. General wear and handling with covers trimmed with decent paper, VG. 75.00
1943 October. Surface creasing, stain to back cover, nice paper, VG. 75.00
1943 December. Two small holes in front cover, nice paper, VG/FN. 90.00
1944 February. 2.5" crease to lower right corner, damp stain to back cover otherwise shows well, FN-. 140.00
1944 April. Stahlmaske cover. Lite wear, very small stain to back cover, nice paper, FN. 200.00
1944 June. Final scarce issue. Death Tiger cover. Lite wear, cream paper, FN. 300.00
1944 June. Final scarce issue. Death Tiger cover. Tear at bottom of cover repaired from verso with tape, else VG-. 110.00

Galaxy
1950 October, #1. Contains stories by Clifford Simak, Theodore Sturgeon, Fritz Leiber, Fredric Brown and Isaac Asimov. Surface creasing and diagonal crease to top right of cover, G/VG. 35.00
1953 January. *The Defenders* by Philip K Dick. Moderate wear, creasing and some chipping, G. 10.00
1953 June. *Colony* by Philip K Dick. Moderate wear and creasing, G/VG. 12.00
1953 June. *Colony* by Philip K Dick. General wear, readers crease, G/VG. 12.00
1953 June. *Colony* by Philip K. Dick, VG. 15.00
1954. Contains *Shell Game* by Philip K. Dick, VG. 15.00

Gangster Stories 1930 Jun

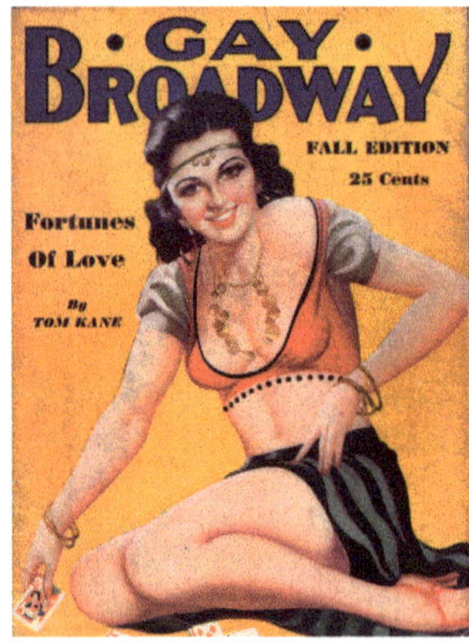

Gay Broadway 1938 Fall

Ghost Stories 1931 May

Giant Detective Annual 1950

1954 October. *A World Of Talent* by Philip K. Dick. Readers crease and some surface creasing, VG-.	15.00
1954 October. *A World of Talent* by Philip K Dick. Aggressive creasing, G.	7.00
1955 November. *Autofac* by Philip K Dick. Moderate wear and creasing, G.	7.00
1955 November. *Autofac* by Philip K Dick. General wear, surface creasing, VG.	15.00
1959 December. *War Game* by Philip K Dick. General wear and some foxing mainly to extremities, VG.	12.00
1963 December. *If There Be No Benny Cemoli* by Philip K Dick. Lite wear, some foxing at spine, VG/FN.	22.00
1963 December. *If There Be No Benny Cemoli* by Philip K Dick. 1" tear, staining to cover, G.	7.00
1964 February. *Oh, To Be a Blobel!* BY Philip K Dick. Readers crease, lite wear, VG.	15.00
1964 February. *Oh, To Be a Blobel!* By Philip K Dick. General lite wear, some foxing at spine, VG/FN.	22.00
1964 October. *Precious Artifact* By Philip K Dick. General lite wear, mild surface creasing, VG+.	20.00
1964 October. *Precious Artifact.* BY Philip K Dick. Lite wear, foxing to spine, VG.	15.00
1969 February. *The War With the Fnools* by Philip K Dick. Lite wear, mild foxing mainly to top edge, VG+.	22.00

Gangster Stories

1930 June/July. 4" & 3" spine splits, 1" paper perished from foot of spine, scarce, G+.	175.00
1931 November. Nbc, spine repair 1 ad page out, scarce, G.	125.00

Gay Broadway

1938 Fall. Second to last issue. Cover art by Earle Bergey. Lite wear, small closed tear above logo, VG+.	75.00

Gay Parisienne

1935 August. Tos, moderate chipping to lower edge and1st few pages, G+.	35.00
1936 April. Tos and interior tape, G/VG.	40.00

Gem Detective

1946 Fall #1. Mild edge wear and few small tears to overhangs, VG/FN.	385.00

George Bruce's Sky Fighters

1932 One Shoot, #1. Rare aviation pulp which rarely shows up for sale. No back cover, some paper perished from spine and general wear to front cover, G+.	250.00

George Bruce's Squadron

1933 November. Amateur repair job Large chip to right corner and edge chipping repaired, FR.	15.00
1933 December. General wear, and nice paper. VG.	75.00

Ghost Stories

1927 July. General lite wear, small chip off at top left corner, mild surface creasing, VG.	165.00
1928 August. Moderate wear, chipping and creasing, G.	60.00
1931 January. Great looking book with tanning paper, FN-.	250.00
1931 February. Cover faded, VG.	125.00
1931 May. Great looking book with tanning paper, FN-.	250.00

Ghost Super-Detective

1940 January. #1. Moderate chipping & wear to extremities, mild flaking, G-VG.	125.00

Giant Detective Annual

1950 Edition, #1 Contains stories by Richard Sale, Paul Ernst, George Bruce, Frank Gruber and many others. General wear and handling, VG+ with nice cream supple paper.	50.00

G-Men

1935 October, #1. 2" tape on spine, Lite wear and some creasing ,VG+	300.00
1935 December #3. General Lite wear, small chip off right edge, very mild flaking to extremities, VG.	175.00
1936 March. Moderate creasing, trim to right edge, G/VG.	35.00
1939 February. Lite wear, FN-.	65.00
1944 Fall. FN-.	50.00

G-Men 1950 Win

Golden Fleece 1939 Apr

Hopalong Cassidy 1951 Win

Horror Stories 1935 Jun

1945 Summer. Lite wear, decent supple paper. VG/FN.	75.00
1946 February. Lite wear, FN-.	40.00
1946 Fall. G-Men 1943 March. General Lite wear, VG+.	25.00
1947 May. G-Men 1947 May. Lite wear, mild crease thru center of cover, VG.	45.00
1947 September. Lite wear, readers crease, VG/FN.	45.00
1948 July. Contains the Dan Fowler story *The Big Break* by C. K. M. Scanlon. Lite wear, some creasing, VG+.	40.00
1950 Winter. Skull cover. Very mild wear, FN.	85.00

Golden Book, The.
1925, January, #1. Lite wear, some mild damage to spine, VG. ... 100.00

Golden Fleece
1938 October, #1. Contains *Roman Holiday* by Talbot Mundy. High grade publishers file copy, NF. ... 400.00
1939 February. High grade publishers file copy, NF. ... 200.00
1939 April. Brundage cover art. Contains *Swords and Mongols* by Murray Leinster. High grade publishers file copy in NF with crease to lower right corner and tanning supple paper. ... 200.00
1939 June. Brundage cover and interior. Lite creasing, sm tip off lower left corner, VG. ... 100.00

Golden West Romances
1949 Oct, #1. Sm tip off crown of spine, some mild chipping, VG. ... 125.00
1949 Dec, #2. 4" tear at bottom edge, mild edge wear, VG-. ... 40.00

Grand, The
1935 August. American edition of British pulp, scarce. Damp staining to staples, G+. ... 125.00

Great Detective Stories
1933 Mar, #1. Moderate creasing to extremities, ¾" x ½" chip off, G/VG. ... 50.00

Gunsmoke Western
1947 January #1. One shot, George Rozen cover art, spine damage, G/VG. ... 35.00

Hopalong Cassidy's Western Magazine
1950 Fall, #1. Canadian edition, FN. ... 300.00
1951 Winter, #2. Canadian edition, NF. ... 225.00
1951 Winter, #2. Moderate damp staining, G/VG. ... 100.00

Horror Stories
1935 June, #4. Lite wear, very mild trim to edge, very nice cream supple paper, FN-. ... 425.00
1935 August. General wear and creasing, few small tears, G/VG. ... 195.00
1936 Apr/May. Moderate creasing, store stamp, G/VG. ... 195.00
1940 August. Bondage cover. Light wear, mild trim, light tan supple paper, VG/FN. ... 325.00

How 7
1928 Jan. Scarce, 4" clean spine split, VG-. ... 175.00
1928 Jan. Scarce, moderate wear, damp staining damage to lower cover with some paper perished, FR. ... 50.00
1928 March, #3. Aggressive creasing, paper perished form cover and spine, FR. ... 25.00

If Worlds of Science Fiction
1952 September. *The Skull* by Philip K Dick. General wear, creasing to covers, G/VG. ... 18.00
1952 September. *The Skull* by Philip K Dick. General wear, creasing to covers, VG-. ... 25.00
1953 September. *The Trouble With Bubbles* by Philip K Dick. General wear, creasing to covers, VG-. ... 15.00
1954 May. *Prominent Author* by Philip K Dick. General wear, some creasing, G/VG. ... 10.00
1954 May. *Prominent Author* By Philip K Dick. General lite wear, creasing to covers, VG-. ... 15.00
1954 November. *Progency* by Philip K Dick. General wear, some creasing, l.r., corner bumped, G/VG. ... 10.00
1954 November. Progency By Philip K Dick. Slight lean to spine, lite wear VG. ... 15.00

Jungle Stories 1931 Aug

Jungle Stories 1943 Feb

Jungle Stories 1948 Sum

Jungle Stories 1949 Fall

1955 April. *Captive Market* by Philip K Dick. General wear, slight spine lean, readers crease, G/VG.	10.00
1955 April. *Captive Market* By Philip K Dick. Lite wear, some creasing, VG.	15.00
1955 August. *The Mold of Yancy* By Philip K Dick. Spine lean, cover a bit dingy, G/VG.	10.00
1958 December. *Null-O* By Philip K Dick. Spine lean, readers crease, G/VG.	10.00
1959 July. *Recall Mechanism* by Philip K Dick. Creasing, price written on cover, G/VG.	10.00
1959 September. *Fair Game* by Philip K Dick. General wear and creasing, G/VG.	12.00
1964 January. *Waterspider* by Philip K Dick. General lite wear and mild readers crease, VG.	15.00

Imagination

1953 February. *Piper in the Woods* by Philip K Dick. General lite wear and mild surface creasing, VG+.	20.00
1953 January. *Mr. Spaceman* by Philip K Dick. General lite wear and surface creasing, VG.	15.00
1953 June. *Paycheck* by Philip K Dick. Lite wear, FN-.	35.00
1953 July. *The Cosmic Poachers* by Philip K Dick. General wear and creasing, G/VG.	12.00
1953 October. *The Impossible Planet* by Philip K Dick. General wear and creasing, VG+.	20.00
1954 July. *The Crawlers* by Philip K Dick. Moderate wear and creasing, G+.	8.00
1956 February. *To Serve The Master* by Philip K. Dick. Moderate wear and creasing, G.	8.00

Indian Stories

1950 Summer, #1. 3 small pieces of tape to spine, moderate tape to back cover, G/VG.	65.00
1950 Winter, #3. Moderate surface creasing, chipping to right edge, G/VG.	40.00

Jungle Stories (Clayton)

1931 August, #1. First issue of this short three issues series by Clayton. All issues very Scarce. Lite wear and surface creasing, very mild trim, nice paper, VG+.	850.00

Jungle Stories (Fiction House)

1941 Winter. Mild wear mainly at extremities, VG/FN.	95.00
1942 Spring. Very small tape to foot of spine, moderate chipping to right edge, VG.	75.00
1943 February. Bondage cover. Lite wear and handling, FN-.	150.00
1943 Summer. General wear and creasing mainly to extremities, VG+.	65.00
1943 Summer. Lite wear mainly to extremities, VG/FN.	100.00
1944 Winter. Lite wear mainly to extremities, VG/FN.	85.00
1944 Winter. Spine ends may have been re-glued, overall a nice copy, shows well, VG.	65.00
1945 Spring. 4.5" crease to top right corner, otherwise a beautiful pulp, VG+.	75.00
1945 Spring. Moderate surface creasing, few small ½" tears to extremities, VG-.	50.00
1945 Winter. General lite wear and mild creasing mainly at extremities, VG/FN.	55.00
1945 Winter. Spine ends may have been re-glued, general mild wear, readers crease, VG-.	55.00
1946 Fall. Moderate wear and creasing, small tape to crown of spine, G/VG.	50.00
1946 Fall. Small paper perished from crown of spine, general lite wear, VG/FN.	75.00
1946 Spring. General lite wear, with tear to foot of spine, VG.	50.00
1946 Spring. Small paper perished from tips of spine, tear to spine VG-.	45.00
1946 Summer. General lite wear, mild chipping to edge, VG+.	60.00
1946 Summer. General wear and creasing mainly to extremities, VG-.	50.00
1946 Summer. Small paper perished from foot of spine, lite wear, VG+.	80.00
1947 Fall. Jungle Stories 1947 Fall. Small lower right corner off, some creasing, VG.	70.00
1948 Fall. General wear, some creasing, VG.	70.00
1948 Fall. Moderate wear and creasing, G/VG.	25.00
1948 Spring. Bondage Cover. Lite wear & handling, grease pencil mark to logo, VG/FN.	95.00
1948 Summer. Bondage Cover. Small paper off foot of spine, lite wear, VG+.	85.00
1948 Summer. Repair to lower left corner, G/VG.	35.00
1948-49 Winter. Back cover loose and chip off, G+.	35.00
1948-49 Winter. General wear and creasing mainly to extremities, VG+.	80.00
1949 Fall. General lite wear, some creasing, VG+.	75.00
1949 Fall. General wear, lower left corner off back cover, VG-.	40.00
1949 Fall. Lite wear, surface creasing, VG+.	80.00

Jungle Stories 1951 Spr

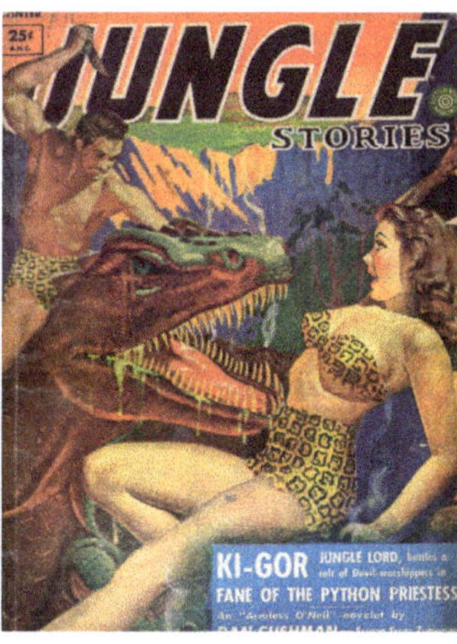

Jungle Stories 1953 Win

Lariat Story 1935 Oct

Leading Western 1945 Jul

1949 Spring. General lite wear and some creasing, VG.	70.00
1949 Spring. Mild wear, slight spine lean, small hole in back cover VG+.	85.00
1949 Summer. Bondage Cover. Bondage cover. General lite wear and cresting, VG.	75.00
1949 Summer. General lite wear, store stamp to cover, VG.	50.00
1949 Winter. Moderate wear, creasing, G/VG.	35.00
1949-50 Winter. Small rubber stamp to cover, shows very well, VG/FN.	95.00
1950 Fall. Bondage Cover. Bondage cover. Mild wear, some creasing to overhangs, white paper! VG+.	65.00
1950 Fall. Bondage Cover. 4" spine split, VG-.	40.00
1950 Fall. General wear, 2" split at foot of spine, some loss at over hangs, VG.	40.00
1950 Spring. Cover separated, back almost loose, FR.	15.00
1950 Spring. General lite wear mainly to overhangs, FN-.	95.00
1950 Spring. General wear and 1.5" paper perished from foot of spine, VG-.	40.00
1950 Spring. Staining to bc, VG.	45.00
1950 Winter. General lite wear, 2" split at foot of spine, VG-.	40.00
1950 Winter. Name stamp to cover, mild wear, VG/FN.	70.00
1950 Winter. Some chipping to right edge, small top left corner off, VG.	40.00
1951 Spring. Bondage cover. Fc loose, G.	20.00
1951 Spring. Bondage cover. Sliver off over hangs, VG/FN.	70.00
1951 Fall. General lite wear, some loss to overhangs, VG+.	50.00
1951 Fall. 4" spine split, VG.	60.00
1951 Fall. Fc almost loose, chipping, G+.	25.00
1951-52 Winter. Chipping to over hangs, 1.5" spine split, VG.	60.00
1951-52 Winter. Front cover loose, G.	20.00
1952 Spring. General lite wear and mild creasing, VG/FN.	65.00
1952 Spring. One third of back cover detached but present, VG.	60.00
1952 Spring. Browning to extremities of covers, VG-.	40.00
1952 Fall. General lite wear, mainly to extremities, VG.	60.00
1952 Fall. 2 1" tears to right edge, some creasing, G/VG.	45.00
1952 Fall. Moderate wear, chip off right edge, interior tape. , G+.	25.00
1953-54 Winter. Dinosaur cover. Lite wear, near fine.	75.00
1953-54 Winter. Dinosaur cover. Moderate creasing to lower right corner area, VG-.	45.00
1953-54 Winter. Dinosaur cover. Surface creasing, some chipping to right edge, G/VG.	40.00
1954 Spring. Covers loose, FR.	15.00
1954 Spring. Moderate wear, top right corner off, G.	30.00
(Also see sets and runs section for a complete set offered)	

Lariat Story Magazine

1935 October. Small top right corner off, 2" tear at foot of spine, VG-	75.00
1947 November. Spine lean, aggressive creasing, G.	15.00

Leading Western

1945 July, #2. Small hole in cover at spine, FN-.	85.00
1945 September. General lite wear, few small tears to extremities, VG+.	60.00
1946 October. Large tear to back cover, G.	20.00
1947 January. Airbrush cover. 2" spine split, G/VG.	25.00

Lone Eagle

1934 Nov. 2.5" tos, some edge wear, VG-.	60.00
1935 October. Zeppelin type cover. Moderate cover creasing, VG-.	50.00
1936 Oct. Readers creases, mild trim, VG.	50.00
1936 Nov. Paper perished form about half of spine, 4.5" split, G.	25.00
1938 Feb. Lite wear, ½" tear to right edge, few sm tears, VG.	50.00
1938 Aug. Mild creasing, few very small tears to extremities, VG.	50.00
1938 Dec. Some damp staining to cover, 2" split at foot of spine, G/VG.	30.00
1939 February. Some creasing to cover, few tears, small damp staining to extremities, VG-.	35.00

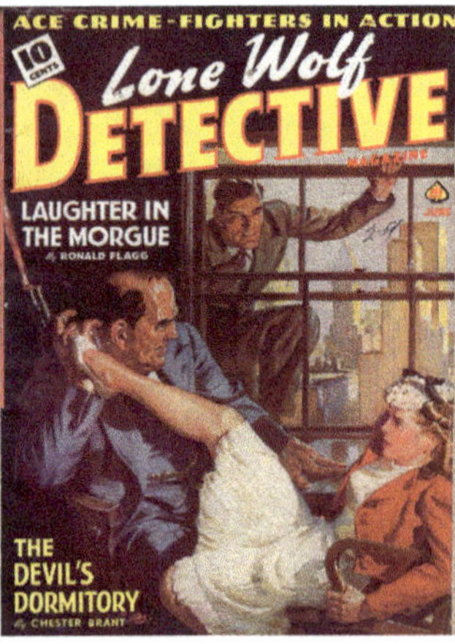

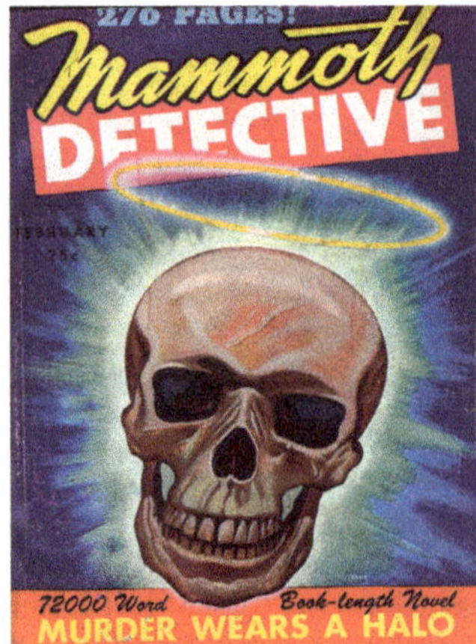

<table>
<tr><td>**Lone Eagle 1940 Oct**</td><td>**Lone Wolf Detective 1940 Jun**</td><td>**Mammoth Adventures 1946 Jul**</td><td>**Mammoth Detective 1944 Feb**</td></tr>
</table>

1939 August. L.l. corner off, some closed tears to right edge, G/VG.	30.00
1939 Oct. Piece off at l.l. corner, some surface creasing, few sm tears to right edge, G/VG.	30.00
1939 Dec. Moderate wear, b.c. almost separated, G.	20.00
1940 February. General wear and handling, sm tear at l.l. corner, VG.	40.00
1940 February. Moderate surface creasing, int. tp, vg-.	35.00
1940 April. Slight spine lean, int tp, lower spine may have glue repair, G/VG.	30.00
1940 June. Sm closed rip at logo, 1" paper perished from foot of spine, VG-.	35.00
1940 August. Lite wear , few sm tears, FN-.	60.00
1940 August. Very sm tear near lower spine, sm closed tears at extremities, VG.	40.00
1940 Oct. Mild center and readers creases, VG.	40.00
1940 Oct. Moderate creasing, edge wear, G/VG.	30.00
1940 Dec. Moderate wear, damp staining, chipping, G.	20.00
1941 April. Piece off bottom of spine and lower left corner. Pin hole thru cover and most of book. G/VG	25.00

Lone Wolf Detective

1940 June, #1. Some surface creasing, mild trim to cover, nice cream paper, VG-.	175.00

Magic Love

1945 Sept, #1. Moderate creasing, 2" tear at spine, G+.	55.00

Mammoth Adventure

1946 July, #1. Lite wear and some creasing with Lite tan supple paper. Iconic cover used on early editions of the Tony Goldstone book *The Pulps*. VG+.	150.00
1946 November, #3. General Lite wear, tan supple paper. VG+.	100.00
September, #2. Some chipping to right edge with tanning supple paper. VG+.	100.00
1947 January, #4. Lite tan supple paper VG/FN.	100.00
1947 July. Lite tan supple paper VG.	75.00
1947 March. Lite tan supple paper VG/FN.	95.00
1947 May. Lite tan supple paper VG+.	85.00

Mammoth Detective

1944 Feb. Skull cover. Contains *Horror in Hollywood* by Robert Bloch. Readers crease, VG.	85.00
1946 March. Hole in back cover, some internal tape. G+.	25.00
1946 May. Moderate readers creases, some chipping, VG-.	40.00
1946 September. General lite wear, VG/FN.	60.00
1946 October. 3.5" tear at top left corner repaired with tape on recto of cover, some chipping, G+	25.00
1946 November. Lite wear, some creasing mainly at over hangs, VG+.	50.00
1946 December. Slight spine lean, lite creasing and wear, G/VG.	40.00
1947 July. Interior tape, general lite wear, creasing, G/VG.	40.00

Mammoth Western

1945 September, #1. 1" x 2" piece off bottom of cover, some chipping, creasing, G+.	25.00
1946 December. Sticker to top right corner, some chipping, G/VG.	20.00
1947 February. Sticker to top right corner, some chipping, G/VG.	20.00
1947 April. ½" off crown of spine, small tip off lower right corner, couple of pieces off bc, G/VG.	20.00
1947 June. Moderate chipping to extremities, some surface creasing, G/VG.	20.00
1947 October. Small lower right corner off, some chipping, G/VG.	20.00
1947 December. Small tip off lower left corner, some chipping and creasing to extremities, G/VG.	20.00
1948 January. Contains *Fighting Man* by Frank Gruber. Pencil writing to cover, piece off bc, G/VG.	20.00
1948 February. Aggressive chipping to extremities, ink marks to logo, G+.	12.00
1948 April. Lite wear and chipping, VG+.	30.00
1948 May. Lite wear and chipping, VG+.	30.00
1948 June. 3" tear at spine, damp staining mainly to right edge, G.	10.00
1948 July. 1" tear to right edge, general wear, G/VG.	20.00
1948 September. 1" spine split at back, lite wear, VG.	25.00

Marval Science 1938 Nov

Marvel Tales 1939 Dec

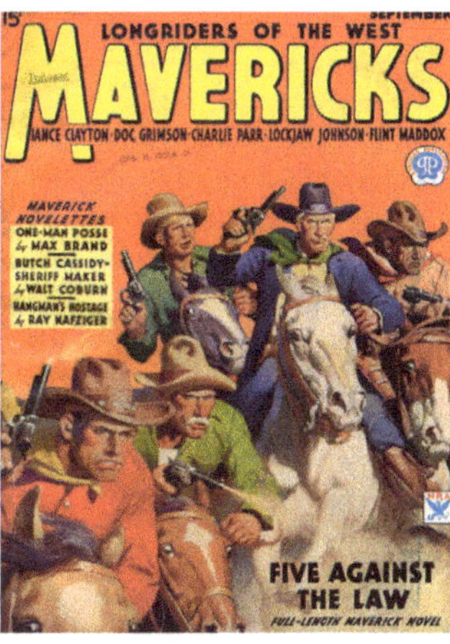

Mavericks 1934 Sep

Movie Action 1935 Nov

1948 October. Lite wear, name in ink at lower left corner, VG.	25.00
1949 July. General wear and surface creasing, VG.	25.00
1949 October. Lite wear, creasing, VG.	25.00
1949 Nov. GGA cover. 2.5" spine split, moderate wear, G/VG.	60.00
1950 May. GGA and rattlesnake cover. ½" paper perished to crown of spine, general wear, G/VG.	60.00

(Also see sets and runs section of catalogue)

Mammoth Western Quarterly
1949 Spring. 456 pages. Scarce. We rarely see these offered. Spine decent, general wear, piece off back cover, some splitting at spine, Lite tan mildly flaking yet still fairly supple paper. VG-.   95.00

Marvel Science Fiction

1951 August. Mild readers crease, FN-.	40.00
1951 November. Matheson, Bradbury, Vance, Asimov. General lite wear, VG+.	35.00

Marvel Science Stories

1938 August , #1. Mild trim to covers, presents well, VG/FN.	195.00
1938 August, #1. General wear, creasing, VG.	95.00
1938 Nov, #2. Paul art, nude cover. Mild wear, FN-.	150.00
1938 Nov, #2. Paul art, nude cover. Mild wear and surface creasing few sm tears to extremities, VG/FN.	100.00
1938 Nov, #2. Paul art, nude cover. Mild wear and surface creasing, rubber stamp to cover, VG+.	85.00
1939 Feb, #3. Mild wear and surface creasing, VG/FN.	100.00
1939 Feb, #3. Cover a bit dingily, dust shadow to right edge, mild readers crease, VG.	80.00
1939 Feb, #3. Moderate wear, creasing, edge trim with nice paper. G+	25.00
1939 April, #4. Nude Norman Saunders cover. Mild creasing, VG.	125.00
1939 August, #5. J.W. Scott cover art. Moderate wear, damp staining, G/VG.	30.00
1950 November. Book trimmed, G.	15.00
1951 May. Digest format. L. Ron Hubbard, Vance, Clarke, Sturgeon. Lite wear and lite readers crease. VG+.	85.00

Marvel Stories

1941 April. Schomburg interior art. *The Iron God* by Jack Williamson. Lite wear, mild chipping to extremities, VG+.	150.00
1941 April. Schomburg interior art. *The Iron God* by Jack Williamson. Wear and few small tears to overhangs, VG-.	100.00

Marvel Tales
1939 December. *The Angel from Hell*. Winged female cover. Lite wear, mild trim, VG+.   195.00

Mavericks
1934 September, #1. Scarce. Small rubber stamps at logo, mild surface creasing, nice paper, VG/FN.   325.00

Mobsters
1953 February. File copy stamped Not Made Ready to back cover, FN-.   250.00

Movie Action Magazine
1935 November. Minor wear to lower spine, 1" tear at lower right corner of right edge, overall shows very well, VG/FN.   395.00

Movie Love
1941 June #1. Rare. Deanna Durbin photo cover. Creasing to cover. VG+.   500.00

Movie Western

1941 July #1. Scarce, Gene Autry photo cover. VG-.	200.00
1941 December #3. Gary Cooper photo cover, lower right corner off. G/VG.	125.00

Mystery Book Magazine.
1948 Summer. General wear, creasing, mild chipping, VG.   25.00

Mystery Novels 1934 Spr

Mystery Novels 1935 Mar

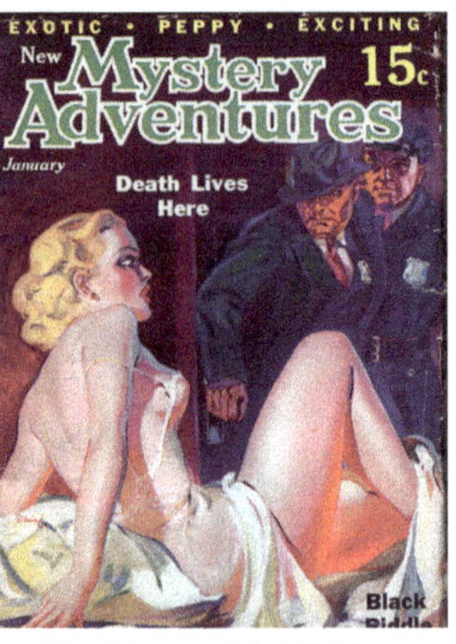

New Mystery Adv 1936 Jan

Nickel Detective 1933 Jun

1948 Fall. Mild damp stain to bc. VG.	25.00
1948 Winter. Fredric Brown, John D. MacDonald. G/VG, store stamp	35.00
1949 February. John D. MacDonald. VG/FN.	45.00
1949 Spring. Mild chipping, creasing, tan supple paper. VG.	40.00
1949 Spring. Some chipping to extremities, VG.	25.00
1949 Summer. John D. MacDonald. Surface creasing, also mild chipping mainly to back cover. VG.	25.00
1949 Winter. Leslie Charteris. Mild damp staining VG+.	30.00
1950 Winter. D. L. Champion, Johnston McCulley. Small chipping to extremities, VG+.	35.00

Mystery Magazine

1940 April. General wear small tip off spine, VG.	65.00
1942 Nov. Mild staining to bottom of front cover, VG.	75.00
1943 May. Final issue. Pencil marks to cover, slight spine lean, VG-.	125.00

Mystery Novels and Short Stories

1939 September #1. Weird menace and gorilla cover, dime size piece off fc and toc missing. Very scarce.	195.00

Mystery Novels Magazine

1934 Spring. *The Saint's Income Tax*. Skull cover. Some chipping & general wear, VG.	125.00
1934 Spring. *The Saint's Income Tax*. Staining and loss of paper to front cover with back cover loose. G.	35.00
1934 Summer. The Saint "The Art of Alibi." . Mild wear and few creases VG/FN.	125.00
1935 March. Skull cover. Tears to top left corner repaired with tape on verso, G+	95.00
1935 July. Contains the Saint story *The Appalling Politician* by Leslie Charteris. Paper pull to right edge, VG.	150.00
1936 February. A very cool "Eye" cover. General wear, 2" tear to top left corner, VG-.	175.00
1936 August. Just Lite wear and handling with very nice supple paper for Fine condition.	100.00

New Detective

1948 March. Skull cover. Loss of paper to top of spine which carries over a bit onto fc, G+.	25.00
1949 May. Contains *Get Out Of Town* by John D. MacDonald and See No Murder by Ray Cummings. Lite Wear, 3" closed tear to bottom left of cover , VG-.	50.00
1950 July. Norman Saunders cover. Lite wear, FN-.	50.00
1951 February. Contains *The Case of The Wandering Redhead* by Leigh Brackett. Lite wear, crease at Lower right area, FN-.	50.00

New Mystery Adventures

1935 March. #1. General wear, some creasing and small right corners off, G/VG.	350.00
1935 December. Bondage operating table cover. Very high demand issue. Top right corner off, readers crease, general wear, excess glue to last page, very scarce to rare, G/VG.	750.00
1936 January. Some loss of paper at top left corner, mild center crease, still shows well, VG+.	675.00
1937 February. Bondage nude cover, 1" loss at top of spine, 2 pieces tos, G/VG.	300.00

New Sports

1948 April 1948 April. General wear, some creasing with tanning supple paper. VG.	25.00
1948 January. Leatherhead Football Cover. Appears to be in unread file copy type condition, VF	35.00
1948 July. General wear, some creasing with tanning supple paper. VG.	25.00
1948 June General wear, some creasing with tanning supple paper. VG.	25.00
1948 November. Football cover. General Lite wear, mild creasing with tanning supple paper, VG+.	30.00

Nick Carter

1935 January. Some chipping to extremities, 1.5" tear at top left mended from verso with tape, VG-.	75.00
1935 Dec. General mild surface creasing, 1" closed tear at spine, VG.	95.00

Nickel Detective

1933 January. 4" spine split, moderate wear, creasing, 1.5" tear, G.	100.00
1933 June. General mild wear and surface creasing, tanning supple paper, VG.	300.00

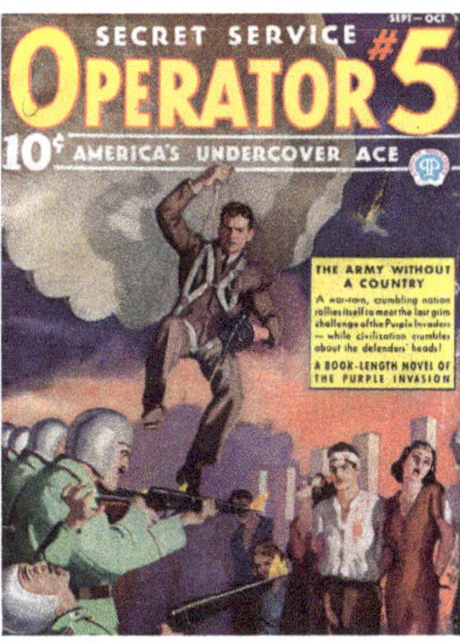
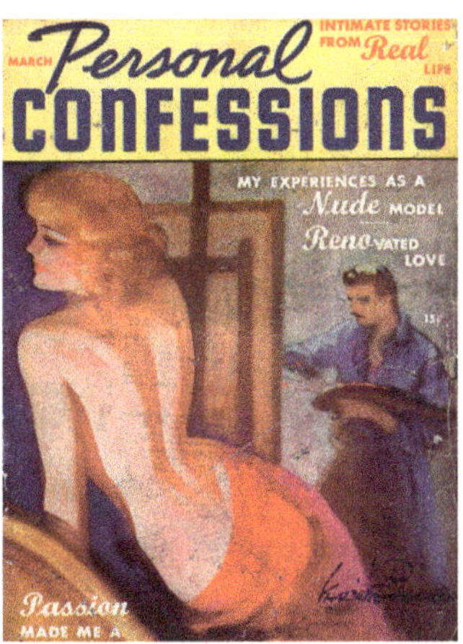

North West Romances 1950 Win	Operator #5 1937 Sep	Personal Confession 1938 Mar	Pete Rice 1935 Mar

North West Romances

1948 Spring. Moderate chipping, small tos, G/VG.	25.00
1950-51 Winter. Mild surface creasing, 1" closed tear to right edge, VG.	40.00

Operator #5

1934 April, #1. First issue of this 48 issue hero run. Aggressive wear and creasing, spine shows restoration and covers may have been re-glued to text block, G.	225.00
1934 May, #2. Moderate creasing, tape to spine, G/VG.	150.00
1934 June, #3. Lower right corner off, half inch off tips of spine, G/VG.	95.00
1934 July, #4. No back cover, tape to spine, general wear and piece off right edge. G.	60.00
1934 August. Tape to edges and spine, interior tape, G+.	90.00
1934 September. Some excess glue to interior covers, spine seems to have repairs, G+.	90.00
1934 October. General wear and chipping to extremities, G/VG.	100.00
1934 December. Skeleton four horseman cover. Store stamp to cover, moderate wear, interior tape, G+.	75.00
1935 February. Moderate wear, creasing, 1. 5" tape to right edge of cover, G/VG.	95.00
1935 January. Moderate wear, creasing, some interior tape, G+.	65.00
1935 March. Moderate wear, creasing, 1" tape at spine, some flaking, G+.	65.00
1935 April. Moderate wear and creasing, pencil marks to logo, interior tape, G.	45.00
1935 June. Some paper perished from spine, some repair seems evident, some interior tape, general wear, G.	45.00
1935 July. General wear, tape full length of spine, G+.	65.00
1935 August. Paper perished from spine and some repair is evident. G+.	65.00
1935 October. Moderate creasing, and trim to right edge, G/VG.	65.00
1935 November. General wear, 1" split to top of spine, VG-.	95.00
1935 December. Tape to cover edges and interior tape, G.	45.00
1936 February. Bondage cover of girl strapped to nose of missile. Rough condition G.	60.00
1937 May-June. Piece off bottom right corner, some flaking to paper, G/VG.	85.00
1937 September/October. Lite wear and small tears to extremities, 1" spine split, VG	175.00
1938 January/February. Back cover loose, some damage to spine, G.	45.00
1939 January/February. Front cover almost loose, back cover re-glued, chipping to extremities, G.	45.00

Orbit

1953 #2. *Tony and the Beetles* by Philip K. Dick. Lite wear, FN.	35.00
1953 #2. *Tony and the Beetles* by Philip K. Dick. Lite wear, small chip off right edge, VG+.	18.00
1954 November-December, #5. *The Last of the Masters* by Philip K. Dick. Moderate surface creasing from someone writing on a piece of paper using this as a writing surface, G/VG.	12.00
1954 November-December, #5. *The Last of the Masters* by Philip K. Dick. Creasing, readers crease, slight chipping to top left corner, G+.	10.00
1954 September-October, #4. *Adjustment Team* by Philip K. Dick. Lite wear, mild crease top corner, VG/FN.	35.00
1954 September-October, #4. *Adjustment Team* by Philip K. Dick. Readers crease and surface creasing, VG-.	20.00

Out Of This World

1950 July, #1. 32 page color comic insert. Moderate creasing, VG-.	110.00
1950 Dec, #2. 32 page color comic insert. Some chipping to right edge, 1" closed tear at logo, VG.	125.00

Parisienne Monthly Magazine

1915 Nov, #5. General wear with very nice supple paper. Scarce to rare pulp title, VG.	175.00

Pecos Kid Western

1950 July, #1. Foxing to covers, general wear, VG+.	60.00
1950 Sept,#2. Pencil marks to cover, G/VG.	25.00
1951 Jan, #3. Sm l.l. corner off, creasing, G/VG.	25.00
1951 March, #4. Lite wear, FN.	60.00
1951 June, #5. ½" off foot of spine, general wear, VG.	40.00

Phantom Detective 1939 Nov

Planet Stories 1939 Win

Planet Stories 1940 Fall

Planet Stories 1942 Fall

Personal Confession
1938 March, #1. Rare. Spine perished, covers separated from text block, FR.   100.00

Pep Stories
1938 June. Earle K. Bergey cover art? Interior coupon cut from classified ads, tape on spine.   25.00

Pete Rice
1935 March. Moderate surface creasing, interior tape, G/VG.   95.00
1935 August. Interior tape, moderate creasing, some damp staining to back cover, G/VG.   95.00
      (Also see sets and runs section for a complete set offered)

Phantom Detective
1935 March. Lite wear, very mild surface creasing, FN+.   165.00
1939 Nov. Bondage Hooded Menace Cover. Chip off at top of cover, lite wear & surface creasing, VG+.   95.00
1940 September. Scarce according to guide. 1" X 4" piece off back cover, moderate trim to book, G/VG.   50.00
1941 October. Some interior tape to inside front cover, outside in great condition with lite supple paper, VG+.   60.00
1944 April. Some chipping to extremities, interior tape, dark tanning paper, G/VG.   40.00
1944 June. Chipping to top left corner of cover, readers crease and general wear, VG-.   35.00
1944 June. Small paper perished from tips of spine, VG+.   60.00
1945 October. General wear, surface creasing, G/VG.   40.00
1946 November. General wear and chipping with tanning supple paper, VG-   45.00
1947 September. Creasing to cover, nice supple paper, VG.   50.00
1947 November. Moderate chipping, lite tan supple paper, G/VG.   35.00
1950 Winter. Lite wear, mild damp stain, VG+.   30.00
1950 Winter. Lite wear chip starting to come loose at the lower right corner, VG+.   40.00
1952 Spring. Lite wear and handling, some chipping to extremities, VG.   40.00

Pioneer Western
1950 December.#1. Color insert. Moderate surface wear, sm piece off spine, G/VG.   40.00

Planet Stories
1939 Win, #1. Partial paper perished from spine, tos, G+.   175.00
1940 Spring, #2. Moderate creasing, tos, G/VG.   75.00
1940 Summer, #3. Lite wear to extremities, FN.   195.00
1940 Summer, #3. Some spine damage and tos, G/VG.   75.00
1940 Fall, #4. Small tos, shows well, VG.   95.00
1940 Winter, #5. General wear and 2 store stamps to cover, VG.   95.00
1940 Winter, #5. Stories by Leigh Brackett, Ray Cummings, Eando Binder and others. Lite wear, some creasing, VG/FN.   100.00
1941 Spring. Some spine damage and tos, trim to edge, G+.   30.00
1941 Summer. Virgil Finlay cover. Sm tos, and 1" at right edge, VG-.   65.00
1941 Fall. Frank R. Paul cover. SM tos, wear to extremities, VG-.   65.00
1941/42 Winter. Hannas Bok cover. Sm tos, grease pencil price to cover, VG-.   65.00
1942 Fall. Mild creasing, date written on cover, FN-,   95.00
1942 Summer. ½" tips off spine, creasing to cover, VG-.   55.00
1945 Fall. No back cover, partial spine, interior tape, G.   15.00
1945 Fall. Tape on spine, moderate trim, G+.   25.00
1945 Spring. Tape on spine, covers starting to separate from book block, G+.   30.00
1946 Fall. Contains *The Creatures That Time Forgot* by Ray Bradbury. Lite wear, some creasing & tp to foot of spine, VG.   60.00
1946 Fall. Contains *The Creatures That Time Forgot* by Ray Bradbury. Damp staining to back cover, VG.   60.00
1946 Spring. Contains *Defense Mech* by Ray Bradbury. Small piece off bc, very sm tp at foot of spine, VG+.   80.00
1946 Spring. Contains *Defense Mech* by Ray Bradbury. Lite wear, creasing, small tears, store stamp to logo, G/VG.   40.00
1946 Summer. Contains *The Million Year Picnic* by Ray Bradbury. 2" spine split, some loss at spine tips, VG-.   75.00
1946 Winter. General wear, creasing, 1" tear on right edge and some tape to foot of spine, VG- .   40.00
1947 Fall. 1" tear to spine, VG.   50.00
1947 Fall. Mild edge wear, FN-.   85.00

Planet Stories 1950 Spr

Planet Stories 1952 Jul

Pocket Western 1950 Sep

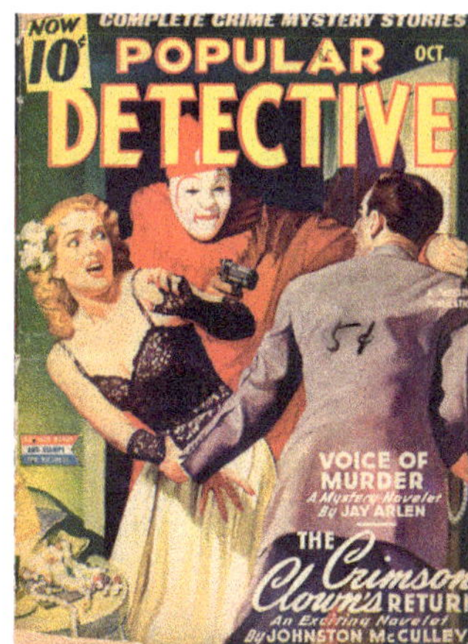

Popular Detective 1944 Oct

1947 Summer. Tape whole length of spine, G/VG.	35.00
1947 Winter. Moderate creasing, lower right corner off, G.	20.00
1947 Winter. Aggressive wear, tearing, FR.	10.00
1948 Spring. Contains *Jonah Of The Jove Run* by Ray Bradbury. Mild wear, mainly at extremities, VG/FN.	90.00
1948 Winter. Contains *Asleep In Armageddon* by Ray Bradbury, Moderate tos, trim to pulp, G+.	40.00
1948 Fall. Contains *Mars Is Heaven!* By Ray Bradbury. Moderate tos, split, G.	20.00
1949 Spring. Contains *Dwellers In Silence* by Ray Bradbury. 2" split to foot of spine, general wear, VG.	65.00
1949 Fall Contains *Enchantress Of Venus* by Leigh Brackett. Lite wear some creasing ,VG+.	45.00
1949 Summer. Pulp trimmed, tos, G.	20.00
1949 Fall Contains *Enchantress Of Venus* by Leigh Brackett. Moderate tos, creasing ,G/VG.	25.00
1949 Winter. Small tos, slight creasing, VG+.	60.00
1949 Winter. Large p.o.b.c., creasing, G+.	20.00
1950 Spring. Contains *Forever And The Earth* by Ray Bradbury. Aggressive int tp to covers, shows well VG-.	55.00
1950 Summer. Contains *Death-By-Rain* by Ray Bradbury. Lite wear, mild center crease, VG/FN.	75.00
1950 Fall. Contains *Death-Wish* by Ray Bradbury. Tos, aggressive trim, G.	20.00
1950 Fall. Contains *Death-Wish* by Ray Bradbury. Tape to whole spine, trim, G.	20.00
1951 July. Contains *Temple Of Han* by Jack Vance. Some tos, general wear, G/VG.	30.00
1951 Sept. Contains *The Incubi Of Parallel X* by Theodore Sturgeon. Moderate wear, damps staining, G/VG.	25.00
1951 Nov. Moderate surface creasing, some chipping, G/VG.	30.00
1952 July. Contains the first published appearance of Philip K. Dick with *Beyond Lies The Wub*. 2" tear to bc, general wear, VG-.	200.00
1952 July. Contains the first published appearance of Philip K. Dick with *Beyond Lies The Wub*. Moderate tape to whole spine, chipping, large tear repaired to cover, G.	95.00
1952 Sept. Contains *The Gun* by Philip K. Dick. Back cover loose, chipping, G+.	35.00
1952 November. Contains *Shannach-The Last* by Leigh Brackett. General wear, 1" spine split, VG.	55.00
1952 November. Contains *Shannach-The Last* by Leigh Brackett. Moderate surface creasing, VG-.	50.00
1953 Jan. Mild wear, FN-.	80.00
1953 March. Lite wear, few small tears and some creasing. VG+.	45.00
1953 March. Lite wear, few small tears small tos, VG.	40.00
1953 May. Contains *The Infinites* by Philip K. Dick. Aggressive wear mainly to bc, pieces missing, G+.	30.00
1953 July. Bc almost separated from pulp, VG-.	40.00
1954 May. Contains *James P. Crow* by Philip K Dick. Moderate creasing some spine damage, G+.	25.00
1954 Fall. Moderate creasing, G/VG.	40.00
1955 Spring. Mild wear, some chipping, VG.	45.00
1955 Summer Contains *Out of the Iron Womb!* By Poul Anderson and *Last Call from Sector 9G* by Leigh Brackett. Lite wear some creasing mainly to extremities for G/VG	50.00

Pocket Western Magazine

September 1950, #1. Readers crease to left edge, else nice condition with lite tan supple paper, VG/FN.	100.00

Popular Baseball

1951 Spring. Lite wear with Lite tan supple paper. FN	40.00

Popular Detective

1940 Oct. 1½" spine split and paper perished, VG-.	50.00
1941 Oct. Contains *Lilies Of Lead* by G. T. Fleming-Roberts. Some pieces off extremities, creasing, G/VG.	25.00
1944 April. Moderate wear and some chipping and small tears to extremities, VG-.	40.00
1944 August. Moderate wear and some tape to cover and interior, G/VG.	30.00
1944 Oct. The Crimson Clown. Moderate wear and handling, moderate tape to bc being held on with tape, chipping, G+.	95.00
1945 Feb. Readers crease, sm tears to extremities, some int. tp to front cover, VG-.	40.00
1945 June. Circus cover. Moderate damp staining to pulp, spine lean. G+.	20.00
1945 August. Lite wear with very nice paper, FN.	60.00
1945 August. Some chipping to edge, lite flaking, VG-.	30.00
1945 Oct. Mild center crease, lite wear, VG+.	45.00
1947 January. Belarski cover art. General wear, creasing, slight spine lean, VG-.	40.00

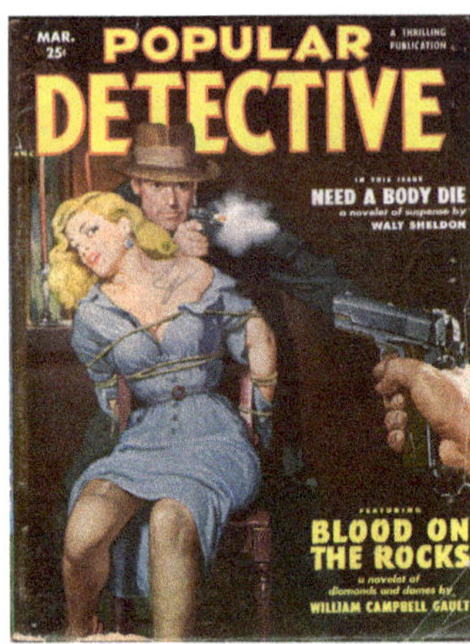

Popular Detective 1951 Mar

Popular Western 1934 Nov

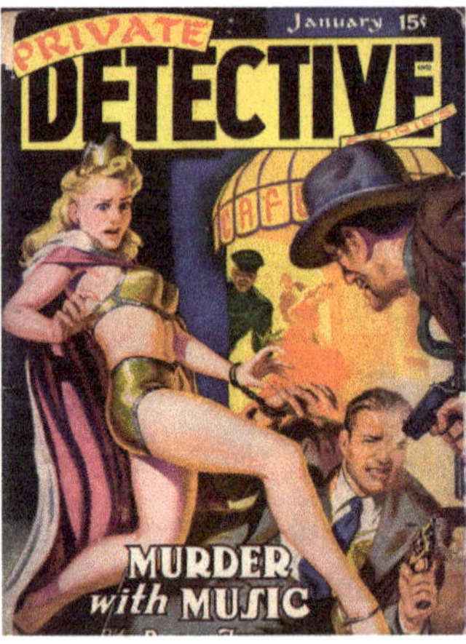

Private Detective 1942 Jan

Public Enemy 1935 Dec

1947 January. *The Grave Must be Deep* by Norman Daniels. General wear and some staining to cover, VG.	40.00
1947 July Contains *Aftermath Of Murder* by Norman Daniels. General wear, G/VG.	30.00
1948 January. 4" split to spine, some chipping to extremities, G/VG.	35.00
1948 July. General lite wear and handling, mild creasing, VG+.	50.00
1948 March. Story by Johnston McCulley. Front cover detached, G.	35.00
1948 May. Contains *Corpse on the Carpet* by Louis L'Amour. Edge wear, some chipping and 1" tear, G/VG.	45.00
1948 November. Contains *The Beautiful Angel Of Death* by Wyatt Blassingame. Belarski cover art. General wear, creasing. Tanning supple paper. Skull in Crystal ball cover, VG.	40.00
1948 November. Contains *The Beautiful Angel Of Death* by Wyatt Blassingame. Belarski cover art. General wear, creasing. Tanning supple paper. Skull in Crystal ball cover, VG	40.00
1948 September. Moderate wear, creasing, small tears and slight lean to spine, G+.	20.00
1949 January. General Lite wear, mild trim with Lite tan paper. VG+.	45.00
1949 July. 4" spine split, creasing with Lite tan supple paper, VG-.	30.00
1949 July. 4" spine split, creasing with Lite tan supple paper, VG-.	30.00
1949 May. Mild wear with small chip off right edge, VG+.	20.00
1949 November. Skeleton cover. Some chipping, creasing and few tears with tanning supple paper, VG-.	40.00
1949 November. Skeleton cover. General wear, some creasing and small tears to extremities, VG-.	45.00
1950 Mar. Chipping off lower edge, mild readers crease, VG-.	40.00
1951 March. Bondage cover. Moderate creasing to extremities and some chipping, VG-.	45.00
1952 January. General wear, spine lean, readers crease, VG-.	30.00
1953 January. General wear, mild readers crease, VG.	40.00
1953 May. Hair pulling cover. General lite wear and great off white paper, VG/FN.	50.00

Popular Magazine

1903 December, #2. General Lite wear, lower right Corner off, Lite tan supple paper, some tape on spine, G/VG Very scarce.	300.00
1929 July 1st. Art by Paul Stahr. Contains *Headlines* by Fred MacIsaac. General wear, hint of flaking. VG-	50.00

Popular Sports

1937 June, #1. Dizzy Dean Cover. Diagonal crease to right side of cover, VG.	125.00

Popular Stories, The

1927 October 8. Jerome Rozen cover art. Creasing and small tears to over-hangs, VG.	50.00

Popular Western.

1934 November, #1. Great looking FN/VF, nice colors to cover, with Lite supple paper. Scarce.	450.00
1950 February. Contains *The Killer from Pecos* by Louis L'Amour. Lite wear, mild trim, FN.	50.00

Private Detective

1942 January. Great showgirl cover (Anderson art?) General wear, chip off top left corner, some chipping to edge, mild flaking, VG-.	125.00
1943 June. Lite wear, few sm tears to extremities, VG+.	60.00
1944 March. 2 large chips off extremities of fc and few sm tears to bc, G/VG.	35.00
1944 Nov. L.l. corner off, general lite wear, VG-.	40.00
1944 Dec. Showgirl cover. 1" closed tear to edge, lite wear, 1 diagonal crease to top corner, VG-.	40.00
1945 August. Some internal tape to cover, medium wear, cream to tan supple paper, VG-	40.00
1945 Dec. Aggressive damp staining damage and large pieces off bc, FR.	15.00
1946 Feb. Large diagonal crease to cover, fc seems to have been re-glued, G.	20.00
1946 July. Lite wear, one medium crease at lower right, Lite tan supple paper, VG+.	50.00
1946 Sept. Center crease, moderate surface creasing, G/VG.	35.00
1946 November. General wear, few small tears at extremities, some surface creasing, VG-.	25.00
1947 Jan. Center and readers creases, edge wear, damps staining, G/VG.	35.00
1947 March. Some pencil marks to cover, NF.	60.00

Public Enemy.

1935 December (#1.) Saunders cover. Lite handling and dust soiling to edges, FN-.	300.00

Rangeland Sweethearts 1940 Oct

Rapid Fire Western 1933 Jan

Red Star Detective 1940 Jun

Red Star Western 1940 Jul

Pursuit Detective Story Magazine
1953 Sept, #1. Contains *The Last Man Alive* By Craig Rice. Readers creases, general wear, VG-.   45.00

Railroad Magazine
1937 April. General Lite wear, some mild chipping to over-hangs, FN-.   25.00
1937 May. General Lite wear, some very mild tears to over-hangs, FN-.   25.00
1937 October. General Lite wear mild tears to over-hangs, FN-.   25.00
1937 November. General Lite wear mild tears to over-hangs, FN-.   25.00
1938 February. General Lite wear mild tears to over-hangs, FN-.   25.00
1938 June. General Lite wear mild tears to over-hangs, FN-.   25.00
1938 May. General Lite wear mild tears to over-hangs, FN-.   25.00
1938 Aug. General Lite wear mild tears to over-hangs, FN-.   25.00
1938 Oct. General Lite wear mild tears to over-hangs, FN-.   25.00
1938 Sept. General Lite wear mild tears to over-hangs, FN-.   25.00
We have additional Railroad Magazines in stock. Your want list is solicited.

Rangeland Sweethearts
1940 October #1. Lite wear with nice off-white paper, VG/FN.   75.00

Range Rider Western
1945 Fall. General wear, some creasing, small tears, lower right corner off, Lite tan supple paper interior.   15.00
1951 April. Lite wear, creasing, lite tanning supple paper interior.   15.00

Rapid Fire Western Stories
1933 January. Pencil marks to fc, some damp staining, G. Scarce title.   60.00

Real Northwest Adventures
1937 March. Moderate surface creasing, G/VG.   95.00

Real Western
1943 June. General wear, some small tears and mild loss of paper at extremities, VG+.   20.00
1948 August. General wear, some small tears and mild loss of paper at extremities, VG+.   20.00
1947 February. General wear, some small tears and mild loss of paper at extremities, VG+.   20.00
1946 August. General wear, some small tears and mild loss of paper at extremities, VG+.   20.00
1948 January. General wear, some small tears and mild loss of paper at extremities, VG+.   20.00
1949 April. General wear, some small tears and mild loss of paper at extremities, VG+.   20.00

Red Seal Western
1937 April. General mild wear and mild surface creasing, great paper quality, VG+.   40.00

Red Star Adventures
1940 June #1. Moderate chipping to right edge of fc, 5" spine split, G.   75.00
1940 Oct, #3. Paper pull below logo, general wear, G+.   85.00

Red Star Detective
June 1940, #1. General lite wear, mild foxing at spine, VG/FN.   200.00

Red Star Western
1940 July #2. Silver Buck app. No back cover, G+.   50.00

Rio Kid Western, The.
1946 December. General Lite wear, mild trim to right edge, Lite tan supple paper interior.   25.00
1948 August. General wear, chipping and water damage, tan supple paper interior. G+.   10.00
1951 May. General wear, some creasing with cream supple paper interior, VG.   20.00

Romantic Detective 1938 Jun

Romantic Western 1938 Jul

Saucy Movie Tales 1936 Aug

Saucy Stories 1936 Apr

Roaring Western Stories
1953 May, #1. VF   75.00

Romance Round-Up
1936 September. #1. General lite wear, creasing, VG+.   125.00

Romantic Detective
1938 February, #1. Date written in "D" of title, couple of lite diagonal creases, very scarce, shows very well, FN-.   495.00
1938 February, #1. 1.5" tear to front cover right edge, 2" split to top of spine, 4" tear to back cover, G+.   195.00
1938 June, #3. Small tears to extremities, some damp staining most visible on verso of cover, very scarce, VG.   450.00
1939 February, Final Issue. One of the few photo cover in pulp magazines. Mild surface creasing,
        few small tears to extremities, mild damp staining to back cover, very scarce, VG.   450.00

Romantic Western
1938 July. Lite wear and handling, FN.   500.00

Romantic West
1951 Annual #2. Mild wear hole at top staple, very small crease to top right corner, FN-.   75.00

Saucy Movie Tales
1936 July. Tos, lite wear, shows very well, VG.   750.00
1936 August. High demand issue, fireman rescues blond cover. Very lite wear, lite tan supple paper, FN-.   1,500.00
1937 December. Dancer cover, Small tape to crown of spine, else shows well, VG/FN.   400.00

Saucy Stories
1936 April, #7. Cover art by Norman Saunders. Lite wear and handling, diagonal crease near lower right corner, near white paper,
        strong spine. A very scarce to rare high demand pulp which is very difficult to find. NF.   2,500.00

Science Fiction
1939 March, #1. Frank R. Paul cover. Lite wear and creasing, small tip of foot of spine, VG+.   125.00
1939 August, #1. Frank R. Paul cover. ½" off crown of spine, general wear, VG.   60.00
1939 Dec. Frank R. Paul cover. Surface creasing, wear to extremities, VG.   60.00
1943 July. Classic Robot Cover. Mild chipping to extremities, 1" closed tear to foot of spine, crease to lower right corner, VG.   150.00

Science Fiction Stories
1954, Volume 1, #2 . Contains *The Turning Wheel* by Philip K. Dick, VG.   30.00

Science Wonder Quarterly
1929 Fall, #1. Great looking copy with 1" tear off crown of spine with nice paper quality. Rarely encountered
        in this condition, VG/FN. Printed with gold ink to cover.   400.00

Sea Novel Magazine
1941 January. FN/VF.   95.00

Secret Service Stories
1928 February, #4. Some interior tape, surface creasing, very scarce, VG-.   200.00
1928 April. 3" spine split at crown of spine, general wear and some loss at overhangs,
        mild flaking to paper, G/VG. Scarce to rare pulp.   250.00

Shadow
1933 April 15. The Shadow's Justice. Amateur color touch to cover, moderate creasing and wear, G+.   200.00
1935 March 15. *Bells of Doom*. 1" tear to right edge, few small tears and creasing mainly to over hangs, VG.   200.00
1936 April 15. The Man From Shanghai. ½" tear to right edge, lite wear, nice paper, VG/FN.   200.00

Science Fiction 1943 Jul

Shadow 1938 Aug 15

Sheena 1951 Spr

Shock 1948 May

1936 Dec 1. *The Seven Drops of Blood*. Two 1" tears to right edge and hole punch cover, VG-.	110.00
1936 July 15. The Broken Napoleons. Lite surface creasing, small tears to over-hangs, nice paper, VG+.	140.00
1937 March 15. Murder House. 2 pieces of tape to spine, some damp staining, trim to right edge, G/VG.	140.00
1937 April 15. The Masked Headsman. Aggressive creasing, 1" x 2" piece out of right edge, FR.	25.00
1938 March 15. *Face of Doom.* Tears, chipping, lower left corner off, FR.	25.00
1938 April 1. *The Crimson Phoenix*. Moderate creasing, 4" spine split at back, G+.	75.00
1938 May 15. Aggressive chipping including interior especially at lower right corner, flaking, FR.	25.00
1938 August 15. Few small tears to extremities, over hang chip off bottom edge, crease at logo, VG.	150.00
1939 February 15. *The Lone Tiger.* 2" repaired tear at top left corner, some creasing, G/VG.	100.00
1939 August 15. Moderate wear and surface creasing, G/VG.	50.00
1939 August 15. *Wizard of Crime*. General wear and handling with Lite tan supple paper. VG-.	70.00
1939 Sept 1. *The Crime Ray*. General Lite wear and mild trim to covers with mild flaking paper. G/VG.	60.00
1940 July 1st . *The Murder Genius*. Lite wear and handling with couple of wear holes at staples, VG+.	110.00
1941 November 15. Some tos, sm hole at right edge, G/VG.	55.00
1941 December 1. *Murder Mansion*. 1" paper off top and ½" paper off foot of spine, tape stains, G+.	35.00
1942 March 15. Tos, dime size piece off spine, large tear, FR.	25.00
1942 April 15. *The Jade Dragon*. General wear, some ink marks to logo, VG-.	65.00
1942 June 15. *The Devil's Feud*. Tos, general wear, G+.	35.00
1943 February 1. *The Devil Monsters* Cool Dinosaur cover. ½" off crown of spine, else VG+.	75.00
1943 February 1. *The Devil Monsters* Cool Dinosaur cover. General wear, minor spine damage, VG.	45.00
1943 April. Moderate wear and some spine damage, some interior tape, G/VG.	35.00
1943 June. Moderate wear and some spine damage, VG-.	40.00
1943 July. *The Golden Doom*. Spine damage, paper flaking, G.	25.00
1948 June-July. *The Lock and Key* by Frank Gruber. General wear with lower right corner off. VG-.	75.00
1948 Fall. Moderate surface creasing, small chip off right edge, back cover dingy, G/VG.	85.00
1949 Winter. *The Magigals*. General surface creasing, some tears and war to extremities, Nice paper, VG.	195.00

Sheena Queen of the Jungle (Stories Of)

1951 Spring, #1. Lite surface creasing and very mild creasing at right edge, VG.	225.00
1951 Spring, #1 General wear and some staining mainly to back cover, VG-.	150.00
1951 Spring, #1 Lower left corner off, few small ½" tears to extremities, G/VG.	125.00

Shock

1948 May, #2. Some bug damage to top right of back cover and last few pages and about an inch paper perished to top of spine, VG-.	75.00

Short Stories

1950 Nov. Lite wear, some creasing, few small tears, mild loss of paper to overhangs, VG.	20.00
1950 Nov. RCMP Cover. General Lite wear, some creasing, few small tears, no back cover, G/VG.	10.00
1951 April. General Lite wear, some creasing, VG	25.00
1952 April. General Lite wear, some creasing, mild trim, VG	20.00
1952 July. General heavy wear, creasing, loss of paper to overhangs, G.	10.00
1952 July. Lite wear, some creasing, some loss of paper to overhangs, 1.5 inch tear to top of spine, G/VG.	20.00
1953 Mar. General wear, creasing, spine splits, Lite tan supple paper interior.	15.00

We have additional Short Stories in stock. Your want list is solicited.

Six-Gun Western

1949 Dec. Air brush cover. Moderate wear, creasing, piece off back cover, G.	20.00

Sky Birds

1932 November. Printed in Canada. 1" closed tear to right edge of cover, lite surface creasing, VG.	45.00
1933 July. Printed in Canada. Slight spine lean, mild surface creasing, VG.	45.00
1933 Oct. Moderate creasing, store stamp, G+.	25.00
1934 April. Moderate damp staining to whole pulp, G+.	25.00

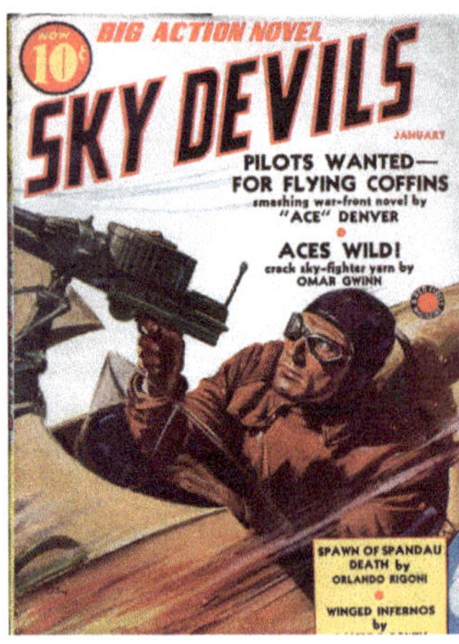

Sky Aces 1938 Jun	**Sky Devils 1939 Jan**	**Sky Devils 1939 Apr**	**Smashing Western 1936 Aug**

Sky Aces

1938 June, #1. Contains *Boomerang Bomber* by L. Ron Hubbard, FN.	295.00
1939 March, #4. Moderate damp staining, G+.	25.00
1940 April. Mild surface creasing, VG+.	60.00

Sky Devils

1939 Jan, #4. Slight spine lean, NF.	95.00
1939 April, #5. General lite wear, VG+.	75.00
1940 February. Severe browning, flaking, FR.	15.00

Sky Fighters

1935 September. Lite wear and 2" tape to interior cover.	50.00
1936 March. General wear, few small tears and couple of chips off edge, tanning supple paper. VG+	50.00
1937 February. Moderate wear and chipping to right cover edge, Lite tan supple paper. G/VG.	25.00
1937 March. General wear, back over loose, tanning supple paper. G/VG.	25.00
1938 November. General Lite wear, few small tears, tanning supple paper. VG+.	50.00
1940 July. General Lite wear, few small tears, tanning supple paper. VG+.	50.00
1941 January. 3 pieces of tape to spine, general Lite wear. VG-.	35.00
1941 March. Tape on spine, shows well, Lite tan supple paper. VG+.	35.00
1941 May. Contains *Kill or Be Killed* by David Goodis. Small hole in logo, VG.	50.00
1941 May. Mild chipping to bottom of cover, nice supple paper. FN-.	50.00
1941 November. Mild chipping to bottom of cover, nice supple paper, FN-.	50.00
1942 July. 1" tear in center of spine, mild wear and nice paper, VG.	40.00
1942 March. Mild wear, nice supple paper, FN.	60.00
1942 November. General Lite wear, some chipping, Lite tan supple paper, VG.	40.00
1948 Winter. Contains *Pirates With Wings* by Louis L'Amour. Some creasing mainly to extremities, VG.	65.00
1949 Spring. Contains *Shroud Lines* by Norman A. Daniels. Lite wear, some small tears, VG+.	40.00
1949 Fall. Tape to verso of front cover with some bleed thru, G/VG.	30.00

Sky Raiders (Series One)

1939 Dec (#5, third issue) FN-.	125.00

Sky Raiders (Series two)

1942 December, #1. Moderate interior tape including a 3" tear repaired from verso, G.	20.00
1943 April, #3. Paper chewed at top of spine, some chipping, G/VG.	60.00
1943 #4. Paper perished from top right corner of pulp, some chipping, G/VG.	40.00
1943 August, #5. Readers and surface creasing, some chipping, G/VG.	40.00
1943 Oct. 1" tear at spine, lite surface creasing, VG.	50.00
1944 Jan. Some loss at over hangs, general wear, G/VG.	40.00
1944 Spr. Some loss at lower spine, ½" tear at right edge, G/VG.	40.00

Smashing Western

1936 August. #1. 1" tear at bottom edge, general lite wear, VG.	95.00

Snappy Stories

1925 Feb 1. Center crease, general wear and creasing, VG-.	60.00
1925 May 2. 2" tear at lower left corner, dust shadows to cover, VG-.	60.00
1925 Aug 2. Circular stain to fc, general wear, VG-.	60.00

Soldiers of Fortune

1931 October, #1. General wear, some mild chipping to extremities, VG-. Scarce.	250.00

South Sea Stories

1939 December, #1. Lite wear, a very nice looking copy, FN-.	250.00
1940 August. Mild trim, FN-.	225.00

Soldiers of Fortune 1931 Oct

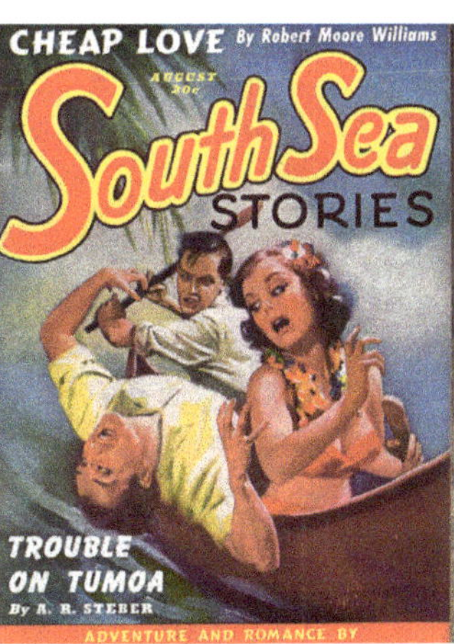

South Sea Stories 1940 Aug

Speed Adventure 1943 Jan

Spicy Adventure 1936 Aug

Speed (Spicy) Adventure Stories
1943 January, #1. H. J. Ward cover art. Small corner off lower left, general wear, creasing, G/VG.   150.00

Speed (Spicy) Detective
1943 January, #1. Lite wear & creasing with small chip off right edge and nice paper. VG+.   250.00
1943 June, #6. General mild wear and handling, some mild creasing to cover, VG+.   75.00

Speed (Spicy) Mystery
1943 July, #5. Cover of blonde about to be torched with gasoline. H. J. Ward cover art. 1.5" tape to logo,
      some chipping to extremities and some damp staining, G/VG.   50.00
1943 Sept. Some loss of paper to lower right edge and Corner, does not affect type, nice supple paper.   40.00
1944 Sept. Moderate chipping to extremities, G/VG.   40.00
1944 Nov. Bondage cover. General wear, few small tears to extremities, VG.   85.00
1945 March. Contains *Timepiece of Death* by Ray Cummings. Spine split, VG.   75.00
1946 March. Last issue of the run. Some writing to toc page, general wear and trim to front cover, VG-.   50.00

Speed (Spicy)Western
1944 September. Mild wear and creasing, VG.   40.00
1944 October. General wear, some chipping, VG.   40.00
1944 November. General wear, some chipping, VG.   40.00
1944 December. 3" spine split, lite wear, VG.   40.00
1945 January. General wear and some creasing, VG-.   35.00
1945 February. Stain to back cover, VG.   40.00
1945 June. Some surface creasing and edge wear, VG.   40.00
1945 July. General wear, small tears to extremities, VG.   40.00
1945 August. Lite wear, small tip off lower right corner, VG+.   50.00
1945 October. Interior tape, moderate creasing and wear, G/VG.   30.00
1945 December. Lite wear, small tip off lower right corner, VG+.   50.00
1946 January. Moderate wear and creasing, top right corner off, G/VG.   30.00
1946 March. Speed (Spicy) Western 1946 March. Lite wear and creasing, FN-.   70.00
1946 November. Minor spine damage, creasing and some small tears to VG-.   35.00
1946 December. December. 2" spine split and some damage to spine, G/VG.   30.00
1947 July. Scarce. General creasing and small tears and some chipping to right edge, VG-.   75.00
1947 October. 1" spine split, 1" tear at spine, chipping, creasing, G.   20.00
1948 January. Back cover loose, chipping, creasing, G.   15.00

Spicy Adventure
1935 April. General mild wear, some surface creasing, VG+   375.00
1936 Feb. 1" & few smaller tears to extremities, some chipping, sm l.l. corner off, G/VG.   225.00
1936 June. General lite wear, mild chipping to overhangs, 1" tear to back cover, VG.   400.00
1936 July. Bondage whipping cover. Surface and readers crease, VG-.   275.00
1936 August. Classic Octopus Cover. Some surface and readers creasing, mild trim VG   550.00
1936 December. General wear and handling, some creasing. VG+   375.00
1937 Jan. Robert E. Howard story *Murderer's Grog*. Slight lean to spine, some surface creasing, mild flaking to paper, VG-.   400.00

Spicy Detective
1935 November. Clear tape to spine, lite tan supple paper, VG-.   295.00
1935 November. Moderate wear, large tear at logo repaired on verso by tape, aggressive int tp, variant B. FR.   175.00
1935 Nov. Large tear, moderate creasing & interior tape repairs, G. This is the scarcer variant "B" cover art.   250.00
1936 May. Mild diagonal crease at lower right of cover, lite wear and mild trim, VG.   350.00
1936 June. General wear and creasing to cover, small amount of paint on the Gunman's left arm, G/VG.   175.00
1936 Sept. General Lite wear Lite tan supple paper. VG.   250.00
1938 Feb. 1" tear to lower left corner, mild flaking, VG-.   350.00
1941 Sept. 1" off foot of spine, general wear, damp staining, some creasing, G/VG.   250.00

Spicy Mystery 1935 Nov

Spicy Western 1936 Nov

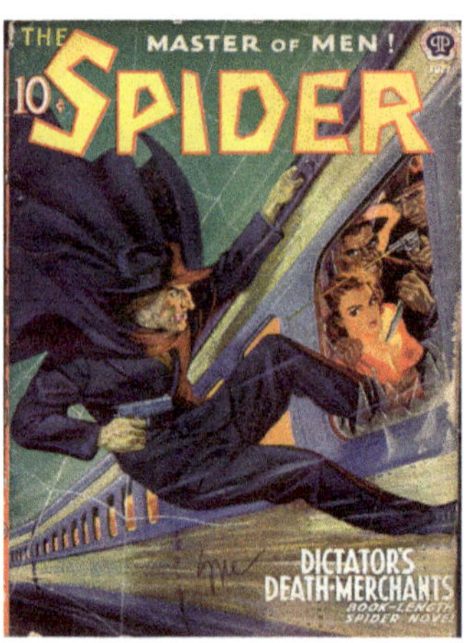

Spider 1940 Jan

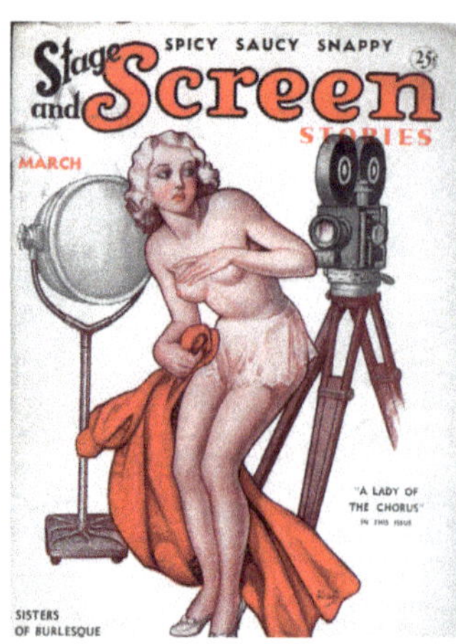

Stage & Screen 1936 Mar

Spicy Mystery Stories

1935 November. Vampire bat monster menaces red head in negligée. Lite surface creasing and mild edge wear, wrinkles to spine, VG/FN. 900.00

Spicy Western

1936 November, #1. Bondage cover by H. J. Ward. First issue of the fourth spicy. Sm tip off top right corner, general lite wear and lite tan supple paper. This is the uncensored cover version. VG+. 1250.00
1936 December. #2. Moderate creasing to cover, VG-. 250.00
1937 October. General wear, some chipping to extremities, G/VG. 100.00
1942 December. Last issue. Re-stapled, G/VG. 75.00

Spider

1934 October. *Builders of the Black Empire*. Mild trim, general Lite wear. Lite tan supple paper. VG/FN. 225.00
1934 April. Snake cover. General wear, pen marks to logo, some interior tape, G+. 150.00
1934 August. Spider, General wear, small tape on spine, last couple of pages starting, G/VG. 95.00
1934 June. Satan's Death Blast. Bondage Bomb Cover! Half of page 5/6 cut out, Pg 125/6 glued to back cover and page 127/8 missing. Spider sty complete, FR. 60.00
1934 May. Skeleton Cover. Some interior tape, general wear and creasing, G+. 125.00
1934 October. Tape at foot of spine, general moderate wear, G+. 85.00
1934 September. General wear, mild flaking, G/VG. 95.00
1935 April. Wraparound re-glued, some color rubbing at spine, G/VG. 75.00
1935 May. General lite wear, VG+. 150.00
1935 June. Lite wear, some readers creases, and internal tape, G/VG. 75.00
1935 October. Some excess glue to insider front cover, general wear & creasing, G/VG. 70.00
1939 March. Lite wear, ½" off foot of spine, VG. 100.00
1940 January. Bondage torture cover. Right corners off, nice paper, G/VG. 85.00
1940 July. One of the high demand "fang" covers. General wear, some chipping & spine split at back cover, VG. 200.00
1942 April. 1" tear and other smaller tears to right edge, G/VG. 85.00

Sports Action

1937 December, #1. Football cover. Lite wear, scuffing, some mild creasing, VG+. 75.00

Sports Fiction

1949 November. Special World Series Issue. wear, few small tears with tanning Paper. VG+. 35.00
1950 January. General moderate wear, 1" tear, tanning supple paper, VG. 20.00

Sports Novels

1946 Dec. Leatherhead Football Cover. FN/VF unread file copy type condition. 40.00
1947 February. Basketball Cover. FN/VF unread file copy type condition. 40.00
1947 November Leatherhead Football Cover. FN/VF unread file copy type condition. 40.00
1948 May. Track Cover. Track Cover. FN/VF unread file copy type condition. 40.00
1948 June. Baseball Cover. Baseball Cover. FN/VF unread file copy type condition. 40.00
1949 March. Contains *Last Chance Cleats* by John D. Macdonald. FN/VF unread file copy type condition. 60.00
1949 November. Boxing Cover. Small chip off right cover edge otherwise appears in unread file copy type condition. 25.00

Sports Winners

1951 October. World Series cover. Half inch tear to right edge, mild trim with Lite tan supple paper. VG+. 30.00

Stage and Screen Stories

1936 March. Bare nipple cover art by Burley. Lite wear with star stamp at logo, very scarce to rare, NF. 1250.00

Star Detective

1935 May, #1. Scarce hard to find issue. Aggressive tape to spine, moderate creasing, interior tape, G. 200.00

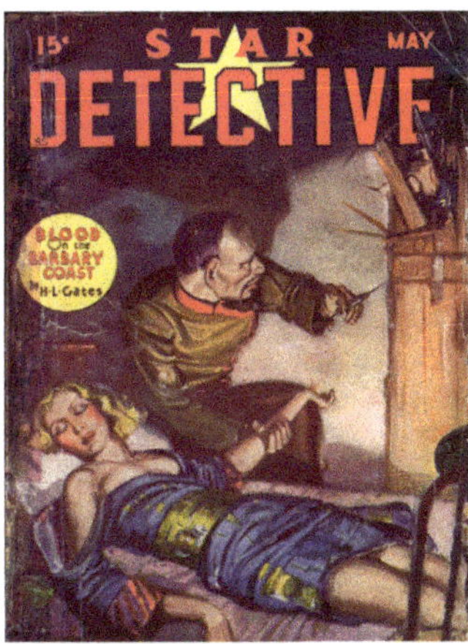

Star Detective 1935 May

Startling Mystery 1940 Feb

Startling Stories 1941 Jul

Startling Stories 1945 Spr

Star Novels Magazine.
1934 July. Skull Cover. General moderate wear and creasing to cover. Canadian printing. G/VG.   75.00

Startling Mystery
1940 February, #1. Piece off bc, general wear, some chipping, small hole to front cover, VG-.   200.00

Startling Stories
1939. Jan, #1. Tos, G+   50.00
1939 Mar, #2. Mild trim, genera light wear, 1" closed tear, VG.   75.00
1939 May, #3. Moderate chipping to right edge, large chip of bc, G/VG.   30.00
1939 July. Small lower left corner off cover, general light wear, VG.   40.00
1939 Sept. Large piece of lower left corner, 2" tos, G+.   25.00
1939 Nov. Ark of space cover. Some spine damage, chipping, store stamp, VG-   60.00
1940 Jan. Moderate wear and creasing to front and back cover, G+.   25.00
1940 Mar. Dime size chip of right edge, VG.   30.00
1940 May. General light wear, VG+.   40.00
1940 July. General light wear, some chipping and sm tears to extremities, VG-.   30.00
1940 Sept. Large piece off tr corner, chipping, 2" tear, FR.   15.00
1940 Nov. General wear, chipping to right edge, sm top right corner off, VG-.   30.00
1940 Nov. General light wear, dime size chip off top edge, VG+.   40.00
1941 Jan. Lite wear, small tears to right edge, VG+.   40.00
1941 Mar. Creasing to lower right corner, general wear, VG+.   40.00
1941 May. Aggressive tape to spine and all edges int and exterior, G.   15.00
1941 July. Contains *Gateway to Paradise* by Jack Williamson, FN.   60.00
1941 July. Contains *Gateway to Paradise* by Jack Williamson, some spine damage, 4" ss, chipping, G+   20.00
1941 Sept. Small holes to cover, tape, store stamp, G+.   20.00
1941 Nov. Large piece off lower edge, moderate trim, G+.   20.00
1942 Jan. Damp staining mainly to bc, some chipping to right edge, VG-.   30.00
1942 Mar. Slight spine lean, mild chipping to extremities, VG+.   30.00
1942 Mar. Moderate wear, 1" closed tear, VG-.   30.00
1942 May. Wraps separated from text block, damp staining. G.   15.00
1942 July. Empire State and Statue of Liberty cover. Tos, 1" paper perish from foot of spine, G/VG.   45.00
1942 Sept. Slight spine lean, readers crease, mild chipping, VG-.   30.00
1942 Nov. Aggressive trim, G.   15.00
1943 Jan. Large chipping to extremities, 2" tos, G.   15.00
1943 June. Aggressive chipping, piece off lower left corner, some damp staining, G.   15.00
1943 Fall. Slight spine lean, some surface creasing, VG.   35.00
1944 Spring. Moderate wear and chipping to lower edge, G.   15.00
1944 Summer. Moderate surface and readers creasing, VG-.   30.00
1944 Fall. Front cover almost separated, G.   15.00
1944 Fall. Large piece from lower right corner, G.   15.00
1945 Winter. Moderate surface creasing, damage to foot of spine, G/VG.   25.00
1945 Spring. Captain Future robot cover & first app of Captain Future in this title. 2" tos, G/VG.   95.00
1945 Fall. Lite wear, 1.5” tear at foot of spine, VG.   30.00
1946 March. Slight damage to spine, cover has slight ripple, VG+.   35.00
1946 March. Cover loose, 4” tear, G.   10.00
1946 Spring. Mild surface creasing, few small tears at extremities, VG.   20.00
1946 Summer. Contains *Planet of the Black Dust* by Jack Vance, medium size chip off bottom edge, VG.   30.00
1946 Fall. FN.   40.00
1946 Winter. Captain Future cover and story, 1" tear through book and spine, G.   10.00
1947 Jan. Some surface creasing, chipping to extremities, G+.   15.00
1947 Mar. Light wear, VG+.   25.00
1947 May. Light wear, mild chipping, VG.   20.00
1947 July. Store stamp at logo, VG+.   25.00
1947 Sept. Contains Lodana by Carl Jacobi, light readers crease, some chipping, VG.   25.00

Startling Stories 1947 May   **Startling Stories 1948 Mar**   **Startling Stories 1949 Jan**   **Startling Stories 1950 Jan**

1947 Sept. Contains *Lodana* by Carl Jacobi, store stamp, moderate creasing, G/VG.	20.00
1947 Nov. Contains *Through the Purple Cloud* by Jack Williamson, light wear and chipping, VG+	25.00
1948 Jan. Contains *The Blue Flamingo by Hannes Bok*, moderate chipping, 1.5" tp at crown of spine, VG-.	20.00
1948 Mar. Fn.	40.00
1948 May. 1" tear at bottom of cover, mild chipping, VG.	20.00
1948 July. Contains *When Shadows Fall* by L. Ron Hubbard and *Hard Luck Diggings* by Jack Vance, light wear, ½" tear to bottom cover, VG.	40.00
1948 July. Contains *When Shadows Fall* by L. Ron Hubbard and *Hard Luck Diggings* by Jack Vance, store stamp, aggressive trimming to cover, Fr.	10.00
1948 Sept. Contains *What Mad Universe* by Fredric Brown, *Shenadun* by John D. MacDonald, *Sanatoris Short-cut* by Jack Vance, mild creasing, few small tears to extremities, slight spine lean, VG-.	40.00
1948 Nov. Contains *Against the Fall of Night* by Arthur C. Clarke, *Ring Around the Redhead* by John D. MacDonald, *The Visitor* by Ray Bradbury, *The Unspeakable McInch* by Jack Vance, moderate tape to end of spine, VG-.	35.00
1949 Jan. Contains *Forbidden Voyage* by Renee LaFayette (L. Ron Hubbard), *Flaw* by John D. MacDonald, *The Sub-standard Sardines* by Jack Vance, light wear, mild chipping, VG+	55.00
1949 Jan. Contains *Forbidden Voyage* by Renee LaFayette (L. Ron Hubbard), *Flaw* by John D. MacDonald, *The Sub-standard Sardines* by Jack Vance, 5" tear to cover, chipping, mild trim, Fr.	15.00
1949 Mar. Contains *The Magnificent Failure* by Renee LaFayette (L. Ron Hubbard), *The Howling Bounders* by Jack Vance, *Marinette's Inc.* by Ray Bradbury and *The Loot of Money* by Clifford D. Simak, general light wear, some tape to bc, corner size piece from bc, G/VG.	25.00
1949 Mar. Contains *The Magnificent Failure* by Renee LaFayette (L. Ron Hubbard), large lower right corner off, moderate wear, G+.	15.00
1949 May. Contains *The Incredible Destination* Renee LaFayette (L. Ron Hubbard), *Immortality* by ohn D. MacDonald, *History Lesson* by Arthur C. Clarke, tears and creasing to cover, G+.	15.00
1949 July. Contains *The Unwilling Hero* by Renee LaFayette (L. Ron Hubbard), *Transience* by Arthur C. Clarke, *The Lonely Ones* by Ray Bradbury, small tos, mild damp staining, VG-.	25.00
1949 Sept. Contains *Beyond the Black Nebula* by Renee LaFayette (L. Ron Hubbard), *A Condition of Beauty* by John D. MacDonald, *The Fires Within* by Arthur C. Clarke, alien dinosaur cover, general wear and creasing to extremities, VG-.	25.00
1949 Sept. Contains *Beyond the Black Nebula* by Renee LaFayette (L. Ron Hubbard), *A Condition of Beauty* by John D. MacDonald, *The Fires Within* by Arthur C. Clarke, alien dinosaur cover, lower left corner off, general wear, G+.	15.00
1949 Nov. Contains *The Ultimate Catalyst* by John Taine, and *The Emperor of the Universe* by Renee LaFayette (L. Ron Hubbard) small name written under logo, light wear, VG.	40.00
1950 Jan. Classic robot, ray gun and space babe cover. Pose was later used on an issue of Vampirella. Contains *The Return of Captain Future* by Edmond Hamilton, light wear, VG+	300.00
1950 Mar. Witch cover, small top right corner off, light creasing, VG.	20.00
1950 May. Contains the Captain Future story, *Children of the Son* by Edmond Hamilton and *Wine of the Dreamers* by John D. MacDonald, top right corner torn off and reattached by tape on verso, G+.	15.00
1950 July. Contains *the Spa of the Stars* by Jack Vance, *Purpose* by Ray Bradbury and *Robot Menace* by Dr. Edward E. Smith, moderate surface creasing, VG-.	25.00
1950 Sept. Classic Flame Girl cover, contains the Captain Future story, *The Harpers of Titan* by Edmond Hamilton, and *Cosmic Hotfoot* by Jack Vance, mild surface creasing, 1" split at foot of spine, VG-.	50.00
1950 Nov. Contains the *Five Gold Bands* by Jack Vance and *Tough Old Man* by L. Ron Hubbard, moderate creasing and chipping, G/VG.	30.00
1951 Jan. Contains the Captain Future Story *Moon of the Unforgotten* by Edmond Hamilton, some spine damage, small piece of bc, general wear, G+	15.00
1951 May. Contains the Captain Future story *Birthplace of Creation* by Edmond Hamilton, general surface creasing, VG.	20.00
1951 July. Moderate surface creasing, mild trim, VG-.	
1951 Sept. Contain *Masquerade of the Vicantropus* by Jack Vance and *The White Fruit of Banaldar* by John MacDonald, light wear, F-.	45.00
1951 Sept. Moderate wear and greasing, some chipping, G/VG.	25.00
1951 Nov. Small hole at logo, light wear, VG.	20.00
1951 Nov. Loss of paper edge and back cover, G.	15.00

Startling Stories 1952 Sep

Startling Stories 1952 Nov

Startling Stories 1953 May

Startling Stories 1953 Aug

1952 Jan. Light wear, small tear to extremities, VG.	20.00
1952 Jan. Moderate creasing, VG-.	15.00
1952 Feb. Small tape to back cover, light wear, VG.	20.00
1952 Mar. Moderate creasing and wear, G/VG.	15.00
1951 May. General light wear, mild readers crease, VG.	20.00
1951 July. Contains *Witch War* by Richard Matheson, readers crease, general light wear, VG+.	30.00
1951 Sept. Contains *The Masquerade on Dicantropus* by Jack Vance, *The White Fruit of Banaldar* by John D. MacDonald, light readers crease, wear ark to lower left corner, VG.	40.00
1951 Nov. Schomburg cover art, contains *The Gamblers* by Mack Reynolds and Fredric Brown, light edge wear, VG/FN.	35.00
1952 Jan. General wear, mild surface creasing, small tips off spine, VG-.	15.00
1952 Feb. Moderate wear and creasing, dime size chip off right edge, G.	10.00
1952 Mar. General wear and surface creasing, small tips off spine, VG-.	15.00
1952 Apr. Contains *Looking for Something?* By Frank Herbert, readers crease, mild wear to extremities, VG.	35.00
1952 May. Schomburg cover art. Moderate creasing, G/VG.	15.00
1952 June. Contains *Sabotage on Sulfur Planet* by Jack Vance, *Dragon's Island* by Jack Williamson, readers crease, light wear, VG.	35.00
1952 July. Contains *All the Time in the World* by Arthur C. Clarke. Rub hole at top staple, ½" off foot of spine, VG.	20.00
1952 Aug. Contains *The Lovers* by Philip Jose Farmer, *Noise* by Jack Vance, mild staining to top of cover, sm corner off l.l., VG.	50.00
1952 Sept. Contains *Big Planet* by Jack Vance, moderate wear and surface creasing, G/VG.	25.00
1952 Oct. Light surface creasing, mild edge wear, VG.	20.00
1952 Nov. Slight spine lean, FN.	30.00
1952 Nov. General light wear, readers crease, VG.	20.00
1952 Dec. Contains *Sale on! Sale On!* By Philip Jose Farmer, FN.	40.00
1953 Jan. Contains *Button, Button* by Isaac Asimov, and *Three-Legged* by Jack Vance, 3" tape on front cover at spine, VG-.	20.00
1953 Feb. Contains *The Monkey's Fingers* by Isaac Asimov, and *Sestina of the Space Rocket* by Philip Jose Farmer, general surface creasing and wear, VG.	30.00
1953 Mar. Readers crease and general surface creasing, price in grease pencil. VG-.	15.00
1953 Apr. Light surface creasing, light foxing at spine, VG+.	20.00
1953 May. Moderate surface creasing, 1" tear at crown and spine, VG.	15.00
1953 June. Contains *Moth and Rust* by Philip Jose Farmer, grease pencil price at logo, mild surface creasing, VG.	30.00
1953 Aug. Contains *The Wages of Synergy* by Theodore Sturgeon, mild wear and surface creasing, VG.	30.00
1953 Oct. Schomburg cover art, general mild wear, VG/F.	30.00
1954 Jan. Contains *A Present for Pat* by Philip K. Dick, moderate surface wear, VG-.	20.00
1954 Spring. Contains *The Houses of Iszm* by Jack Vance, mild readers creasing, VG.	25.00
1954 Sum. Light wear, FN-.	30.00
1954 Fall. General slight wear, some creasing, VG.	20.00
1955 Sum. Skull cover. Moderate wear and creasing, VG-.	15.00
1955 Win. Contains *Human Is* by Philip K. Dick, loss of paper at top right corner and edge, G/VG.	20.00
1955 Fall. Readers crease, general wear, VG-.	15.00

Stirring Detective & Western Stories

1940 November. #1. Small piece off foot of spine, FN-.	350.00

Stirring Science Stories

1941 Feb. #1. Contains the poem *Always Comes Evening* by Robert E. Howard, general moderate wear, small piece of tape and some interior tape, G/VG.	95.00
1941 April, #2. Hannes Bok cover art, some creasing and wear to edges, readers crease, G/VG.	60.00
1941 June. #3. Hannes Bok cover art, moderate wear mainly to right edge and lower corner, G/VG.	60.00
1942 March. Fourth and final issue and scarcest of the run. This issue is bedsheet size while the other three were regular pulp size. Chipping to two corners and some creasing to spine. Cover by Bok, VG-.	200.00

Stories Annual

1955 #1. Mild wear to over hangs, FN.	75.00

Strange Detective

1938 Nov/Dec. Lite wear, mild creasing mainly to over hangs, VG+.	175.00

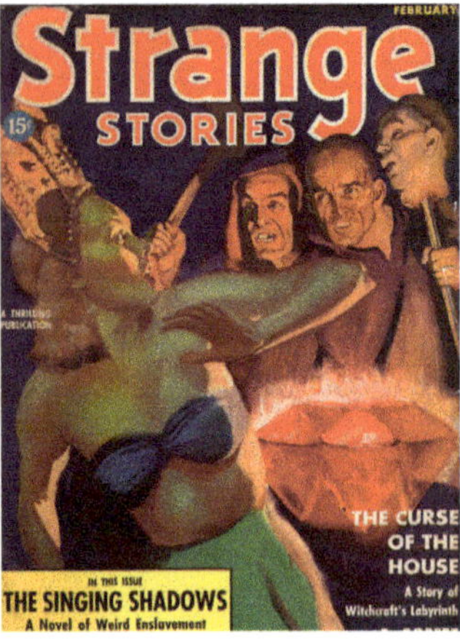
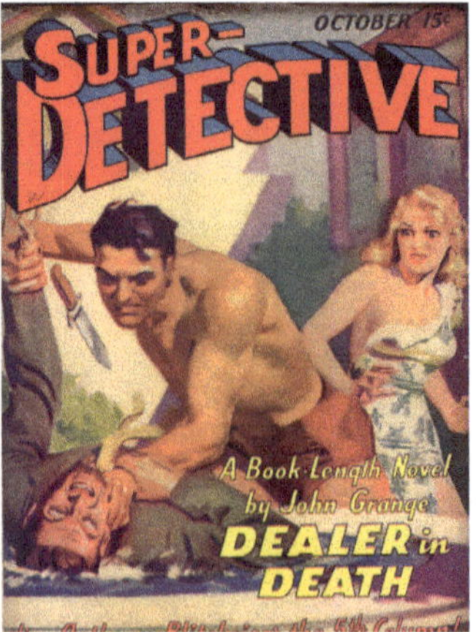
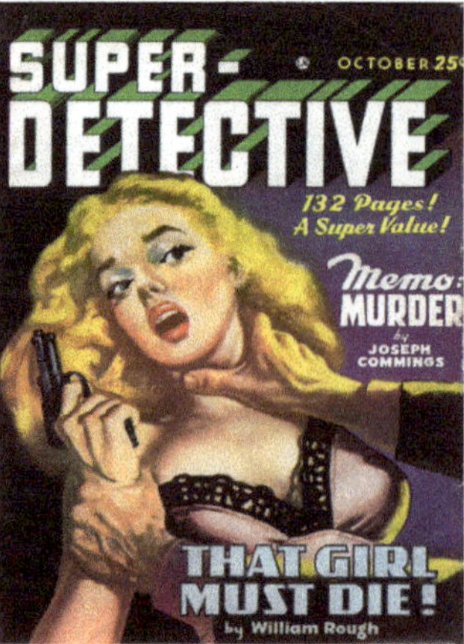

Strange Detective 1938 Nov   **Strange Stories 1939 Feb**   **Super Detective 1940 Oct**   **Super Detective 1950 Oct**

1942 Nov. Skull cover. Chip off right edge, int. tp, G/VG.	85.00
1943 January. General wear, some surface creasing, VG.	125.00
1943 March. Classic Invisible Man Cover. Store stamp and mod creasing to cover, VG.	200.00

Strange Romances
1939 Jan, #1. Small tip off top right corner, mild surface creasing, VG+.	300.00

Strange Stories
1939 February. #1. General lite wear, some creasing, VG.	175.00
1939 April, #2. Some chipping to right edge, few small tears, VG+.	100.00
1940 October. Multi-skull cover. General wear and few chips to extremities, VG+.	175.00
1941 February. Moderate wear and creasing, G/VG.	50.00

Super Detective
1934 November. ¾ cover, FR.	40.00
1935 April. Scarce early bedsheet size issue from the first series of this title. General wear, surface creasing, some writing to back cover. VG-.	375.00
1940 October, #1. General lite wear, nice paper, FN.	500.00
1941 December. Super Detective 1941 December. Lite wear, some interior tape, VG.	175.00
1943 February. Corner off bc, some chipping, VG-.	95.00
1944 Aug. Moderate wear chipping, G.	20.00
1950 October. Final issue. Mild wear and lite creasing, VG/FN.	150.00

Super Science Stories
1940 Mar, #1, Nbc, creasing and small tears to right edge, G+.	40.00
1940 Mar, #1. Moderate creasing and trim to right edge, G.	30.00
1941 Jan. 1" tear to right edge, mild readers crease, VG.	40.00
1941 May. Front cover almost loose, G.	15.00
1941 Nov. Contains *The Biped, Reegan* by Alfred Bester, moderate chipping, some creasing, G/VG.	30.00
1942 Aug, #1. Contains *Pendulum* by Ray Bradbury and Henry Hasse, logo on toc colored in, moderate creasing and chipping, G/VG.	
1942 November. Contains *The Imaginary* by Isaac Asimov. Slight spine lean, readers creases, G/VG.	25.00
1943 May. Classic Finlay cover. SM hole at left logo, some creasing, VG-.	50.00
1949 January. Contains *The Silence* by Ray Bradbury. Moderate creasing and chipping, G+.	20.00
1950 May. Contains *By The Stars Forgot* by John D. MacDonald. 1" split at crown of spine, VG+.	60.00
1950 July. Contains *Half-Past Eternity* by John D. MacDonald & Vengeance, Unlimited by Fredric Brown. Lite wear and surface creasing, VG	50.00
1951 April. Readers and surface creasing, VG.	30.00
1951 April. Moderate trim to right edge, G+.	15.00
1951 August. General wear , chipping to edges, G+.	15.00

Super Western
1937 August. #1. Norman Saunders cover art, FN.	175.00
1937 December. Norman Saunders cover art. Damp staining, sm chip off lower edge and l.l. corner, G/V.	50.00

Sure-Fire Western
1936 November. #1. Smudge market top of cover, o/w a nice looking Pulp. VG.	125.00
1936 November. #1. Piece off front cover, general wear and creasing, G.	45.00

Suspense Magazine
1952 Winter 1952, #4. Contains *The Screaming* by Ray Bradbury. VG.	25.00

Sweetheart Stories
1928 Oct 23. Mild readers and surface creasing, VG+.	35.00
1935 Sept. Moderate creasing, VG-.	25.00

Super Western 1937 Aug

Tailspin Tommy 1936 Oct

Tattle Tales 1935 Oct

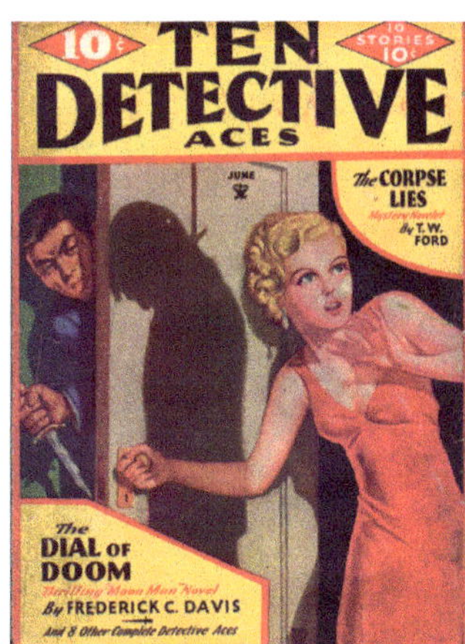

Ten Detective Aces 1935 Jun

Tailspin Tommy
1936 October, #1. Very scarce. General wear and creasing, some doodling to first page
    and bc, some pencil marks to fc, VG-.   750.00

Tattle Tales
1935 October. H. J. Ward Cover art. Mild wear and handling with mild dirt to white extremities.
    Half inch closed tear at top left corner, VG+.   350.00
February No year given but according to one site this is a British edition from 1938 . Quintana cover art.
    Great color to cover and nice paper quality, FN.   295.00

Tender Love Stories
1953 May, #1. Sliver off top right corner, mild wear, VG+.   60.00

Ten Detective Aces
1935 June. Moon Man appearance. General wear and some surface Creasing, VG.   85.00
1937 Nov. Normal Saunders cover art, Diagonal crease to top of cover, wear to extremities, VG-.   60.00
1945 Jan. Norman Daniels, Frederick C. Davis. Moderate creasing to cover, VG.   45.00
1941 Dec. Norman Saunders cover art. Contains *The Corpse Walks Out* by Frederick C. Davis.
    Some marks and creasing to cover, VG.   45.00
1942 April. Saunders cover art. Stories by D. L. Champion, Norman Daniels, Frederick C. Davis. Lite wear, small tears, VG+.   45.00
1946 Dec. Contains *Trigger Snare* by Frederick C. Davis. Lite wear, few sm tears to edges, VG+.   45.00
1946 March. Lite wear ad some creasing , small tears to extremities, VG.   45.00
1946 June. Slight spine lean, moderate creasing, VG.   45.00
1947 Nov. Lite wear and creasing, VG+.   45.00
1948 Sept. Moderate creasing and some edge wear, G/VG.   35.00
1949 Jan. Center crease, sm tears to extremities, mild spine damage and lean, VG-.   40.00
1949 March. Norman Saunders cover art. General lite wear, few small tears to overhangs, VG+.   45.00

Ten Story Gang
1938 August #1. Nice looking book, few small tears in overhangs, tanning supple paper, FN.   500.00

Ten Story Love
1937 March, #1. Lite creasing to cover, VG/FN.   100.00

Terence X. O'Leary's War Birds
1935 March. First issue. 2" tp to foot of spine G/VG.   250.00
1935 April. 4" spine split, G/VG.   200.00
1935 June. 1" tape on spine, some creasing, back cover dingy, VG-.   200.00

Terror Tales
1934 November #3. Moderate wear, creasing , some chipping, small tears at extremities, G+.   95.00
1935 November. General wear, moderate creasing, 1.5" tear to bc, G/VG.   150.00
1939 September. Classic *Mates For The Bat Man* bondage cover. General wear and creasing,
    some chipping to overhangs, VG-.   300.00

Three Star Magazine
1928 August 1. 2" tear mended on reverse, general wear, creasing, G/VG. Rare.   200.00

Three Western Novels
1948 June, #1. Norman Saunders cover art. Mild readers crease some int. tp to mend few tears, VG-.   95.00

Thrilling Adventures
1932 June. Moderate wear and surface creasing, G/VG.   50.00
1933 Jan. Contains cover and story *Kwa and the Ape People* by Paul Regard. Some interior tape,
    edge wear with tanning supple paper, VG.   200.00

Ten Story Gang 1938 Aug

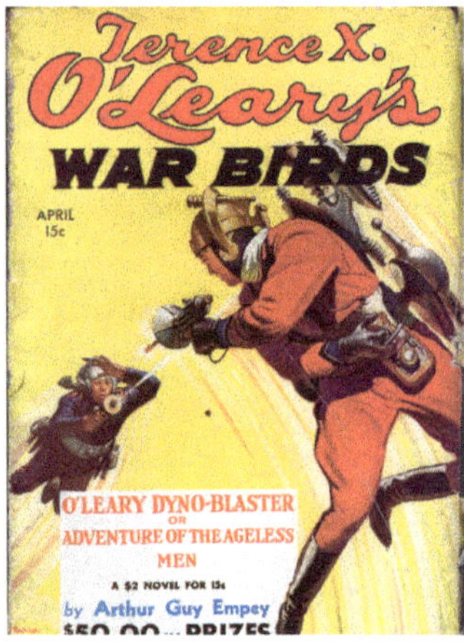
Terance X. O'Leary's 1935 Apr

Terror Tales 1939 Sep

Three Western Novels 1948 Jun

1935 March. Mild wear to extremities & mild chipping to bc, VG+.	95.00
1936 August. Fc loose creasing, chipping, G.	20.00
1937 January. Lite wear, FN-.	85.00
1937 March. Moderate wear, creasing some damp staining, G/VG.	50.00
1939 April. Contains *Incident At The Border* by Hugh B. Cave. Slight spine lean, few small tears and some creasing with lite tan supple paper. VG.	100.00
1939 May. Pencil marks to cover, 1" tear to right edge, general wear, G/VG. 25.00	
1940 January. *East of Gorontalo* by Louis L'Amour. 1.5" tear at bottom of cover, VG.	125.00
1941 January. Moderate trim to cover and 1st few pages, tos, G+.	20.00
1941 April. 1" split to lower spine, few creasing, VG-.	60.00
1942 April. Damp staining to spine area, chipping, G/VG.	25.00
1942 June. 1942 June. Lite wear and handling, FN-.	85.00
1943 Nov. Final issue. Contains *Wings Over Brazil* by Louis L'Amour. Few sm chips, VG+.	100.00

Thrilling Baseball

1949 Summer, #1. FN	95.00
1949 Summer, #1. Lite surface creasing, mild chipping, VG+.	65.00

Thrilling Detective

1931 November. #1 No back cover, partial spine, scarce first issue, G+.	295.00
1931 Dec, #2. Hooded menace cover. L.l. corner off bc and last 2 pages affects a few words, VG-.	140.00
1932 February, #4. Contains 1st appearance of Mr. Death. General wear and creasing, 1" tear at right edge, small tape to crown of spine, G/VG.	175.00
1933 February. Pile of Skulls Cover. Pile of skulls cover. General wear, some damp staining mainly to back cover, VG-.	175.00
1933 November. General wear, moderate chips off right edge, creasing, G/VG.	50.00
1934 January. Skeleton cover. Moderate wear and creasing, G/VG.	45.00
1934 March. 1st appearance of The Green Ghost by Johnston McCulley. Tos, some chipping. G/VG.	395.00
1935 July. Green Ghost story, last appearance. General wear and creasing, G/VG.	150.00
1935 November. Return of Raffles. Lite wear and handling, tanning to extremities VG+.	95.00
1937 January. Snake cover. Store stamp to cover, trim, VG.	40.00
1938 December. Slight spine lean, some small tears, mild damp staining to lower right corner, VG.	60.00
1939 April. 1" missing from crown and foot of spine, spine split, general Lite wear. VG.	50.00
1939 May. Mr. Death story. Lite wear and creasing, VG+.	95.00
1941 July. Moderate surface creasing, small int tp, VG-.	35.00
1944 September. Hooded skulls cover. Moderate wear, creasing, chipping, slight spine lean, VG-.	85.00
1944 December. Mild surface creasing, Canadian edition, VG/FN.	35.00
1945 March. Candid Camera Kid final appearance. .5" X 1.5" piece off lower left corner, G/VG.	40.00
1945 June. General lite wear, readers crease, VG.	40.00
1945 September. Bondage cover. Moderate wear, some chipping, VG.	40.00
1946 May. Moderate creasing, some chipping, VG-.	30.00
1947 April. Moderate surface creasing, 1" tear to bc, VG-.	30.00
1947 August. Contains *Dead man's Trail* by Louis L'Amour. Some chipping and sm l.r. corner off, VG-	60.00
1947 October. Moderate tears, creasing, 2" X 3" piece off lower left corner of back cover, G/VG.	20.00
1947 December. Skeleton cover. Louis L'Amour. Lite wear, small lower right corner off, VG+.	60.00
1949 February. General mild wear and surface creasing, VG+.	30.00
1949 April. Mild loss at spine tips, some creasing, VG.	25.00
1949 August. Contains *The Man Without A Head* by D. L. Champion. General wear, some chipping, VG-.	50.00
1951 February. Contains *Murder Comes Home* by D. L. Champion. Lite wear &surface creasing, VG/FN.	50.00
1951 February. Moderate wear, some staining to covers, G/VG.	25.00
1951 August. ½" tear, else very nice with lite tan supple paper. VG/FN.	45.00
1951 August. Moderate chipping, fading to cover, G/VG.	25.00
1951 December. Moderate wear and surface creasing, G/VG.	20.00
1952 June. Contains *The Importance Of Being Ernie* by John Carol Daly. General wear, creasing, VG+.	50.00
1953 April. Moderate readers and surface creasing, VG-.	25.00
1953 Summer. Mild wear mainly at extremities, white paper, VG/FN.	50.00

Thrilling Detective 1931 Dec

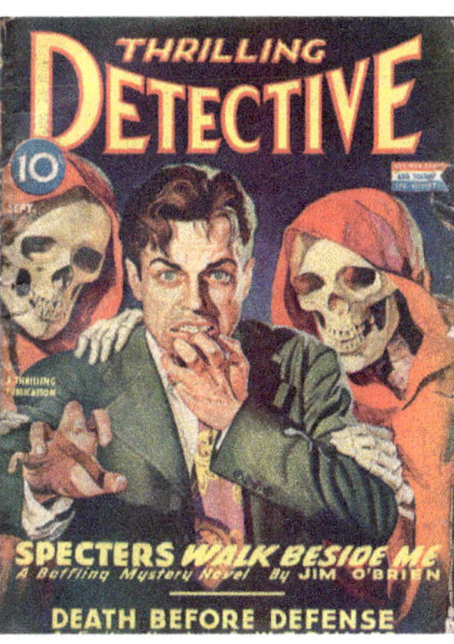

Thrilling Detective 1944 Sept

Thrilling Mystery 1936 Apr

Thrilling Mystery 1937 Apr

1953 Fall. Last issue. FN.	95.00

Thrilling Football

1940 Fall. Aggressive chipping to extremities, G+.	15.00

Thrilling Mystery

1936 April. Bondage & snake cover. Small chip off edge, mild wear, Great cover. FN-.	250.00
1937 April. Giant spider menace cover. Some loss of paper to top of spine at the fold and some damp staining. VG-.	195.00
1937 June. Bondage cover. Mild damps stain seen mainly inside cover, VG/FN.	175.00
1937 September. Snake cover. General wear, creasing, VG.	115.00
1938 January. Mild paper perished from spine, store stamps to cover, VG-.	65.00
1939 July. Bondage cover with nude statue in background. Chip to right edge, lite wear, VG.	125.00
1940 July. Wild Skeleton cover. Contains *Hybrid of Horror* by John Coleman Burroughs. Large tear to cover and moderate chipping to extremities, G.	60.00
1941 May. Chipping to edges, tanning supple paper. VG-.	70.00
1942 January. Bondage, hooded menace cover. 1.5" tape to cover, chipping, some damp staining mainly to bc, G/VG.	85.00
1942 January. Mummy bondage with skull cover! A beautiful Fine or better with great cream paper.	250.00
1944 Spring. Moderate chipping, flaking paper. G/VG.	40.00
1944 Summer. Contains *The Jabberwocky Murders* by Fredric Brown. 1" tear at spine, mild surface creasing, VG/FN.	175.00

Thrilling Ranch Stories

1935 July. Lite surface creasing, VG/FN.	25.00

Thrilling Sports

1936 September, #1. FN.	150.00
1944 Spring. FN.	30.00
1944 Winter. Chipping, trim, G/VG.	15.00
1947 Spring. Surface cresting, trim to right edge, G/VG.	15.00
1948 September. Lower right corner off, flaking to interior paper, G.	10.00
1949 Fall. Lite wear, VG/FN.	25.00

Thrilling Spy Stories

1939 Fall, #1. General wear, mild center crease, VG.	95.00
1940 Spring. Few sm chips off extremities, VG+.	95.00
1940 Summer. Small paper off foot of spine, some int. tp. G/VG.	55.00

Thrilling Western

1936 January. FN.	40.00
1946 November. Lite wear, stain to logo, Lite tan supple paper interior.	20.00
1947 April. Lite wear, small hole at spine, mild trim to right edge, Lite tan supple paper interior.	20.00
1948 November. Lite wear, mild trim to right edge, Lite tan supple paper interior.	20.00
1949 August. Lite wear, Lite tan supple paper interior. Near Fine.	25.00
1949 August. Lite wear, tanning supple paper interior.	20.00
1949 March. Lite wear, mild trim to right edge, Lite tan supple paper interior.	20.00
1953 March. Lite wear, tanning supple paper interior.	20.00

Thrilling Wonder Stories

1936 August, #1. Lite wear and surface creasing, VG/FN.	250.00
1936 August, #1. Readers crease, some writing to cover, some chipping, VG.	125.00
1936 August, #1. Moderate creasing, slight spine lean, wear to extremities, G+.	75.00
1936 October, #2. Classic "worm creature" cover. General wear and handling, some creasing, VG.	100.00
1936 October, #2. Classic "worm creature" cover. Moderate wear, creasing, tos. G	50.00
1936 Dec, #3. Creasing to cover, few small tears to extremities, G/VG.	45.00
1936 Dec, #3. Aggressive trim to right edge of cover, two small tears thru book at spine, FR.	15.00
1937 February. Sm tp to spine ends, lite wear, VG.	60.00

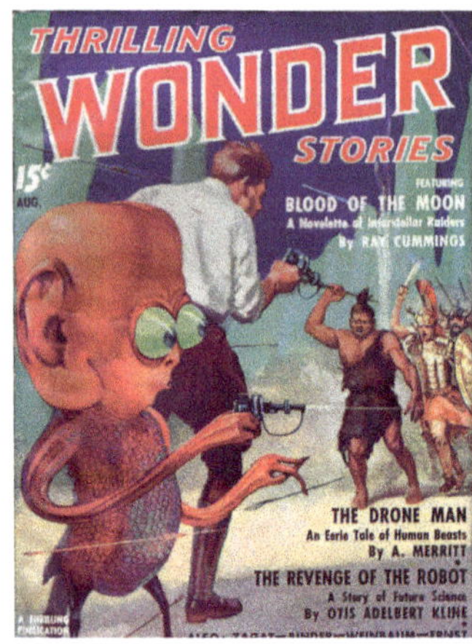   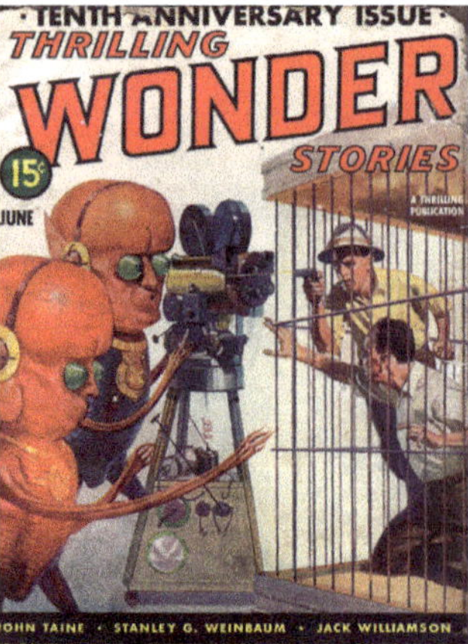

Thrilling Wonder 1936 Aug	**Thrilling Wonder 1937 Oct**	**Thrilling Wonder 1938 Aug**	**Thrilling Wonder 1939 Jun**

1937 April. General lite wear, small tear at spine, VG.	60.00
1937 April. Lower left piece off corner, readers crease, G+.	35.00
1937 June. Mild readers crease, NF.	95.00
1937 June. Damage to bottom of cover and several pages in margin, with no text affected, G.	20.00
1937 August. Lite wear and creasing, VG+	70.00
1937 August. Slight spine lean, surface creasing, VG.	60.00
1937 August. Spine lean, moderate surface creasing, G/VG.	45.00
1937 October. Dinosaur cover. Lite wear, NF.	100.00
1937 October. Dinosaur cover. Readers crease, Names in pencil to cover, VG+	75.00
1937 October. Dinosaur cover. Moderate wear and creasing, 1" x 1" piece off bc, G.	30.00
1937 December. Some surface creasing, sm chip off right edge, VG.	60.00
1937 December. Some writing in ink to cover, some chipping, VG-.	50.00
1938 February. Mild creasing, smallish dark spot at logo, VG.	60.00
1938 February. Small corner off bc, few small tears to over hangs, VG-.	50.00
1938 April. Back cover almost loose, moderate wear, G.	25.00
1938 June. Sm tape to foot of spine, lite wear mainly to extremities, VG.	60.00
1938 August. Mild creases to bottom right corner, shows very well NF.	85.00
1938 August. ½" off foot of spine, some chipping to extremities, VG.	60.00
1938 October. NF.	85.00
1938 October. Lite wear, one diagonal crease at lower cover, VG/FN.	75.00
1938 October. Moderate wear and surface creasing, quarter size chip off bottom edge, G/VG.	45.00
1939 February. Lite wear and surface creasing, slight spine lean, VG+.	70.00
1939 February. General wear, large diagonal crease, 2" open tear to right edge, G+.	30.00
1939 April. Few small tears to extremities, lite wear, 1.5" closed tear to left edge, VG.	60.00
1939 April. Surface and readers creasing, VG-.	50.00
1939 April. Top right corner off, nbc, FR.	20.00
1939 June. General wear and surface creasing, some chipping to right edge, VG-.	50.00
1939 June. Moderate wear and creasing, G+.	30.00
1939 August. Dinosaur cover. Surface creasing, 1.5" tear at bottom edge, G/VG.	50.00
1939 August. Dinosaur cover. Moderate creasing and edge chipping, sm tp to foot of spine, G+	30.00
1939 October. Lite wear, small chip off right edge, VG/FN.	85.00
1939 October. Readers and surface creasing, 2 ¾" tears to right edge, VG-.	50.00
1939 October. Moderate wear, rubber stamp to cover, G/VG.	45.00
1939 December. Small lower right corner off, general mild wear, VG-.	50.00
1940 January. Mild trim, some int. tape, few spots of paper from spine, VG-.	40.00
1940 February. Mild center crease, few small chips off extremities, VG-.	40.00
1940 February. Large piece missing to lower right corner, G/VG.	30.00
1940 February. Label of Bonnett's Magazine dealer to right edge, lower right corner off, moderate wear, G.	15.00
1940 March. Mild trim to right edge, int. tp, small writing to cover in ink, G/VG.	30.00
1940 April. Tos, mild trim to right edge, int. tp. G/VG.	30.00
1940 May. Spine lean, lite wear, VG.	45.00
1940 June. Contains Dr. Cyclops by Henry Kuttner. Movie tie-in cover art. 2" tear at logo, general wear, G/VG.	85.00
1940 July. Spine lean, surface creasing. Giant turtle man cover later used on a Jimmy Olsen comic cover, G/VG.	85.00
1940 August. Slight spine lean, few small tears to right edge, VG.	45.00
1940 September. Sm tp at crown of spine, int. tp., and tp to bc, G+.	20.00
1940 September. Large 2" x 1.5" piece off top right corner, G+.	20.00
1940 October. Lite readers and surface creasing, VG+.	55.00
1940 November. Miniature Dinosaur cover. Loss of paper to lower right edge of cover and text block, G/VG.	30.00
1940 November. Miniature Dinosaur cover. Moderate rim to right edge, rubber store stamp, G+.	20.00
1940 November. Miniature Dinosaur cover. Moderate surface creasing, large corner off lower right corner, G.	15.00
1940 December. Mild trim to two edges, interior tape, G+.	20.00
1941 January. General wear, some creasing, VG.	45.00
1941 February. FN.	90.00
1941 February. Some creasing an tears to bc, mild chipping to right edge, VG-.	40.00
1941 March. Giant octopus cover. 4" tear repaired with tape to front cover, chipping, G+.	30.00

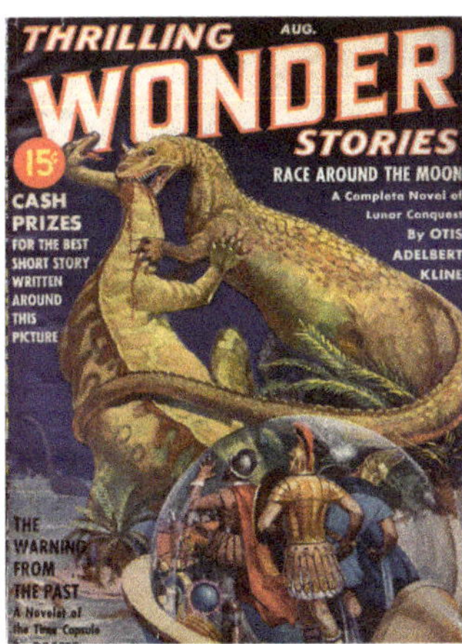

Thrilling Wonder 1939 Aug

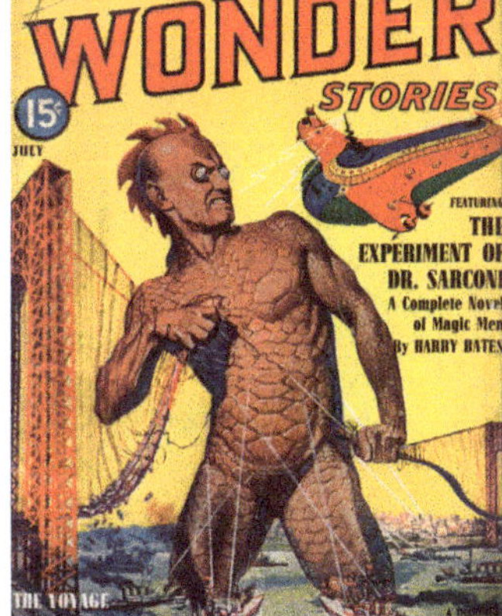

Thrilling Wonder 1940 Jul

Thrilling Wonder 1944 Fall

Thrilling Wonder 1945 Sum

1941 April. FN.	90.00
1941 June. Mild creasing to lower right corner, VG+.	55.00
1941 August. General wear and creasing, mild chipping to right edge, VG-.	40.00
1941 October.1" tear to bottom of cover, some chipping, couple of scratches at lower left corner, G/VG.	30.00
1941 October. Mild trim to edge, tape at foot of spine, G+.	20.00
1941 December. Moderate chipping, G/VG.	30.00
1941 December. Two large pieces off cover, moderate surface creasing, G.	15.00
1942 February. NF.	80.00
1942 February. Slight spine lean, mild chipping to extremities, VG+.	55.00
1942 April. Lite wear and chipping, VG+.	55.00
1942 April. Slight spine lean, store stamp to cover, moderate trim to entire pulp, G.	15.00
1942 June. Large 1" x 2" piece off right edge, G.	15.00
1942 August. Readers and surface creasing, few small tears to extremities, G/VG.	30.00
1942 October. General lite wear, some chipping to extremities, VG.	45.00
1942 October. General wear, some chipping , some paper perished from bc, G+.	20.00
1942 December. Small top left corner off, VG.	45.00
1943 April. Readers crease, moderate trip to right edge, VG.	45.00
1943 April. Moderate damp staining, evident mainly to covers, VG-.	35.00
1943 April. Aggressive tape to outside and inside covers, G	15.00
1943 June. Moderate surface creasing and trim to right edge, G/VG.	30.00
1943 August. Lite center and readers creases, VG-.	35.00
1943 Fall. 1" x 1.5" piece off right edge, G.	15.00
1944 Winter. Readers and surface creasing, VG-.	30.00
1944 Winter. Slight spine lean, moderate edge chipping, G+.	20.00
1944 Fall. Slight spine lean, mild wear, VG+.	55.00
1945 Winter. General lite wear, VG+.	55.00
1945 Winter. 1.5" tear at spine, damp staining to lower right corner, some chipping, VG-	35.00
1945 Spring. Readers crease, moderate surface creasing, G/VG.	30.00
1945 Sum. Contains *The World-Thinker* by Jack Vance, and his 1st appearance. Lite surface creasing, few small tears to bottom edge, VG	200.00
1945 Fall. Small ¼" x ¼" piece off right edge & also bottom edge, VG.	45.00
1945 Fall. Moderate wear and creasing, G+.	20.00
1946 Summer. 3" tear at top left corner, small piece off lower left corner, G/VG.	20.00
1946 Fall. Small piece off crown of spine, general lite wear, VG.	30.00
1947 February. Lite wear and few small tears to lower edge over hangs, VG+.	40.00
1947 April. General wear and surface creasing, G/VG.	20.00
1947 April. Moderate wear, chipping and small tears, G+.	15.00
1947 June. Sm int. tp, moderate chipping, wear, G+.	15.00
1947 August. Moderate wear, G+.	15.00
1947 October. General wear, some creasing, VG.	30.00
1947 October. Readers creasing, 1" tear to right edge, G/VG.	20.00
1947 October. About 1/6th piece off back cover, G+	15.00
1947 December. Contains *The Irritated People* by Ray Bradbury. FN.	90.00
1947 December. Contains *The Irritated People* by Ray Bradbury. Bc loose, chipping, G.	20.00
1948 February. Contains *The Shape of Things* by Ray Bradbury. Readers crease, general lite wear, VG.	40.00
1948 April. 1" split to rear at foot of spine, general wear, VG.	30.00
1948 June. Contains *And The Moon Be Still As Bright* by Ray Bradbury. 1.5" spine split re-glued, VG-.	40.00
1948 June. Contains *And The Moon Be Still As Bright* by Ray Bradbury. Moderate creasing and wear, G/VG.	30.00
1948 August. Contains *The Earth Men* by Ray Bradbury. Lite chipping to right edge, VG/FN.	60.00
1948 August. Contains *The Earth Men* by Ray Bradbury. Back cover loose, chipping, G.	20.00
1948 October. Contains *The Square Pegs* by Ray Bradbury. Moderate chipping, G/VG.	30.00
1948 December. Contains *240,000 Miles Straight Up* by L. Ron Hubbard, *A Child is Crying* by John D. MacDonald and *The Off Season* by Ray Bradbury. Readers and surface creasing, general wear, G/VG.	40.00
1949 February. Contains *The Weapon Shops Of Isher* by A. E. Van Vogt and *The Man* by Ray Bradbury. Aggressive tape to front cover and partial spine, G.	20.00

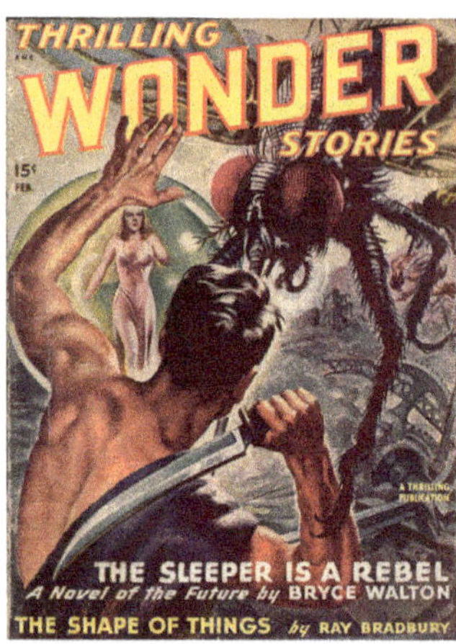

Thrilling Wonder 1948 Feb

Thrilling Wonder 1948 Aug

Thrilling Wonder 1950 Feb

Thrilling Wonder 1950 Dec

1949 April. Contains *The Concrete Mixer* by Ray Bradbury. Wear hole at lower staple, lite wear, VG.	45.00
1949 April. Contains *The Concrete Mixer* by Ray Bradbury. Nbc, tp to whole spine, G.	20.00
1949 April. Contains *The Concrete Mixer* by Ray Bradbury. Ll corner off, Lite creasing, VG.	25.00
1949 June. Contains *Like A Keepsake* by John D. MacDonald. Lite wear and few small tears to extremities, VG.	45.00
1949 June. Contains *Like A Keepsake* by John D. MacDonald. Readers and surface creasing, lite wear, G/VG.	30.00
1949 August. Contains *The Naming Of Names* by Ray Bradbury, *Amphiskios* by John D. MacDonald. General lite wear, small tears to extremities, VG.	45.00
1949 August. Contains *The Naming Of Names* by Ray Bradbury, *Amphiskios* by John D. MacDonald. Front cover coming loose, some paper perished from spine, G.	20.00
1949 October. Contains *The Planet Makers* by L. Ron Hubbard, *Kaleidoscope* by Ray Bradbury. General surface creasing, edge wear, G/VG.	40.00
1949 December. Contains *A Blade of Grass* by Ray Bradbury. Moderate wear and creasing, G/VG.	30.00
1949 December. Contains *A Blade of Grass* by Ray Bradbury. Moderate wear and creasing, tos, G+.	25.00
1950 February. Contains *Payment In Full* by Ray Bradbury, *Spectator Sport* by John D. MacDonald. Few tears repaired with tape on verso of cover, tp at tips of spine, G+.	25.00
1950 April. Contains *Journey For Seven* by John D. MacDonald. Lite surface creasing, few sm tears to extremities, VG-.	35.00
1950 April. Contains *Journey For Seven* by John D. MacDonald. Tears to extremities, dime size piece off at spine, G+	25.00
1950 June. 1" x 1" lower right corner, some damp staining, G/VG.	20.00
1950 August. Contains *New Bodies For Old* by Jack Vance, *Battling Bolto* by L. Ron Hubbard. 1.5" tear at spine, VG.	55.00
1950 August. Contains Battling Bolto by L. Ron Hubbard and *New Bodies For Old* by Jack Vance. Mild trim, VG+.	60.00
1950 October. Contains *Shadow On The Sand* by John D. MacDonald. Readers and surface creasing, VG-.	35.00
1950 October. Contains *Shadow On The Sand* by John D. MacDonald. 5" tear to lower spine and into cover, G.	20.00
1950 December. Mild chipping off extremities, few small tears, VG.	30.00
1950 December. Moderate creasing, wear and chipping, G/VG.	20.00
1951 February. Contains *Overlords Of Mars* by Jack Vance. Lower right corner off, moderate creasing, G/VG.	15.00
1951 February. Contains *Overlords Of Mars* by Jack Vance. 2" tear at foot of spine, some damage to spine also, G+.	12.00
1951 April. Moderate wear, some small tears and a 1" tear to right edge, G/VG.	15.00
1951 August. Contains *The Dome* by Fredric Brown. Sm top right corner off, some chipping, creasing, G+.	15.00
1951 October. Contains *The Plagian Siphon* by Jack Vance. ½" x 1" piece out of right edge, G/VG.	20.00
1951 December. Small tear in cover at price, VG.	20.00
1952 Feb. Contains *Abercrombie Station* by Jack Vance. Some chipping, small tears, VG.	25.00
1952 April. Readers and surface creasing, VG.	20.00
1952 June. Contains *The Foxholes of Mars* by Fritz Leiber. Moderate creasing, G/VG.	25.00
1952 August. Contains *Cholwell's Chickens* by Jack Vance. Mild surface creasing, small tears to edges, VG.	25.00
1952 August. Contains *Cholwell's Chickens* by Jack Vance. Moderate creasing, lower right corner off, G+.	15.00
1952 Oct. Contains The Kokod Warriors by Jack Vance. Mild surface creasing, VG.	25.00
1952 Oct. Contains *The Kokod Warriors* by Jack Vance. Moderate creasing, some damp staining to cover, G+.	15.00
1952 December. Lite wear, mild wear to extremities, VG.	20.00
1953 April. Contains *Mother* by Philip Jose Farmer. Moderate creasing and wear, G/VG.	25.00
1953 June. Small rub hole at top staple, small tape to spine ends, G+.	12.00
1953 August. Mild creasing, some paper perished from over hang at bottom of cover, VG.	20.00
1953 August. 4.5" tear at spine, G+.	12.00
1953 November. FN.	40.00
1954 Spring. 1" x 2" triangle top right corner off, G+.	12.00
1954 Fall. Mild surface creasing, VG.	20.00
1954 Fall. Moderate readers and surface creasing, G/VG.	15.00
1954 Winter. Contains *Prize Ship* by Philip K. Dick. Moderate chipping and surface creasing, G+.	25.00
1954 Summer. Contains *Time Pawn* by Philip K. Dick. Couple chips off extremities, moderate surface creasing, G/VG.	35.00
1955 Winter. Small paper pull on cover, chipping to right edge, G/VG.	15.00

Tip Top Semi-Monthly

1915 August 10. Lite wear, dust shadow at spine, VG.	95.00
1915 November 25. Tos, general wear, creasing, G+.	75.00

Triple-X 1931 May

Triple-X 1931 Jul

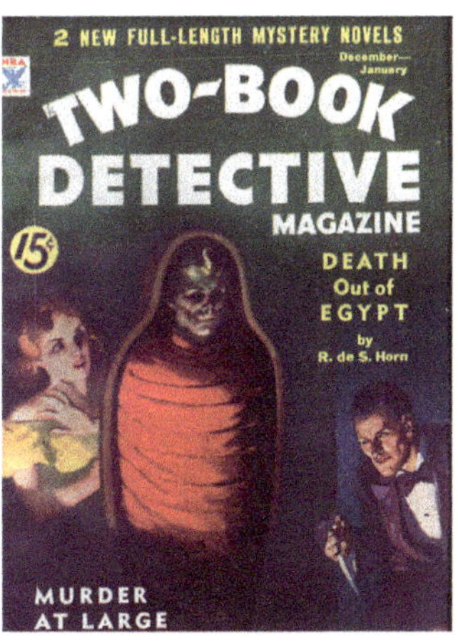

Two-Book Detective 1933 Dec

Two-Book Detective 1934 Jul

Top Notch Magazine

1913 July 15. Lite wear, few small tears, VG/FN.	95.00
1916 February 1. Lite wear, VG/FN.	95.00
1928 March 1. 6" clean tear near spine, G.	30.00
1928 September 15. Moderate creasing and few small tears to right edge, VG.	60.00
1928 November 1. Slight edge loss at bottom left, some spine damage, VG-.	40.00
1929 January 15. Moderate creasing and few small tears to edge, VG.	60.00
1931 November 1. 2 tears to right edge, VG.	60.00
1932 Sept 15. Lower right corner off, some chipping, 1" spine splits, G+.	40.00
1936 May. Period based oriental menace cover. Lower left corner off, nice paper, VG.	60.00
1926 June. Aggressive chipping, taped tears, FR.	20.00
1936 July. Moderate creasing, some spine damage, G/VG.	40.00

Top Western Fiction Annual.

1950 (#1.) Small tape to foot of spine, otherwise VG+.	30.00

Treasury of Great Western Stories

1972 (#9.) Last issue? FN/VF unread type condition with great paper.	25.00

Triple-X (Triple-X Western Magazine)

1924 June. #1. Very scarce, issue rarely turns up. General wear, 2" tear at bottom left of cover, some chipping to bc. VG.	750.00
1927 Sept. Scarce early issue. Lite wear, FN-.	250.00
1930 October. Small chip off crown of spine, lite over all wear, lite tan paper, VG/FN.	300.00
1931 May. Lite wear and creasing mainly to extremities, nice cream paper, VG/FN.	300.00
1931 July. Parkhurst cover art. Lite staining to back cover, dust shadow at spine, VG+.	250.00
1931 August. Lite wear, some dirt to back cover, lite tan paper, VG/FN.	300.00

Two-Book Detective Magazine

1933/1934 Dec/Jan, #3. Mummy cover, scarce. Mild readers crease, FN-.	300.00
1934 Feb/Mar. General wear and creasing, large amount of interior tape to front and back covers, G/VG.	85.00
1934 July. Very lite wear, few small tears to overhangs, FN-.	250.00
1934 September. General wear and creasing, Interior tape, VG-.	200.00

Undercover Detective

1938 December, #1. Moderate wear & creasing, some chipping, G+.	125.00

Underworld

1927 May #1. Scarce. Moderate wear, creasing, tape stains and some chipping, G.	250.00

Universe Science Fiction

1953 June, #1. Contains The World Well Lost by Theodore Sturgeon. Also stories by Murray Leinster and Robert Bloch. VF unready type condition.	35.00

Unknown (Unknown Worlds)

1939 September. Dime size piece off front cover, large tear mended on reverse with tape, G+.	40.00
1940 February. Death's Deputy by L. Ron Hubbard. Mild wear, 1" ss, VG.	100.00
1940 April. Contains *The Indigestible Triton* by L. Ron Hubbard. Mild wear and some creasing, VG-.	100.00
1940 April. Contains *The Indigestible Triton* by L. Ron Hubbard. Aggressive wear, tape, FR.	30.00
1940 May. Contains the conclusion of Reign of Wizardry by Jack Williamson. General mild surface and readers creasing, VG.	45.00
1940 May. Contains the conclusion of *Reign of Wizardry* by Jack Williamson. General wear, large pobc, G/VG.	35.00
1940 June. Moderate tape to spine. G/VG.	50.00
1940 June. 2" spine split with some loss of paper, VG-.	60.00
1940 August. Contains It by Theodore Sturgeon. Some tos, general wear, G/VG.	40.00
1941 February. The Crossroads by L. Ron Hubbard. Moderate wear, staining to logo & some staining, G+.	50.00

Underworld 1927 May

Unknown 1940 Apr

Variety Story 1938 Oct

War Stories 1931 May

1941 April. Contains *The Haunt* by Theodore Sturgeon. Sm tp to spine ends, lite wear, VG.	50.00
1941 June. Contains *Yesterday Was Monday* by Theodore Sturgeon. Moderate wear and creasing, G+.	40.00
1940 December. Contains *Typewriter in the Sky* by L. Ron Hubbard. Lower right corner off, 1" tear to cover, G/VG.	45.00
1941 February. Contains *The Crossroads* by L. Ron Hubbard, *Shottle Bop* by Theodore Sturgeon. 1" x 2" corner off lower right corner, G/VG.	50.00
1943 August. Front cover loose, G.	20.00
1943 October. Some chipping to edges, G/VG.	30.00

Variety Love Stories

1938 November, #1. Small tear at right edge, NF.	95.00

Variety Novels

1938 September, #1. General lite wear and some damp staining to back cover, VG+.	60.00

Variety Sports Magazine

1938 September, #1. Wrinkling to bc, else a sharp copy, FN-.	85.00

Variety Story Magazine

1938 October, #2. Lite surface creasing, FN-.	150.00

War Birds.

1933 March. Creasing to cover and over hangs, VG.	60.00
1933 April. Splitting to spine and wraparound loose from text block, G.	40.00
1933 October. Diagonal crease to lower right area, VG.	60.00
1934 October. Mild trim to right edge, mild creasing to cover and interior with Lite tan supple paper, VG+. Terence X. O'Leary appears.	75.00
1934 September. Trim to right edge, some creasing to cover with Lite tan supple paper. VG+ Terence X. O'Leary appears.	75.00
1935 December. 1935 December. Lite wear and mild creasing to cover with decent supple paper, VG.	45.00
1937 February. Tos, int. tp., moderate creasing, G.	25.00

War Novels

1928 October. Moderate creasing, 1" tear, G/VG.	65.00

War Stories

1931 May. Mild creasing, few small tears to extremities, VG.	75.00

Weird Tales

1930 October. Contains verse by H. P. Lovecraft and verse by Clark Ashton Smith. Small piece of tape to crown of spine, small piece of tape on edge of inside fc, nice over-hangs, VG-.	200.00
1931 July. Contains *The Outsider* by H. P. Lovecraft. Some int. tp., 1" off foot of spine, creasing, G/VG.	200.00
1931 Sept. Great Solomon Kane story *The Footfalls Within* by Robert E. Howard. Some chipping to edges, bc loose Some paper perished from crown of spine, G+.	200.00
1932 March. Robert E. Howard verse, Clark Ashton Smith. Lite wear mild surface creasing, VG/FN.	195.00
1934 February. Great Brundage cover art. Contains *The Valley of the Worm* by Robert E. Howard. Tos, general wear, G/VG.	150.00
1934 June. Contains *The Haunter of the Ring* by Robert E. Howard. Aggressive wear, 4" perished from spine, FR.	40.00
1935 August. First Doctor Satan by Paul Ernst. General wear and surface creasing, slightly fading spine, Brundage cover art, VG-.	125.00
1938 August. Content by Robert E. Howard and H.P. Lovecraft. Rubber stamp to cover, one crease to lower right corner, great Brundage cover, shows well. VG+	250.00
1938 October. Contains *The Other Gods* by H. P. Lovecraft. Rusty staples, damp stain to fc, creasing. G/VG .	65.00
1939 May. Verse by H.P. Lovecraft. Contains *Almuric* pt 1 by Robert E. Howard. Tos, general wear, 3" paper perished from spine, G+.	75.00
1939 May. Nbc, tos, top left corner off, FR.	25.00
1940 January. 4" tear at spine, G/VG.	50.00

Weird Tales 1931 Jul

Weird Tales 1931 Sep

Weird Tales 1938 Aug

Western Raider 1938 Aug

1940 March. Verse by H.P. Lovecraft. Embossed seal to cover, hard to see, shows well, VG+.	95.00
1941 March. Brundage cover art. 2" tear in cover at spine, VG.	95.00
1941 May. Contains pt. 1 of *The Case of Charles Dexter Ward* by H.P. Lovecraft. Moderate damp staining, VG-.	85.00
1941 May. Contains pt. 1 of *The Case of Charles Dexter Ward* by H.P. Lovecraft. Top left corner off, large tear mended with tape, chipping, G/VG.	50.00
1942 May. Contains *Black Bargain* by Robert Bloch. ½" off foot of spine, general wear, VG.	75.00
1943 January. Contains *The Eager Dragon* by Robert Bloch. Supple browning paper, VG.	75.00
1944 March. Contains *The Trail of Cthulhu* by August Derleth. Some fading, 2" paper perished from spine with splitting, G.	40.00
1945 November. Scarce Canadian edition with variant cover art. Store stamp to "W" in logo, NF.	125.00
1947 January. Contains *The Handler* by Ray Bradbury. ¾" tear to right edge, mild damage to spine, G/VG.	35.00
1947 March. Contains *Sweets to the Sweet* by Robert Bloch. Faded spine, general wear, sm l.l. corner off, VG.	60.00
1948 Sept. Contains *Fever Dream* by Ray Bradbury. General wear and surface creasing, G/VG.	45.00
1949 May. Contains *But Not The Dream* by John D. MacDonald. Mild readers crease, lite wear, VG.	60.00
1949 July. Contains *Floral Tribute* by Robert Bloch. SM tape to spine ends, VG.	60.00
1950 July. Contains *The Weird Tailor* by Robert Bloch. Lite wear and handling, VG+.	50.00
1950 November. NF.	75.00
1951 Nov. Contains *Dagon* by H. P. Lovecraft. "V' shape tear in cover about 1" long, VG-.	45.00
1952 May. General lite wear and handling, VG.	45.00
1953 March. Finlay GGA cover. Small tape to spine ends, VG.	60.00
1953 Sept. 1st digest format issue. Readers crease and some creasing, VG-.	35.00
1954 January. Lite surface creasing, VG+.	45.00
1954 March. FN.	60.00
1954 May. Readers crease, lite wear, VG-.	35.00
1954 Sept. 1" spine split, mild wear, VG-.	30.00

West

1928 Oct 20. Mild chipping to extremities and mild damp staining, VG-.	45.00
1928 Oct 27. Sm tp to foot of spine and interior tape to versos of covers, VG-.	45.00
1928 Nov 10. Interior paper darkening to extremities, G/VG.	35.00
1935 October. Lite wear, crese to top right corner, VG/FN.	35.00
1946 Oct. Contains *Zorro Raids A Caravan* by Johnston McCulley. Mild spine lead and center crease, VG.	40.00
1947 Jan. Contains *Zorro's Moment of Fear* by Johnston McCulley. 1" X 2.5" piece cut from fc, G-.	15.00
1947 Dec. Contains *Zorro Fights For Peace* by Johnston McCulley. Aggressive tape to covers and versos, G.	20.00
1948 March. Contains *Zorro Meets a Wizard* by Johnston McCulley. Mild surface creasing and wear, VG.	40.00
1948 Sept. Contains *Zorro Shears Some Wolves* by Johnston McCulley. Spine fading, some wear to extremities, VG.	40.00
1949 Nov. Contains *Zorro Gives Evidence* by Johnston McCulley. Moderate creasing to cover, G/VG.	30.00

Western Love Story

1938 May, #1. Lite wear and handling, few small tears to extremities, small piece off top of spine, VG.	150.00

Western Raider

1938 August. #1. Rare. Mild trim to front cover, FN-.	400.00

Western Rangers

October 1953 #1. 1st issue of this short run 6 issue Popular Publications title. Lite wear and handling, VG+.	75.00

Western Romance Anthology

1948. Only issue. General wear, 1" tear to right edge, VG-.	75.00

Western Yarns

January 1938, #1. Lite wear to extremities with nice supple lite tan paper, VG/FN.	150.00

Whisperer

1937 March. 6" tear at spine, chipping and some tape on spine, G+.	75.00
1940 December, #2. Small tips off spine, some surface creasing, lite tan supple paper. VG	100.00

Wide-Awake 1916 Jun 10

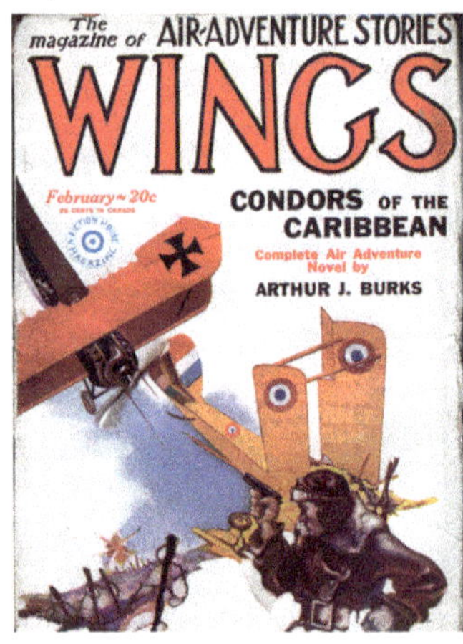

Wings 1929 Feb

Yellow Book #76

Zoom 1931 Aug

1941 February, #3. General lite wear, 1" split to crown of spine, VG+.   150.00
1941 October. General moderate wear, mild creasing VG-.   85.00
1941 December. ½" off crown of spine, mild wear , lite tan supple paper. VG.   100.00
1941 December. General moderate wear, creasing, chipping to edges, G/VG.   70.00

Wide-Awake Magazine.
1916 June 10. Scarce to very scarce last issue of the run. Lite wear, creasing, VG+.   250.00

Wild West Stories and Complete Novel Magazine
1936 April. Dime size chip off right edge, general Lite wear and creasing some flaking to paper. G/VG.   25.00
1937 February. Some markings to cover, general wear, VG-.   25.00

Wild West Weekly
1928 July 21. Wild West Weekly 1928 July 21. Interior tape, 1" tape to right edge, creasing, G/VG.   60.00

Wings
1928 August, #8. Moderate wear, creasing, writing to cover, tos, G+.   95.00
1929 January. General moderate wear, some chipping to extremities, G/VG.   125.00
1929 February. Cover art by E. K. Bergey. Moderate wear, some spine damage, G/VG.   150.00
1930 February. Moderate wear, some tape to spine, large chip, G/VG.   95.00
1935 April/May. Large paper pull to lower left corner, else nice, VG-.   95.00
1945 Fall. Erasure marks at logo, general wear mainly to extremities, VG-.   70.00
1945 Fall. Front cover loose, G.   25.00
1946 Win. Surface creasing, mild spine damage, G/VG.   35.00
1949 Fall. Great Norman Saunders good girl art cover. General lite wear, some creasing, VG.   75.00
1951 Spr. Moderate chipping to lower edge, G/VG.   30.00
1952 Spr. Large corner off top right cover, some chipping, G.   20.00

Wizard
1940 October, #1. Moderate surface creasing, some oxidation mainly to right edge, G/VG.   85.00
1941 April, #4. Moderate handling, interior covers darkening, G/VG.   60.00

Whisperer
1940 December (#2) Small tips off spine, some surface creasing, lite tan supple paper, VG.   100.00

Wonder Stories Quarterly
1931 Summer. Lite wear, 2" split at rear of spine, VG.   75.00

World Adventurer.
1934 January, #1. Some tape, creasing with mild flaking paper at extremities. G+.   200.00

Yellow Book
V 19 #74. Semi-nude cover. 4" tear to back cover, VG.   85.00
V 25 #75. Cir 1933? Small hole at left cover near spine, very sexy cover appears to be Enoch Bolles. Same cover as
       #98 on the Galactic Central site. VG+.   100.00
V 26 #76, GGA cover. 1" closed tear at top of spine, sharp copy, VG+.   100.00
#90. Store stamp to cover, general wear, damp staining, 4" tear mended on verso with tape, G+.   50.00
#91. Line drawn cover, slight loss of paper from spine, VG.   75.00
#92. Line drawn cover, back cover shows mild damp staining to extremities, VG.   75.00

Young Love
1936 Dec, #1. Large piece off toc page, G.   50.00

Zoom
1931 August. Rare. Moderate wear, creasing, some glue repair to spine, G/VG.   1,500.00